Take This Heart of Stone

by
Carol A. Thomas

AmErica House
Baltimore

Copyright 2001 by Carol A. Thomas.

First printing

ISBN: 1-58851-860-4
PUBLISHED BY AMERICA HOUSE
BOOK PUBLISHERS
www.publishamerica.com
Baltimore

Printed in the United States of America

Dedications

This book is dedicated
to all my precious
grandchildren and Godchildren
who bubble over with life ...

to my husband Tim,
who fills my life with love...

and to God,
who is the author of all life.

In Memory of
Guy Condon

Acknowledgment

With deep affection, my appreciation goes out to numerous family members, friends and colleagues for believing in me, encouraging me and spurring me on to write. With special thanks and gratitude to my board of directors who allowed me the time to write this novel. Wow... we did it!

This book could not have been written were it not for my Lord and Savior Jesus Christ who drew me to the pregnancy center and allowed me to personally be involved with the many courageous women who sought resolution to their past abortion.

It has been my joy to be there as they took that soulful journey of healing and restoration in Christ. My prayers continue on behalf of the many other women who have not yet taken that journey. God is waiting and He delights in you.

Dear Reader,

Thank you for your interest in reading this novel. Before you begin there are a few things I would like to share with you. Although this is a work of fiction it is based on real life experiences.

You are about to enter into the world of abortion. But not the political world where the battle to keep "a woman's right to chose" legal is headline news. This novel takes you into the lives of four women who have suffered greatly because, at a vulnerable time in their lives, they succumbed to the choice of abortion only to have traded one crisis for another. These are women who could be one of your friends, a sister, a niece or a favorite aunt. Each of these four women are a composite of two people who I have come to know while leading post-abortion Bible studies since 1992.

As you are taken through the symptoms and effects of post-abortion syndrome (PAS) I want you to know that I chose to highlight only the most common manifestations of PAS and those journeys traveled by the average woman participating in such a Bible study. There are both more extreme and destructive symptoms of PAS as there are truly miraculous incidents of healing. I chose the middle ground because to do otherwise would invited skepticism or seem too far-fetched.

For those readers that have experienced abortion but have not yet received healing, I have written with you in mind. But this is not a Bible study within a novel. I purposely did not address several relevant chapters usually found in PAS Bible studies. Please know that this was not done to add to your suffering. It is because I strongly encourage you to seek out help in a group setting.

My reason is this. Abortion hurts us the most when we keep it a tightly held secret. It is those areas of our life that we keep hidden in the darkest corners of our soul that need to be brought out into the light for healing to begin. It is my hope that this book would give you the strength and courage to seek out a Bible study designed to walk you through the healing process.

Some readers may have never heard about PAS while others will have a limited knowledge. It is my prayer that you would come to a better understanding of abortion and how it can destroy both the innocent unborn baby as well as the mother and the other people involved.

Whether or not you are a woman or whether or not you have had an abortion, I believe this book speaks universally to the hurts and struggles in all our pasts. Most of life's sufferings bring with it the wide range of reactions from denial, anger, bargaining, broken relationships, stagnation, depression, inability to forgive or accept forgiveness and the human attempts to lessen the pain. Although the focus is PAS, the focal point is Christ.

For all who have been hurt and need healing, Jesus Christ has His hand extended out to you. Find a way to take His hand and allow Him to guide you through to the other side of pain and turn your painful experience(s) into something He can use for good. Many churches now offer wonderful Bible studies designed to deal with specific issues of human struggle and sorrow. May this book help you to know that God is able to do exceedingly abundantly beyond what we can imagine.

In His grace,

Carol A. Thomas

Section One:

Life

Chapter One:
Renee

Renee saw the light flash on her office phone before it even rang. Quick to respond she answered before the first ring even finished beckoning her. Every minute in Renee's life was meant to count for something. As a news-reporter for a recently recognized, albeit small town, newspaper Renee instinctively knew her chance to grab the brass ring, the coveted Society of Professional Journalists Award, could be just one phone call away. She was ready. She knew the price she had paid to get this far. She knew how hard she had worked accepting any assignment, being gracious when harshly critiqued, putting in long hours, refining her style, dealing with the guys that felt women should be in Customer Service...even Sales but not reporting and yes, even kissing up to Haggerty, the chief editor.

Renee, although a youthful 28 years old, carried herself with the confidence of a seasoned journalist. It was rare to see the energy of youth combined with the wisdom earned only after years of experience. Yet, what people saw first, before reading any of Renee's work, were her alert brown eyes that gave you the sense that she didn't miss a thing. They may have noted the smooth ebony tone of her African-American heritage, but her eyes, her poise, her ability to draw people in transcended any racial barriers that may have existed or been allowed to take root and germinate.

Renee herself had often said that being black was less of an issue than being a woman. She attributed the lack of prejudice to her childhood where she grew up in a community that was not merely accepting of each other but that epitomized the true sense of the word community. She had never experienced the cruelty of racism. Because of this Renee rarely recognized the subtle bigoted remarks or reactions. But she definitely experienced the hostile man-woman tensions in the workplace.

Her educated, well thought out, often-pondered explanation came down to, "Men were jerks!" As a woman, she was smarter, stronger, harder working, and more versatile than any of the men she had ever worked with or for. She thought their preening and prowess was laughable. On a personal level Renee felt men did more to mess up her life than to augment it...with the exception of her father, of course, and her son, whom she was raising to be an exceptional young man...far more evolved than those she knew.

What astounded Haggerty, though he never told her, was Renee's ability for taking what she saw with those eyes, running it through her mind and putting it into print in a way that struck the hearts of the community. He knew, in watching her for these past years, that she was a tough gal, her eyes were on the prize, she had one goal...to succeed and she fought anyone who got in her way. He knew that small town politics...and yes, small town minds, would have been a hindrance to any other woman trying to make her mark through news reporting. But not Renee. Just cross her and...

"Renee Stanwell here," she answered. After listening and scribbling on the always-available notepad Renee pushed back her chair, grabbed her recorder while ending the conversation, "I can be there in five minutes. I'll bring Mike with me."

It was Renee's habit to check the photographer's assignment roster every time she came into the office. She wanted to know who was on the schedule during her shift. Larry, who did great work but was a sloppy-dressing, chain-smoking, foul-mouthed pig was Renee's last choice to partner with on a story. Jake, Pete and Felecia were your average, point and shoot photographers. They got the picture but it never seemed to speak to Renee. She felt bad in a way about Felecia. It took years before the paper hired a woman photographer and Renee wanted to support Felecia's efforts but, not at a cost to Renee's own career. Heck, this isn't a sorority; this is the real dog-eat-dog world.

Then there was Mike, a veteran, the older guy who most people chose last. He took the kind of shots Renee would take, if she had an once of creative talent when it came to cameras. Mike's pictures were her words. More then once Renee felt that the paper shouldn't even print her words, just Mike's pictures. Although she knew better than to voice that thought! To Renee, Mike was part of the formula in her ticket to the top. Anytime his name was on the roster, she requested him.

She dialed his extension, "Hi Mike...ready to make me look good? We've got a drive by shooting over at the Center City Mall. I'm on my way to the elevator, meet me at the garage." In one sweeping motion Renee slung her knapsack-briefcase over her shoulder, pivoted, took several long graceful strides toward the exit, pushed open the press rooms door while calling over to the receptionist, "Mary, put me "out" until late afternoon. Mike and I are covering the drive-by over at Center."

"Wait Renee," Mary injected, "I was just putting a call through to your desk. Here, let me put it on the lobby line." Renee knew Mary was the most efficient person within the entire paper's staff. Mary recognized voices, remembered names, phones numbers and even birth dates of everyone, past and present, and their families. If Mary stopped Renee to take a call, it needed to be answered.

"Renee Stanwell here."

"Renee, Hi...it's Liz," an all too familiar voice said, "I have Jay here. He came in after recess complaining of a tummy ache. Poor baby...what a nice, respectful young man he is. I was holding off calling you to see if it was over exertion. You know, it's such a hot day outside and the children do play so hard and well you know..."

Renee was automatically rotating her hand, signaling Liz to get to the end of her explanation. She loved Liz, the school nurse – who was always so sympathetic to Renee being a working mom – but her sweetness could be a little too much at times. This was one of those times.

"...running a slightly elevated temperature. Nothing to worry about mind you but, as you know, that means we must call a parent."

Renee jumped in when Liz paused to take a breath, "Liz, hate to rush you but I've just been called out. I'll have my mom come get Jay." She mouthed to Mary to get her mother on the line.

"Oh, but he was asking for you Renee and..."

"Give him a hug for me will you Liz. Mom will be there in just minutes...gotta go. Bye...and Liz, thanks...you're the best."

Without missing a beat, Renee hung up from Liz and picked up the blinking line before it even rang. "I'm getting faster at this with every call!" She told herself. Renee needed a little more self-encouragement to cover up feeling guilty about passing Jay along to her mom...again.

"Hi mom. Look, I've just been called out and Jay's over in Liz's at the school office with a slight fever. Could you run over and get him."

"Let's see honey," her mom responded, thinking out loud, "I guess I could pick up groceries later and the dry cleaning has already waited a week, what's one more day? Sure, it's not a problem at all. You go do a good job and leave Jay to me."

"Thanks mom, I'll try to be there before dinner time. Bye." Waiting for the elevator Renee felt worse having spoken to her mother. *Why is she always so giving? Why doesn't she just tell me that I have my priorities all screwed up, that Jay needs me...that I'm his mother...his only parent...and should be there for him.* All at once the weight of her knapsack seemed overwhelming as her shoulders sagged and her body began to lean against the wall for support. She caught herself in mid-lean, straightened up her knapsack and glanced to see if Mary was watching. As the elevator approached Renee took a deep breath and re-focused. *This is all for Jay...To give him a good life, send him to camp this summer, give him swimming lessons, take him on a fun, kid-vacation.* By the time the elevator door opened, as far as Renee was concerned, the phone calls hadn't even happened. Connecting with Mike and getting out to the mall filled her mind. She was in full control again.

"Mike, hey...ready? This could be it...eh... the big one? Can you do it?"

"You know I'm always ready...and together we can't be beat!" They jumped into the company van, Mike knowing Renee preferred to drive, and sped out to the mall arriving an instant before the ambulance. It wasn't until later, while lying in bed unable to fall asleep, that Renee wished she would have let Liz ramble on or had taken the time to ask her mom how dad was feeling, or had been delayed somehow for a mere five minutes. If she had been delayed, the first casualty would have left in the ambulance and she would not have seen that woman.

When they arrived at the mall, it was late morning, mid-week when the mall is usually fairly quiet. But today was the one-day-only-sale at the Bon and shoppers streamed in and out of the mall. It amazed Renee how many people were so absorbed in their spending frenzy that they didn't notice the commotion, while others seemed to live for the chance to see a disaster. The latter were typically under foot in the way.

Using her high-brow Briton accent, acquired from two years abroad, Renee spoke with assured authority while using the weight of her knapsack to nudge bystanders out of the way, "Pardon, Daily Journal...pardon...excuse me...coming through."

Although this was the first drive-by shooting in their small town, she and Mike had both seen blood and human wreckage before. The cries and screams of the injured did not put them off. Mike was instantly in position moving deftly in and around the scene, his camera clicking like a heart beat. Renee stood back for a second, carefully surveying the players.

As the ambulance positioned itself, the police directed the EMT's to the most severe casualty. Another police officer, having just finished talking to a distraught young man, proceeded to try and disperse the crowd to allow the EMT's room to work. Renee, seeing that Mike was covering the EMT activity, decided to talk to the distraught young man. He was now pacing, unsuccessfully trying to light a cigarette and muttering when Renee approached. She hadn't even formed her first question when he began crying as a confession poured from his mouth.

"I did it. It's all my fault. Oh God...oh God...what have I done?" His chest heaved as he gasped between wracked sobs.

Still using her British accent but softening her inflection Renee asked, "You shot her? Why?"

Startled that there was someone else near him, he looked at Renee from behind dazed, tear filled eyes. In the few moments it took him to register that someone had asked a question, Renee realized he was just a kid...sixteen...maybe seventeen. What possessed him to shoot another human being? She had to probe into his psyche.

"Was it gang related? Revenge?" When he didn't respond Renee backed off and tried a friendly route. "What's your name son. You can talk to me...it'll be okay."

Slowly her questions reached his mind. *Something was wrong. Who was she? Why was she saying he shot Tessa? He loved Tessa.*

Renee watched his mind catch hold of her inquiries and waited.

"Shot Tessa..." His words were labored as he began to explain. Tessa? Why did you shoot her?"

"No. No! I didn't shoot her. I love her."

It struck Renee that her assumption was wrong. Of course it was wrong. *This kid couldn't be the shooter...he wouldn't be standing here...he'd be in custody! Pull yourself together Renee. Okay, if he's not the... he's the boyfriend.*

"Are you Tessa's boyfriend?" He nodded affirmatively, relief entering his face. "What's your name?"

"Leo...my name's Leo." He was desperate to explain, "We skipped school for the sale. I wanted to buy something for the baby...ya know, to wear home after it's born. Tessa thought I didn't care about the baby. I do care. I wanted to show her."

"Tessa's pregnant? How old are you two?"

"Old enough," Leo said with pride, then sheepishly, "Sixteen...Tessa too. I mean it wasn't a planned thing or nothin'...but it's our baby...so, well...you know." Momentarily distracted, his face had lit up when he spoke about Tessa and the baby.

A piercing wail erupted from the ambulance reverberating deep within Renee. As the ambulance doors closed, Tessa cried out, "My baby..." Again, this struck a chord of identification...the heart rendering lamentation only a woman can feel, even a 16-year-old child, as she cries out for her unborn.

"Renee are you okay?" Mike was at her side. Leo was running to Tessa...chasing the ambulance as it was cautiously making its way through the crowd. A police officer gently intercepted him with a fatherly arm guiding Leo to a waiting car.

"Fine Mike...sure I'm fine. Did you hear her? Whoa that was intense."

"I heard her. I was there when they told her the baby might not make it. Just under four months along...jeez. The shot could have hit her anywhere. But she gets it right in the stomach. Makes you want to take justice into your own hands!"

Renee interviewed others, bystanders, witnesses, Officer Sam who believed the public should have all the facts. She and Mike were just about to wrap things up and head back to the office when Sam waved them down from his cruiser. "Thought you'd want to know...it's just become a homicide."

"Tessa?" Renee offered, though her gut told her otherwise.

"No, the baby. Tessa's got a chance...if she'll fight. Take care now."

As Sam drove off Renee handed Mike the car keys. Without a word, they returned to the office.

It was midnight. Renee, lying in bed, unable to sleep, couldn't even remember the rest of the day. But, she could not shake the awful, penetrating wail. It carried all the weight of her own sorrow buried for years now...or so she thought. *I should have let Jim spend the night. Having him here beside me would have helped...or at least distracted me. No, then in the morning I would have to listen as he brought up marriage again. God I wish I could turn off my mind.*

At 2 a.m. Renee startled herself out of a partial sleep with a scream. Finally she could not stop the memories from flooding her semi-conscious mind. Lying bathed in her own sweat, tears hidden just beyond her eyes, she gave in to the haunting images.

* * *

She was 19, studying abroad in jolly ol' England...a lifetime dream comes true. And Alex...ah Alex. So handsome, debonair...so English. She could listen to him talk for hours. If she left England with anything, she wanted to leave with an English accent. Funny, she came to broaden her experiences, which would help make her a better writer, and now her goal was to master an English accent. Oh she wanted to walk with that air about her as well. Dignified.

It wasn't too dignified starting each day with your head in a toilet that's for sure. She knew when you went to Mexico you couldn't drink the water without getting sick, but England? It probably wasn't England, since she'd been there eight months. It was probably her quick get-away with Alex to Paris and all that rich food. Well, if it didn't pass soon, she'd have to find a doctor.

A week later, feeling foolish because she just couldn't shake this bug, she asked Alex to recommend a doctor.

"I say, touch of the flu is it then?"

"More then a touch, I've been sick every morning for two weeks," she explained.

winced, caught himself, then questioned, "Flu my dear...or something more...shall I say, *delicate*?"

His expression and choice of words snapped her brain into overdrive, as the truth became obvious, she was pregnant.

She gasped audibly, "Oh no!"

His expression became tender as he reassured her, "Not to worry Pet...I'm here for you. I know of a straight up facility..."

It was a week later when the "bad dream" became a nightmare that would relentlessly haunt Renee for the rest of her life. She didn't know that Alex was more than a very busy statesman...he was married. *Here for me...how...we can't get married. Here for me...he's a liar. My only solid connection in England is a liar...who knows of a decent...no...straight up facility to handle the problem!!! I can't tell mom and dad, it would kill them...all they did to get me here and I get pregnant by a married man.*

Renee walked from the shower the next morning and stood before the full-length mirror gradually bringing the palm of her hand down along her stomach. She didn't look any different than she had a day ago, but she had aged a thousand years. *It's time to grow up and deal with this. Lots of the girls on campus had been where she is and handled it by having an abortion. It was no big deal. It's legal in England with no big stigma like in the states. Mom and dad will never have to know. And Alex...to blazes with him and his "facility" I don't need him.*

That was it. The next day Renee had an abortion, took a day to recoup then finished out the year, traveled some, submitted articles to various publications, and headed home. One, two, three...what's the fuss. She was fine. She had even gotten several articles printed and hey, she spoke like a true Brit.

Renee had been home a week when her mom joined her in the den, sitting next to her on the couch by the window overlooking the backyard where Elmer, their golden retriever, was playing fetch with her dad.

"How's my daughter doing?" she asked lovingly with a touch of concern.

"Okay I guess. Still feeling a little sluggish – must be jet lag."

"If that's all it is...good. I just wanted you to know it's great to have you home. You've grown up a lot in two years and..." Her mother hadn't finished her sentence when Renee began sobbing uncontrollably

16

and fell into her mother's arms.

"What is it Renee dear...what's wrong?"

"Nothing Mom, really. Just homesick I guess. You know 2 years away. I don't know...everything feels so different. I feel different."

For a month Renee cried continuously for seemingly no reason. She had no motivation, couldn't eat and spent most of her days curled up in her bed. Her mother, tender and compassionate, ministered to her only child while trying to understand what was burdening Renee. Wisely, she chose not to push Renee with questions but to wait on her daughter's timing to speak. This never happened, leaving Renee's parents without any inkling as to the cause of Renee's dark period, as they came to call it. How could they know when Renee herself only briefly saw into the pit of her despair where the truth was revealed...a truth too traumatic that in order to survive Renee instantly shoved the revelation deep into the abyss of her being.

The moment of knowledge – a glimpse at the awful truth – was a transitory episode which both revealed and concluded Renee's month long-period of darkness. She was alone in the modest colonial house that had been home for her entire life. The stillness of the evening broke through her quiet pain, prompting Renee to wander from the safety of her bed.

Depleted from a month of inner turmoil, Renee shuffled through the familiar hallway by rote, patting Elmer on his head, checking the message machine...with no intention of listening to the messages if there were any...rifling through the mail and ending up in the kitchen. Turning on the lights she reacted to the brightness, studied her surroundings as if in a stranger's house, then began opening cupboards. A few minutes later, her arms hugged a sleeve of crackers, chunky peanut butter, a knife, and an apple to her chest. With a stiff robotic motion, Renee shuffled back toward her sanctuary...her bedroom. The sound of her slippers scuffing along the polished wood hallway echoed back into her consciousness but she didn't have the strength nor the desire to lift her feet as she continued toward her door.

Along one side of the hall hung an ornate mirror, a gift handed down through generations of Stanwells. Renee paused to look at the pathetic hag that faced her with greasy hair, matted and kinky, hanging across her face, eyes red rimmed barely held up by dark half moons

17

beneath, a torn and tattered T-shirt that was beyond the rag bin. *When was the last time I brushed my teeth?* But the questioned faded before she had the energy to think back for an answer.

Climbing into bed, she let her slippers fall from her unbathed feet, her bundle of supplies toppling onto the bed. *Maybe I should have a plate or napkin to avoid crumbs?* Again, the thought passed before it could be answered. Little efforts were monumental tasks. When she began to spread the chunky peanut butter on a cracker and it crumbled in her hands, tears teemed from within her giving way to loud sobs that escalated into vocal cries of anguish. Unexpectedly Renee heard her own voice screaming, "My baby...I killed my baby."

The sound of her voice shocked her. When the words she heard penetrated everything inside her, she froze. In a flash she saw her wounds laid bare and fought fast to deny what she was seeing...it was just too horrific. With great effort she pushed the vision back into her subconscious. Exhausted, she slept.

The next morning her parents were pleasantly surprised as Renee, showered, dressed and looking like their daughter again, joined them at the breakfast table. Her dad mentioned that he had bumped into Haggerty at the Rotary dinner the previous night and that the paper was looking for a cub reporter. By the end of the week Renee was gainfully employed at the Daily Journal.

Chapter Two:
Jill

Russ looked at his wife and knew he was the luckiest man alive. Twenty years with Jill and his love for her had never wavered. She was as beautiful today as when they had met as awkward ninth graders. Well, he was the awkward one. Jill was all bounce and smiles. As the new kid in town, Russ felt he belonged every time she'd pass by him and smile at him. It was all he could do to get his grades where they needed to be so that his parents would allow him to try out for the football team. He barely had time to make friends, but Jill's smile cured all his longings to connect. He made the team, she turned up on the cheerleader squad and the rest is history. Here he stood, having just said good-bye to close friends who helped them share their twentieth anniversary. He was a man who had all a person could ask for in life.

"Sweet pea, the dishwasher is pretty full, should I turn it on, or do you have more?" he called out from the kitchen to the patio just off the family room. He noticed that Jill hadn't heard him because there was music still softly playing outside. Russ stood at the counter just wanting a moment longer to watch the woman he loved plump up the cushions on the wicker settee.

He started to walk around the counter and across the family room toward the sliding glass doors, when Jill shifted to gather up a glass off the small table. His stomach constricted anticipating what Jill would do next. *Please baby, don't drink it. We've had a wonderful twentieth. Let's make this one last all night.* His thoughts swirled unrestrained through his mind until he felt bile coming up from his gut. *Stop this man, you can't freak every time Jill is near alcohol.*

Jill turned and saw Russ just as he had regained control. "Wasn't it a lovely evening honey?" she said as she placed the glass on a tray with other straggler dishes and proceeded toward the family room.

Russ took the tray from her, set it on the counter and took Jill in his arms. "The best...because I've had you to love for all these years." He hesitated, waiting to see if she would pull back at all. When she didn't he tightened his embrace as she gave in and let him enfold her completely in his arms. These were the moments that he would sell his soul for – having Jill surrendered within his arms.

Jill whispered in his ear, "Trudy gave me a nice, flimsy little surprise for you tonight. Go get comfy in bed and I'll join you in a few minutes. I just want to finish up down here."

Russ's heart raced with anticipation. Trudy had a terrific sense of flair. Any thing she bought would surely make an impact. "You got it. I'll be waiting. You will model it first, of course?"

Jill murmured in his ear, kissed him lightly before releasing herself from his embrace and headed back out to the patio. Russ went upstairs to take a quick shower and await his bride who he heard outside the bedroom window on the patio below. Jill was singing along with the music as she rearranged the lawn furniture. He must have dozed off because, when he looked at the clock, more then an hour had passed. There were no sounds from below, yet Jill was not in bed with him.

Russ threw his robe on to investigate. Coming down the stairs he turned away from the living room toward the back of the house where the patio still radiated the soft glow from the last candles. Not finding Jill, he blew out the candles, walked into the family room, closing the sliding glass door behind him, and went back towards the living room shutting off lights and music along the way. The knot in his stomach subtlety made itself known as it grabbed hold of his side and yanked. Massaging his side as he walked Russ tried to think calming thoughts. These were abruptly stifled with the sound of glass breaking in the living room. As he entered, he saw Jill fast asleep on the couch, her arm having just swung out from under her to knock over a glass, the last of its red contents staining the carpet. A bottle of Merlot, a gift from Jill's' parents *(wouldn't they ever heed his warnings)* sat emptied on the table next to a toppled wine glass.

A pain shot up through his chest, causing Russ to gasp. Jill stirred, mumbled but did not awaken. Lovingly, Russ bent down, carefully placed his arms under Jill, lifted her up then carried her to bed. *Happy twentieth. Now I have to face tomorrow morning. Oh Lord, give me strength.*

Why should he expect that this morning would be any different than the "mornings after" in the past? Russ had run through every variation in responses he could conjure up over the years. None forestalled the storm nor resolved the private guilt he felt. At a time when Jill, not yet his wife, had needed him the most he had failed her. It fit that he should reap retribution for the suffering he brought into her life. A suffering that in twenty-two years had not abated.

* * *

Russ and Jill were high school seniors. It was the end of fall semester. Russ was waiting to hear from a few football scouts who had sounded really interested in him and Jill was applying to a few local community colleges not quite sure what she wanted to do with her life after Centennial High commencement.

As they wandered, hand in hand, through the mall surrounded by seasonal decorations and bumping into friends at every turn, Russ noticed Jill wasn't her smiley self. Russ bought her a pop and caramel corn, her favorite, then guided her to a bench out of the stream of shoppers. Sitting close he asked, "What's on your mind, sweet pea, you look so glum."

"Sorry, I thought I was hiding it pretty well. Guess not." Her pause lasted far too long, alerting Russ that this was no small tiff with her parents. He waited, not having a hint of what the problem might be.

"I'm a week late," she almost whispered.

*Late...late for what. Her college application had been sent...*Russ stopped mid-sentence as the blood drained from his face. "Late, like in your period?" he prodded.

"Yes." Jill's pleading eyes rested fully on his, watching, waiting, wondering. He was her knight in shining armor. She could always count on Russ, no matter what. She felt safe, loved, protected. She trusted him fully as she had from the day they met right up until now...this day was no different. She knew he would shift closer, put his arm around her shoulder, pull her into him and tell her what to do.

But he just sat there, stunned, staring, not speaking. Panic gripped her. "Russ, what should we do? I might be...I might be..."

"Pregnant? Oh Jill not now. How can this be. We were so careful. It's our last year...our whole lives are ahead of us."

"Tell me what to do Russ. What should we do? Oh Russ hold me,

I'm so scared." And he did. But, he was scared too. This was a bad dream that could only get worse.

At practice he confided in Pete, his best friend. "Wow man, heavy. This could ruin everything for you – and Jill. What are ya gonna do?"

"Man, I don't know – I mean, my life is over."

"Yeah, you got that right. Wait, have you talked to Buddy lately? Remember he knocked up that girl from Westside High? But he took care of it."

"Took care of it? What do you mean?"

"Abortion. It's legal now you know. As Buddy tells it, Fairfield County has a clinic just for abortions."

"But isn't that killing a baby...our baby?"

"Well, if it was a baby. Buddy said its just a mass of tissue, it's nothing for months...until, like just before the kid's born. Then it's a baby."

"Yeah, that makes sense. Who would do an abortion on a baby? Thanks Pete, I owe you. Hey, keep this between us?"

"Man you got it. Holler if you need help...ya know money, whatever."

"Thanks. Later." Although he was two hours early, Russ headed straight to the mall where he was supposed to pick Jill up after work. Her spirits lifted when she saw Russ walk confidently into the boutique. She knew he had solved their problem.

* * *

After twenty years and one day of marriage, Russ looked into the barren eyes of his wife knowing that her womb was also barren...would never bear a child. He had pronounced the death sentence on their only child and now lived with Jill, a woman destroyed from the inside out...a woman desperate for the gurgling mews of a precious newborn that will never come forth from their union.

Hung over, with no effort to hide her contempt for him, she spat out her venom, "Happy twenty years of barren wedded bliss my murdering husband. How are you this fine morning?" Her face was so contorted with hate she looked like evil incarnate. But Russ had accepted, long ago, that this was not Jill, this was poison being let from her soul, a purging of sorts that hopefully would one day end.

"Ah Jill, baby – you know how sorry I am. What more can I do to make it better?'

"It's in God's hands now," she said, shifting to self-contempt, "Only He will know when it's time to stop punishing me. No matter how many times I ask Him to forgive me and let me have one more chance – every month is His reminder of how much He loathes me."

"You were doing so well, Jill, what happened?"

"Trudy's pregnant. Her sixth...her sixth and God won't let me have even one. She's so damn bubbly, like a kid...you'd think it was her first. I can't stand to be around her. And what do I get on my twentieth anniversary – my period!!"

Russ could sense she was sliding into self-pity but felt helpless to stave off the avalanche of emotions.

"Why Russ? Why couldn't you have been man enough to go with me to my parents? Tell them...Find a way to have the baby. You never asked me what I felt. Once Pete gave you the out, that's all there was. What about me, Russ?" Now she was shouting, "What about me!"

He went around the counter to hold her, calm her. She began to pull away but was too distraught to resist. "Jill, I'm sorry. I thought...oh who cares what I thought. I'm sorry. You know, sweet pea, I wouldn't do anything to hurt you. I didn't know. It wasn't a quick out...really. Believe me I didn't know. Jill. Oh baby...please..."

The sobbing spasms lessened as Jill allowed Russ' love to penetrate her sorrow. Resigned to her destiny, she once more turned the blade in their hearts: "We killed our only child Russ. We don't even know if it was a boy or a girl."

As he had done on numerous other occasions, he tried once again to encourage Jill to seek help, "Should we go talk to Pastor Andy. I know he could help."

"Right. And how long do you think it would be before they asked you to step down as a Deacon? Then mom and dad would know – and who knows who else. Do you want to be the one to stand before our friends and tell them we killed our only child? I can just imagine the hell we'd be living in then – like this isn't bad enough."

"Come on babe, you know Andy isn't like that. You know his heart. He'd help...you know that."

"Andy might but...No Russ, I couldn't chance it. Not to mention it could destroy our business. No, it's just not worth it. I've gotta get out of here. I'm going for a run."

"Here, drink some water first. You don't want to dehydrate," Russ said as a peace offering.

"Well I do want to run the booze out of my system." She smiled reluctantly and Russ chose to believe they had weathered the storm but knew Jill was just shutting down again, turning off all her emotions. This was not the end. Would it ever end, he wondered.

"Meet you at the office later?" she said in her cheerleader fashion as she jauntily headed down the hall and out the front door.

"You got it," he said and poured himself another cup of coffee. Maybe this one he'd be able to stomach.

Entirely engulfed in her own pain and bitterness, Jill hadn't heard his last conciliatory comment. *Run. If I just run, this will all go away.* She hit the pavement hard and didn't slow down or stop until the burning in her lungs and calves distracted her from the grief-laden heartache.

Chapter Three:
Gail

A sharp, staccato voice billeted from the back door, "Pauly! Brian! Get in this house now before I kick your *#@*@!"

"Mom take it easy on them. They're just kids."

"Kids my *#@*@. They're in school now. They oughta know how to follow rules."

"Mom please don't use such harsh language...The kids..."

"*#@*@ if your daddy was alive, you wouldn't be giving me any lip."

"Mom when daddy was alive he was either raging drunk, hitting anyone in his path, or out trying to get drunk. Come on; help me make a salad. Relax. Leave the kid raising to me. After all, they are mine." Gail looked up to see that John had come home. She wondered how much he had heard. When he rolled his eyes in sympathy, Gail felt lighter. Thank God he didn't have to work late. The evening would move along nicely with him home. Her mother was always more subdued, putting on her best, when John was around.

"Hi sweetheart." He gave her a peck on her forehead. As if just noticing Gail's mother, he said, "Mildred, how is my favorite mother-in-law doing today?"

She blushed like a teenage with a crush and twittered, "Peachy John...just peachy."

Gail wanted to vomit at how phony her mother could be. But why waste the energy! Tomorrow morning John would be taking her mother to the airport on his way to the office. *"Will miracles never cease?"* she said to herself and smiled. John caught her smile, bent close to her ear and, reading her thoughts said, "Just 16 hours to go. Hang in there, you're doing great."

Piqued that someone was getting more attention than herself, Mildred interrupted, "Oh John you didn't say anything about my new hairdo?" She proceeded to brush a non-existent strand of hair from her temple, while batting her false lashes at him.

"My God," Gail thought, *"she's actually flirting with my husband...and right in front of me! If she puckers her lips I will puke."*

John graciously played along, as if overtaken by her beauty, very much aware that Mildred had very few redeeming qualities inside or out, "I believe you look ten years younger, Mildred."

Gail was thankful that John didn't take everything her mother did as seriously as she took it. Gail knew, when it came to her mother's visits, by the end of it, all her buttons would be pushed. This year was no different. Sixteen hours and counting, then mom would be on her way, the kids would be off to school and Gail would have a few hours all to herself.

Now if, between she and John, they could just keep mom from tearing down the kids, no more damage would be done to their tender hearts. Mildred was the unsurpassed queen of the personal dig, her aim was precise, her timing perfect and her choice of words – always crude – could pierce a stone and draw blood. The two older kids, Patrick, a quiet but undaunted thirteen-year-old, and Mandi, who had turned sweet sixteen last Thanksgiving, had learned how to deal with their grandmother. But Gail's sweet, innocent twin six-year-olds didn't stand a chance alone with their grandmother. Gail and John were diligent to shield the boys continuously. But, it was Mildred's nature to keep trying, maneuvering for a shot at them. It was like she hated children. Which, to hear her tell it, was quite the opposite.

Okay Gail, chill. You did your daughterly duty for the year. The week's almost over. The boys came through it unscathed. And admit it, it's been a kick to watch John lovingly keep mom under control. Gail wondered if any part of her life, going to church, the children praying at mealtime and before bed, the gentle loving manner John had with the kids even though the two older ones weren't his own, if any of that spoke to her mom, made an impression at all. She questioned whether her mother had a spiritual side or ever gave thought to God, the meaning of life or what happens when you die.

If anyone needed Jesus, her mother surely did. And to think, Gail would have been worse off than her mother was today if it weren't for Christ. Silently she lifted her mother up to the Lord, *"Oh Father, you know my heart was hardened but you kept chipping away at it until I saw you and your love for me. Please don't give up on mom. She needs you too. Chip past that crusty exterior, there's got to be a soul inside her somewhere. Please find it Lord. Thank you."*

Finally, morning arrived. Breakfast was hectic; Mandi's favorite blouse wasn't ironed; Brian spilled juice on his homework – Gail chuckled thinking of the teacher's reaction. Pauly and Patrick fought over who got to sit on the one empty counter stool. And Mildred just realized luggage didn't pack itself. John's calm stroll into the kitchen seemed to settle everyone down. Moments later the kids scattered in different directions to catch the bus or hook up with friends for the walk to school. Well, everyone except for Mandi, still in her room primping, who was their never-on-time child.

Mildred was in the guestroom, which would transform back into Patrick's room, grumbling over how her clothes had expanded and no longer fit in the two large suitcases. With the strength of someone minutes from freedom, Gail stuffed the last of her mom's belongings into the bulging baggage and stealthily shut both triumphantly saying, "You're ready Mom. Nothing to it!'

Mildred, hating to be outdone, recanted, "Glad to get rid of me I bet, so you can spoil those brats of yours."

Gail was not going to be bated. Although her eyes couldn't contain her anger, she smiled sweetly, turned and headed back to the kitchen reminding herself, *"Just 10 minutes and the day is mine...all mine!!"*

Mandi even though late, lingered at the car to say good bye to grandma who had suddenly metamorphosed into Mandi's dearest living relative. John had just given Gail his customary I'm-leaving-for-work smooch when Mildred, wanting to refocus the spotlight onto herself, interrupted, "Oh come on you two. Don't you get enough at night. Give it a rest. Gail, you never change. You'd think you invented sex the way you buzz around John. With eight pregnancies, your first at sixteen, I know you haven't stopped screwing since you learned what your..."

Gail quickly turned from John's embrace and cut her mother off, "Mom please!!!"

Mildred looked wounded, then with an innocent, what-did-I-say voice changed the subject, "John, dear, help me put this treasured picture Brian made me in a place where it won't get damaged."

"I'd like to damage you, mother. Stuff you in the trunk and run the

27

car into the black depths of the river. You vicious, spiteful..." Gail's thought's were interrupted by Mandi, "Mom...Mom you okay?" she said softly. When she got Gail's attention and saw color come back into her mother's face, she knew the crisis had passed, "Mom can I bum a few bucks for lunch? I didn't have time to make mine."

"Famous last words," Gail said, with a conspiring smile as she dug into her pocket for a few dollars. "Here you go, Mand, now get moving."

John closed Mildred's door, lovingly squeezed Gail's hand then went around to the driver's side and they were off to the airport. Gail wandered back into the house wondering how much John had caught in her mother's last remark. All too often, with a bustling household, John half-listened to what was being said. Gail prayed that was the case this morning.

The full brunt of having had her mother as a houseguest for far too many days hit Gail as she entered the kitchen and saw the remnants of chaos from the morning. She refilled her coffee cup and went to hide in her favorite overstuffed armchair which in the evenings she silently acquiesced to John.

John...dear John. He didn't know all there was to know about her past. It wasn't that she had tried to hide it from him, well, maybe to some degree. It was, well, it was in the past. When she met John and their relationship clicked, she didn't want her past to overshadow their future. Yet, it nagged at her that there was this vast wasteland that held onto her heart, a part of herself she had never shared and therefore could not share with John. There had been one time when the topic of abortion came up that Gail shared, briefly, about her first abortion. John had been understanding and said all the right things. But, yet, Gail could not bring herself to tell-all.

* * *

It was late, really late. Gail was counting on her father being passed out in front of the TV, which would allow her to sneak down the hall and get to her bedroom. The next morning he wouldn't admit to being soused by asking what time Gail had come home.

Gail knew if she didn't make curfew, she had to stay out even later hoping that her father would be drunk and dead to the world. For a fifteen-year-old this would seem to be a great advantage. Gail, for all intents, really didn't have a curfew. Unfortunately her friends did, which meant she had to hang out alone, usually in the nearby schoolyard twirling on a swing, passing time. That's where she had met Rick. He was seventeen with, pretty much, no place to call home. His mom had died when he was fourteen and his dad had remarried a year later.

Rick grew up fast; grew up as in "men don't cry." "Come on kid you've got your whole life ahead of you." "Meet Patsy and her two darling daughters, we're getting married." Suddenly Rick was noticed less than a fly on the wall. The darling daughters got his bedroom, "You're old enough to have more privacy." Which equated to a makeshift bedroom down in the basement by the furnace. "It'll keep you warm this winter."

It astounded Rick that adults could smile and lie at the same time. Why don't they just say what they really mean, *"You're in the way Rick. I have a new wife, a new family, so be a good kid and disappear."* Rick tested his invisibility by skipping school – no reaction; by letting his grades drop – no reaction; by getting expelled – still no reaction; then by finally missing family gatherings – no reaction, no questions, no nothing, He no longer existed, until he met Gail.

At first he saw her as a kid, not even sixteen, but she'd been through some stuff. She knew how he felt. They would twirl on the swings together talking for hours. He felt like her big brother. Sometimes he thought he could be a big brother to Patsy's two darling daughters, but Patsy was right there scowling like Rick might steal their innocence. Gail was his family. They laughed, wrestled, argued and even cried together. The crying part changed things between them, though.

It was his tears that flowed first on Mother's day when his dad gave Patsy the delicate crystal vase his mom had always pointed out in the gift store whenever Rick was with her when she was shopping for a present. "Look at this Ricky..." she would say drawing his attention through numerous displays of fine china; displays he was afraid to be around because he was in that awkward surge of adolescence and feared he might easily send a fragile piece of glassware crashing into bits as he lumbered past. "See Ricky, this one is my favorite. I love the lacy delicate etching that gently climbs up to just below the lip of the vase. One day your dad will see this and know how much I would cherish it. We have the same taste. Just add a little extra money and one day," she would say dreamily.

The house was empty when he walked in just before dark on that mother's day. The last rays of sun shone through the picture window catching the cut glass and throwing reflections brilliantly into his eyes. Walking toward the mantle to see the object that created such a spectacular fragmentation of light, he halted halfway across the room as if the light itself pierced his heart. The vase, his mother's long awaited, never-received gift, holding one single red rose was on the mantle surrounded by two handmade cards from the girls: and a card from his dad. Stunned, Rick walked over, lifted up the handmade cards trying to feel something, anything. Then he forced himself to read the eloquent words of love on the remaining card from his Dad. Inside the bold stroke of his father's pen hurt just as much as the words proclaiming undying love, "My dearest Patsy, I saw this vase and knew it was you, a reflection of my love for you."

Rick forgot that "men don't cry."

He didn't remember getting to the schoolyard. He just remembered being there, with Gail rocking him and murmuring soothing words as he emptied the river of tears held in for far too many years. After his tears, a desolate chasm remained. Life had taken everything Rick had. A deep inner need craved acknowledgment that he even existed. Rick, wanting to feel that life still had meaning, held onto Gail, breathing in her scent, taking on the beat of her heart as if willing it to make his own heart beat again. He lost himself in the warmth of her body; an assurance of life.

She didn't stop him when his starved soul sought solace through touch. She sensed his desperate hunger to feel alive and denied him nothing. Gail gave herself over to him without hesitation. She gave her life to him, as she would have for any friend in such pain. The fact that her giving included sex had no distinction. In her heart she knew you did not draw lines when it came to a friend's tormented anguish.

The bond forged in those early morning hours became the mainstay for two young adults lost in a world that did not understand them or even recognize them. It was a world spinning out of control as they tried to etch out their own identity, their own lives. United as one, the task was made less fearsome, more attainable. No longer alone they stood as a breakwater that quelled the raging dysfunction of authority that continually swept over their lives. Now, at least, when they could come up for air, they could see the hope proffered by the blue skies above. They clung to each other and that hope.

Strange, they never verbalized this turn in their relationship as love. Maybe because too many words in life had held so little truth. They didn't talk of the future or dream dreams. Just having endured another day brought a sense of satisfaction, of mutual comfort. Yet, the roots of this unspoken love took hold and began to blossom in their lives. Rick began to care about his life, his future. He applied himself at school making sure he got there on time, with all his homework and assignments fully completed. When his teachers recognized his change in attitude they cheered him on, glad to see a once promising student rise up from the ashes.

Unfortunately, Rick's turn-around came a little too late to bring his GPA up to college entry standards. When college was eliminated as an option, Rick began to look into the military. The more he talked to recruiters the more he realized this could work out even better than college, since the military would help pay for his education later on.

Gail too began to bloom, taking effort to dress nicer, enjoying the pleased look when Rick saw her. Although school was not her favorite past-time, she put more effort into her classes and learned she had an aptitude for numbers, math. She used this ability to help Rick plan the financial aspects of his future in the military.

When she turned sixteen, her first job as a cashier quickly turned into lead evening cashier because her station always balanced to the penny. Gail used her knack for numbers to help fellow workers and found affirmation when long-time employees came to her for assistance.

She especially loved Sylvia, an older woman about her mother's age, but so unlike her mother. Sylvia was warm and caring. The qualities you would expect in a real mother. She always had an encouraging word for Gail and a light-hearted way of teasing her.

"Gail...There's a really handsome young man heading your way,

31

with a smile glowing on his face."

Gail would look up to see Rick walking towards them. It was wonderful the way Sylvia – everyone at work – was like family, and Rick was accepted as part of them. When Rick graduated, Sylvia even bought him a gift, an eel-skinned wallet. A few months later, when he headed off to boot camp, Sylvia was always by Gail's side with a tissue to catch Gail's tears. "I miss him so much Sylvia. Six weeks feels like forever!"

"I know honey. It is forever, almost. But you keep writing to him and in no time he'll be home. Imagine what it has to be like for him. He's not even around any friends. Give him my love in your next letter."

"I've got a letter right here. I send one every day. I don't want him to be lonely."

Every night Gail would twirl on her swing and relive the times they had shared on the playground. Then she would go home, close herself up in her room and write to Rick as if he were right there and they were talking. She knew Rick being gone must really be upsetting her, because every morning it was hard to get out of bed. She always felt sick. Then she threw up a few times. The only clue that this was more than loneliness was when she missed her period.

She felt so dumb thinking that nausea was a sign of a lonely heart. My God, she might be pregnant. But the panic was instantly replaced by awe. She might be carrying Rick's baby.

"Gail...Gail...!" Her mother was pounding on the bathroom door wondering, why is she even up this early. "What are you doing in there. Are you puking. You sound like your father after a binge. Have you been drinking?"

"No Ma, just something I ate. I'll be out in a sec."

That afternoon Gail took the city bus into town and went to the family planning clinic for a pregnancy test. Upon hearing it was positive, she did not go into shock like many of the other young women. She sat in the afterglow of knowing for sure that she and Rick had made a baby – their baby.

The counselor at the clinic started talking to Gail about abortion pointing out that Gail was so young...her whole life was still ahead of her. Gail was half listening, planning her life raising this baby with

Rick. "... And so let me schedule you for an abortion."

"What? A what?" Gail was abruptly brought out of her reverie.

"An abortion. I can schedule you for tomorrow. Oh wait, we're booked solid tomorrow, it will have to be the day after."

"I don't want an abortion! I want this baby," Gail protested.

"Well, dear, you sound so sure but you are only sixteen. Have you thought about that? And what about your parents and Dick's parents?"

"His name is Rick and he'll want this baby too. Who cares about our parents!" Gail said as she stormed out of the little room, through the waiting area and onto the sidewalk nearly colliding into an elderly man slowly making his way down the block.

"Oh, sorry." Gail said feebly but the man just regrouped and continued on his way.

Gail took a breath, headed toward the bus and began preparing the conversation in her head that she would have with her mother when she got home. Oh how she wished she could call Rick and talk to him first. Her only means of communication was by letter. He would be so happy to hear her news. But first she had to deal with her mother.

For Gail, pregnant at sixteen, there was no outpouring of panic, but rather an underlying sense of the next step, the only step; to protect their child within the womb of her devotion. Gail expected her mother to react. She could even hear the cussing and bellowing that would occur. But Gail was confident she could stand her ground. It would only be two and a half weeks until Rick graduated from boot camp and he could step in and help deal with her father.

What she didn't expect was her father to be home and fully enraged, the by-product of consuming a bottle of cheap whiskey and two six packs since being fired at noon. Once again the world raged, thrusting itself into the emotional sanctuary Gail had perfected. Still not having fully comprehended the severity of the situation, Gail blurted out her news, "Stop fighting. Listen, please. I'm having a baby."

Her father, fully taken over by his alcoholic demons, turned toward Gail and thundered with threats that teetered on the edge of violence needing a target... Rick. He'd exact payment in blood from that sniveling boy. Where was the low-life anyway, his muddled brain mused briefly, as he took a swing, barely missing Gail.

Meanwhile, Gail's mother quivered in fear. Spittle shot from her father's mouth as his verbal defilement expanded to include both women. Gail could sense by his lumbering demeanor that he had just about exhausted his fury. This would be the moment to quietly ease away from him.

Placing her arm around her mother's shoulder, she led her slowly out of the room, hearing her father stumble out the front door, probably headed to the local bar. There was nothing more to fear for now. Chet, the bartender, would escort her father home at closing time and plant him on the back stoop to sleep it off.

As Gail directed her mother to the couch murmuring soothing words her mother was ranting about how her dad had been fired and didn't need further pressures to deal with, like Gail letting herself get pregnant. Gail knew the routine. Her mother would regain a sense of control, belittle Gail for a few minutes, then turn mushy and apologize for the brutal actions of her father.

At first, this seemed like the worst possible time to have brought up Gail's pregnancy, but in fact, with her mother being defensive and trying to pretend they were a perfect family, this may work out for the best.

"Mom, I feel sorry for dad losing his job. I understand. I really do. Uh... but, I need your help too."

"Sure dearie...You know momma's always here for you."

Gail hated when her mother did the "aren't we a nice family" routine, but right now she needed the odds stacked in her favor. Her mother had this way of trying to contort her face into one that looked like she cared. But, it always looked more like a rubber Halloween mask made even more surreal by the unkempt hair sprouting from every part of her mother's scalp.

"I'm...Well, I..." This was harder than when she had rehearsed it on the way home. Finally Gail just spit out the words, "This baby...My pregnancy, I want it."

Her mother's rubber face of softness instantly hardened. In between the eruption of swear words, Gail, stunned, tried to calm her mother.

"This is a good thing mom. Rick loves me. He'll be happy. It'll be just fine."

"You saw your father. Out of work, hurting. This is too much for the poor man to bear. It's too much for him, too much. And me, what about me? While you two were out screwing around, did you ever think of me? All that I do to keep this family together? This will be the end of us."

Gail hadn't counted on her mother's innate sense of self-preservation. While Gail was wondering what her pregnancy had to do with her mother and father, after all it wasn't their baby, her mother turned even more vicious.

"Oh and do you think Mr. and Mrs. Uptown are gonna embrace the slut who got knocked up and will ruin their son's future? Get real, girlie."

"It's his step-mom..."

"I don't care who it is. You're the slut! Don't you think the whole town will soon be talking about your poor father losing his job? Now you get knocked up. What's that supposed to do for us?"

"Mom, I love Rick and he loves me!" she said as firmly as possible.

"Well, dearie if you do love him, do the right thing for everyone. End this pregnancy. It'll only destroy all of our lives...Including your precious Rick's. I mean really, do you want to hold him back just as he's getting going in life. He could be thrown out of the service, be brought up on statutory rape charges. Is that what you want for lover-boy's future?"

She would not have expected that her mother had the wits to manipulate events and subtlety plant fear for Rick's safety and his future within Gail's subconscious, but that night Gail laid awake rerunning her mother's harsh words. The grain of truth buried within all that her mother had said began to surface, "...It'll destroy all of our lives...Including your precious Rick's." She had been so wide-eyed happy about carrying Rick's baby she never thought about the reality of how this would effect Rick's life. Without a doubt, she knew Rick would do the right thing; be there for her. But now it was her turn to be there for him. Being there meant doing what was necessary *not* to ruin his chances in life.

By morning Gail was resigned to the real-life solution and had given up her pie-in-the-sky, little girl fantasy about having a baby. Her mother was already at the breakfast table, having been up early to drag her father into the bedroom, after finding him dead asleep on the back porch. Gail placed the business card from the family planning clinic right down in front of her mother. "Here, make the call."

Her mother, realizing that her father would not remember the previous evening's revelation and subsequent tirade, was pleased that Gail had agreed to get rid of the evidence and by doing so not add to the burdens fate had so cruelly bestowed upon her.

Gail poured herself a cup of coffee, her first, foregoing the childish glass of milk she drank every morning up until then. *"Welcome to the real world,"* she told herself as she silently sipped the bitter liquid. It tasted just like life.

Chapter Four:
Mandi

Mandi knew that her mom knew that she was always late. Rather than it becoming a source of irritation between them, her mom had made it their special inside witticism by lovingly chiding and teasing Mandi.

But the morning her grandmother left (*Thank God...Gee was it okay to thank God for something like that? It wasn't very loving. Well, neither was her grandmother who always seemed to enjoy hurting her mother. So, yes, thank God she was gone*)...but that morning Mandi had other reasons for delaying her trek to school. Mandi was a sophomore at Chapel Hill Academy. She loved her friends there and was grateful not to be in the overcrowded local public school Highland High School, except for Kip.

Kip was a junior at HHS. No, Kip was more than just a junior... He was the best-looking and the coolest guy Mandi had ever seen. In the words of Nicole, her best friend, "He's the man!" Up until Kip, Mandi barely noticed guys. Yet many were her friends, especially at youth group where she was always surrounded by guys; probably because she loved sports and could handle a basketball as well as any of the guys. They liked shooting hoops with her, treating her as both a sister and a competitor. They knew better than to give Mandi any leeway based on her gender. One friendly action on an opponent's part usually ended up equaling two points for Mandi's team!

The night Ryan brought Kip to youth group, three months earlier, Mandi was so captivated by Kip's presence that she tripped over her feet all evening on the court. Nicole made an excuse to pull her out of the game and save her reputation.

"Mandi, what has gotten into you? You were a total klutz out there." Then she caught Mandi's forlorn look.

"Kip? A new guy comes to youth group and you go ga-ga. He isn't even that cute."

"Nicole...Look again." Mandi had found her voice and was

becoming somewhat rational. "See how his hair falls over his left eye and that quick head move he does to flip it back in place. He's just adorable."

"Oh yeah...Hair in the eyes... Always tops on my stud list!" Nicole said jokingly, but she knew Mandi was serious. It was Nicole who was known to move from one *I'm-so-in-love* crush to another. Mandi never seemed to be stirred by guys. This was gonna be fun!

Just then the ball flew right past them. As it bounced off the wall behind them and rolled past Nicole, she stopped it with her foot and picked it up. Kip and Ryan, sweating and gasping for air, came over to retrieve it.

"Not so quick Ryan," Nicole said teasingly, "first let us welcome your friend."

"Huh? Oh, yeah... Kip this is Nicole and Mandi one of the best free throwers in the game."

"Well I wasn't worth much tonight," Mandi was able to choke out.

"You wouldn't know it by me. I saw how you handled the ball. Come on back in and help us out. We're down by four points," Kip said.

Mandi was just about to beg off when Kip did that flip-of-the-hair move. She could not resist his request.

That was three months ago and every week since Kip had come to youth group. He even listened to the topic Pastor Dale taught on and bowed his head when everyone prayed. Mandi knew he wasn't a Christian and that when she would be allowed to date (a thousand years from now) she would only be allowed to date Christians. But, up until now, she had never been attracted to any of the guys at church or school so that rule had never come face to face with reality.

Besides, there was nothing about the guys at school that attracted her. She had known most of them all her life. Even if she enjoyed them, had lots of laughs at youth group and retreats, they were so serious all the time...Too mature, careful to think before they acted. Or they were control freaks. Treating her as if girls were less and guys ruled! Kip was totally different, exciting but nice at the same time. He treated her like she was a princess. He never took her for granted.

Getting to see Kip "accidentally" created a predicament since they attended different schools. Mandi solved this problem by delaying her trek to school by 5 minutes. In doing so she passed HHS where Kip was usually hanging around the front steps waiting for the first warning bell to ring. If he saw her, which he usually did, he would call out her name and wave. What better way to start a day.

Mandi remembered how she tried to build up the courage to stop and chat with him but there were generally four or five other people she didn't know hangin' with him. Several didn't look too friendly. Then one day Kip broke away from the crowd to talk to her. He actually left HHS grounds and walked her to her campus.

"I think he runs with a rough crowd," Nicole, who also attended HHS, commented, "But I could be wrong. He seems nice and he's a friend of Ryan's. So what do I know?" She did not want to put a damper on her best friend's first crush. Nicole wondered if she acted as weird when she was hot for someone. This was totally entertaining watching Mandi get all bent out of shape.

Of course, each day Mandi delayed heading off to her school in order to have a few minutes with Kip she risked Mr. Stuart's wrath if she was late. The next time meant her parents would be contacted. But, Kip was worth it. Mandi was sure he liked her. He always requested her on his team and sat next to her during Bible study time. That's gotta mean something. Nicole, all encouragement when it came to love, had felt there was potential. Mandi hadn't put a lot of stock in Nicole's opinions concerning guys. As much as she loved Nicole and Nicole was, for sure, her best friend ever, Mandi knew Nicole didn't have an ounce of sense when it came to guys! But, Nicole had been right. A few months after Kip began coming to youth group, she and Kip were going together.

When Mandi was around Kip, or even thought about him, her heart vibrated like a fooze ball table awakening every inch of her being. This was love at its electrifying best. Yet, at times questions flooded Mandi with doubt.

What Mandi really wanted to do was talk to her mom. She knew the part about Kip not being a Christian would be sticky, but she and her mom could talk about anything...So why not this? Unfortunately, with grandma visiting and the house in an uproar, there never seemed to be a right moment to bring up the subject. Maybe now that grandma had left (thank God, again) she could sit down and talk to her mother.

Chapter Five:
Karen

Karen was mid-sized, middle aged and mid way between her desk and her office door when the phone rang at the Mid City Pregnancy Center. But those are about the only things in Karen's life that were midway. Everything else was overflowing.

She loved Jesus abundantly. She had boundless energy when doing God's work in her job as the director of a crisis pregnancy center. And she was turbo-charged with excitement planning the upcoming marriage of her daughter. But, let's get back to the phone.

"Good morning, Mid City Pregnancy Center. This is Karen, may I help you." Karen tried not to sound either too cheerful, in case the caller was facing the panic of a possible unplanned pregnancy, nor too business-like, in case the caller was young and easily intimidated. This always meant catching her breath and counting slowly (one...two...three...) to herself just before answering the phone, since everything else she did was done quickly.

"Do I need an appointment for a free pregnancy test?"

"It's always helpful. Would you like me to set you up with one?"

And so the day began. As Karen sorted through the mail and messages on her voice mail, she also fielded calls. This was her fourth year at the Center and she felt this year was looking hopeful. The recent volunteer training had yielded ten women who wanted to serve as peer-counselors assisting young women who come in for the free pregnancy tests and were facing a possible unplanned pregnancy. Ten...count 'em! That's the best class yet. And what a wonderful group of women. Karen stopped right in the middle of opening an envelop to reflect on how great her God was.

"Oh Father... thank you for how you provide. Thank you for burdening each of these women and drawing them to serve you here at the center. Thank you for your provision in every single aspect of the work we do here. I pray that this brings glory to your name."

She continued opening the mail, most of it represented the donations by individuals and local churches that kept the Center operating. Always in heartfelt awe at how people she didn't even know would monthly write out a check to the Center, Karen had vowed from day one to pray over every check that came into the office. That is what she was doing when Jill called.

(One... two...three...) "Hello, Mid City Pregnancy Center, this is Karen, may I help you?"

"Uh, hello. I, uh, have a question."

Karen both heard the hesitancy in the caller's voice and was also sensitive to the nudge of the Holy Spirit that this was not a pregnancy call. Forgetting the stack of unopened mail and the many messages that sat on Karen's list of people to call, Karen became focused solely on the timid voice reaching across the lines. Soothingly she tried to draw out the caller, "Yes...How can I help you?"

"Uh, someone spoke at my church a few months ago about a Bible study you have." She paused and Karen recognized the normal reluctance to say "the post-abortion Bible study." Just to say the word "abortion" was like shouting their guilt to the world. It's what kept far too many women captive in the emotional wasteland of their soul.

Karen murmured, "Uh hum..." letting the caller know she heard, but not wanting to jump in too soon, letting a bit of silence help prompt the caller to continue. She knew this was not an easy step for the caller but an important one.

"Uh... I would like to be part of it... the Bible study."

Although the caller hadn't said much, Karen knew it was time to give her a little breathing room. "My name is Karen, What is your first name?"

She remembered the first time she had asked a woman her name and perceived the terror in the silence that followed as the woman contemplated giving out her full name. From then on Karen began to clearly ask for only the woman's first name. She could get more details later on in the conversation when the woman became more comfortable and felt safe talking with Karen. But right now they were virtual strangers and even with a phone between them post-abortive women tended to be experiencing a great deal of emotional turmoil the first time they called out for help.

"Jill."

"Jill," Karen repeated with a tone of affirmation, "I'm glad you called. What church do you go to?"

"Central City Bible Fellowship"

"Oh, that's a good church. Well, Jill, let me start by asking a few questions. Is that okay?" Karen knew the last time anyone from the Center had spoken at CCBF was 6 months ago. Jill had been struggling to make this call for many months now.

"Okay..."

"I know this is difficult to talk about. I also know how much it took for you to call. I've been where you are Jill and let me assure you, God is walking right along side of you." Karen paused to allow Jill to turn her heart toward God. "Now... How long ago was your abortion?"

"About twenty-one years ago. I was...uh, eighteen."

"What are you struggling with the most about your abortion?" Karen had learned that most women are in pain, yet can't define how that affects their lives. She begins with this question to help move the caller into the emotional aspects surrounding her past abortion. Later on Karen will assist the caller in better identifying the symptoms of post-abortion syndrome that are present in her life and how those symptoms manifest themselves in hurtful patterns.

"Guilt...That's the biggest. I know God is punishing me for aborting. I cry all the time. I just celebrated my 20th anniversary a month ago... if you want to call it that. But it ended in tears."

Again, nudged by the Spirit, Karen asked, "Was your husband the father of this child?"

"Yes," Jill said meekly, feeling doubly exposed.

"Jill, let me first say that God is not punishing you. He loves you and wants to heal you from all the pain you have been suffering. I know that this is hard to grasp right now, but you have done the first most important thing by calling here today." Again, Karen paused to let God's truth find its way into Jill battered emotions. "Can I tell you a little bit about this Bible study and the gentle loving God you will meet when you participate?"

"Yes. I'd like that."

Karen smiled up toward Heaven, having discerned that God had just tenderly touched Jill's heart making her more open and receptive to the work of healing He wanted to do in her life. They talked for another 15 minutes. At the end of the conversation, Jill felt safe enough to give Karen her complete name, address and phone number to be contacted for the next Bible study. Karen made sure to bring some closure to the deeply hidden feelings that Jill had shared.

"Jill, we've just spent time digging into the past, feelings you've tried to keep stuffed down for many years. Be good to yourself this afternoon. These are real feelings but don't forget, even though it's been painful to talk about them, God is at work and He can bring restoration to your soul. Can I pray for you before we go?"

The conversation ended in prayer and Karen felt God had strengthened Jill for the days ahead. She spent a few minutes allowing God to refresh her after having shared Jill's anguish. Then she called Paula, a gal who had gone through the post-abortion Bible study several years ago and since then had helped lead groups with Karen.

"Hello," came the soft, kind voice of her friend.

"Paula...hi this is Karen. How are you?"

"Great. But the better question is how are *you*, mother of the bride to be!!!?"

"I have writer's cramp from addressing all the invitations! Oh but it is so much fun. This is the big wedding I never had and my little girl's wedding as well. Is it okay to live vicariously through your kid?"

"You bet. It's the best way to live. Of course, I have it easy... my kids aren't even close to the teen years. Ask me again in 10 years! So what's going on?"

"Well, I just got off the phone with another gal who wants to take the Bible study. That makes 6 women waiting. Did you have a chance to look over the intake forms I sent you on the other 5 gals? And how is Vince about you co-leading another Bible study?"

"You know I'd love to. As far as Vince goes, this is softball season and what with practices and games it seems like he's gone more than he's home."

"Is it getting to you?"

"You know me, I would love to have him here all the time. But I know how much he loves to play ball. Lucky for me it's seasonal. I'm just trying not to get uptight like I did last year."

"Well maybe his team won't keep winning and having to go on to play in other districts and states!"

"Now there's a prayer! But whether Vince is here to watch the kids or I get someone to come in, I can do it. When do you want to do this study, days or evenings?"

"It looks like Mondays would work best, as early as possible. I'm freshest in the morning. After the class it takes awhile for my brain to regroup and start functioning as director again."

"I know what you mean. I just do simple, non-taxing errands after a class. Not to mention refueling with a latte. I can do 9:30. Is that early enough?"

"That sounds good. Let's target ...two weeks from now. We'll run for ten weeks taking us to the end of June."

"I'll begin making the calls. Anything more I should know about these ladies?"

Karen and Paula chatted for a good half an hour as Karen discussed the main aspect of the conversations she had with the women interested in the Bible study and Paula made notes on the forms. Each knew how skittish most women were about publicly (even if in a small Bible study group) talking about their abortion. Paula wanted her calls, inviting the women to the study, to be bathed in prayer and exude hope and kindness.

Karen highlighted her most recent conversation, "Jill is the gal that just called. She's 39 and was a senior in high school when she aborted. She's married to the guy who was the father of her baby and they have not been able to conceive since that first pregnancy."

"Then she must feel like God is punishing her?" Paula added.

"Big time. Not only that, she's well-known in her church and they own a local business. So she's scared to death about people finding out about their secret."

"Whew. It must have taken a lot of courage for her to call," Paula observed.

"That's what I thought. But what she said was that it took a lot of pain. The pain was finally so unbearable she knew she had to do something. Boy did I feel her distress, even though I know, I've seen how God works and heals, this is scary. She also admitted to a drinking problem...another deep dark secret. That's how she numbs her pain."

"You know *I've* been there. But I know what you mean. It seems like so much needs to be done in order for any healing to occur. I get

44

nervous. We're not AA or anything. What if drinking becomes a problem? Well I guess we depend on miracles."

"Jill sure needs one." Karen didn't go any further, knowing that Paula was not asking a question, just venting her qualms. "Did you get a chance to look over Renee's file?"

"She's the career lady...a single mom, with a little boy?"

"That's her. What a great English accent. I enjoyed talking to her. She's really upbeat and high energy, but she did let down her guard a few times and I could hear the tears."

"Yes, here's her file. Let's see her abortion was nine years ago. Looks like she's still out trying to prove herself to the world."

The essence of Karen's discussion with Renee about a month ago was coming back to her, "It was something to hear her be both tough then sensitive. She felt she had handled her past abortion pretty well but something happened recently that brought is all boiling over and she can't stop the memories from flooding forward."

"Her '*dealt with it*' ends up equating to '*being very good at stuffing it*.' You and I both know how that just compounds the suffering. I'm glad she's ready to really deal with it. Is she a Christian? There's no church listed on her file."

"Uh...Did I scribble something on the bottom section under comments?"

"Just, 'childhood.'"

"That's right. Renee went to church as a child with an aunt or grandmother. But that all ended before her teen years."

"Does she know this is a Bible study?"

"Absolutely. I asked her if she had ever done a Bible study before. She hadn't. She did say she believes there is a God although she figures He's pretty upset with her about now. I explained that this was not a Bible study where God will be shaking His finger at her condemning her for what she did. Quite the opposite. She will come to know God in a more intimate way and learn how loving He is and how He wants the best for us. She said she'd give it a try."

"Wow... this will be something. Wait 'til she first connects with Jesus!"

"I know. I think this will be a good group of women."

"Now what about Kalli. She's only twenty-two and her abortion was

45

just a few years ago. Do you think she's ready to deal with this?"

"Ya know I am so used to women taking five...ten...fifteen years to be able to come forward and get help. After talking to Kalli, I was so thrilled with this younger generation. They are less inhibited about dealing with their stuff. They just lay it right out on the table and know in order to move ahead they can't stuff it. So, yes... I think she's ready. It'll be different because she is younger. But can you imagine how much more emotionally healthier she will be for facing this early on rather than all the devastation we see from years of suppressed sorrow, grief and guilt."

"When I remember holding all that pain in for eight years, it was such a heavy burden. You're right, it's good that she's facing it now rather than after five or ten years of berating herself.

"Of the other files I have here, two were clients in for a pregnancy test who both have an abortion in their past."

"Right...I never spoke to either of them. The notes are just what the volunteer wrote from information the gals shared while taking the pregnancy test. You'll be their first contact since then."

"The last person then, is Gail. She's early 40s, 4 kids and... Wait this says 4 abortions?"

The number got caught in Paula's throat. Karen remembered her similar reaction the day she had spoken with Gail. It wasn't a judgmental reaction. It was a sense of defeat. Karen had seen women fight back from the emotional desolation caused by one abortion. What must it feel like to be Gail, with four abortions?

"I had the same reaction. I don't know what to say, Paula. We have to remember that restoration is God's work. Our part is to stay in prayer for these women. Beyond that, you and I can't heal them."

"Man, a lady with 4 abortions and a closet alcoholic who can't have kids. That's a lot. I'm glad you're leading this with me."

"Paula, it is truly up to God and if those women will allow Him to work," Karen said both to reassure Paula and to remind herself. "We can only keep pointing them to Christ. We've seen what He can do. I'm ready to let Him work again, through this Bible study."

"Well...if you're ready, so am I."

"Good...Start making those calls and touch base with me in a few days to let me know how things are coming together."

"Sure thing."

"Well, I'd better get back to earning a living!"

"And I'd better get back to being a mom. We're headed off to the park to see a puppet show. Catch ya later."

Karen took a moment to re-file the information on the women who would be contacted about the upcoming study then went out to review the appointment book and to see how the rest of the day was shaping up.

Section Two:

Death

Chapter Six:
Wounds, Scars and Abscesses

Having spoken to most of the women who would be attending the group and having heard Paula's description of the others, Karen felt like she knew each one personally. Meeting them and putting a face to the person added another dimension to the relationship. Women and young girls come through the Center's door all day long. Some are scared they might be pregnant, some are gathering material for a school paper or presentation, and others are donors or potential volunteers. But those who are struggling from a past abortion have an awkward hesitancy that reminds Karen of a trapped animal ready to bolt and run. Even the few, who know how to face the public and can muster up a confident demeanor, are given away by their eyes: darting, frightened.

When Karen and Paula talked about being in prayer, it was for this reason; it was for that step through the Center's door that each woman must take on her own. Karen and Paula are well aware of the obstacles that will be thrown across their paths in trying to get to the Center...in taking that step to break out of their chains of bondage. Every time a Bible study is scheduled and for every week it is meeting, the Center's prayer calendar, sent out to the faithful prayer warriors, requests prayer for the women in the group and the topic they will be discussing.

In truth, then, even though each woman who walks through the door feels alone, she is not. God has brought this day into being and drawn her to this group. He is mightily at work and in the weeks ahead, each in their own timing, the women will see His hand clearly on their lives.

But before that, starting with this first gathering, Karen and Paula will see their walls, their defenses, their pain for which they have no words sufficient to describe. There will probably also come a day when Karen or Paula, or both, will wonder if this study will even help.

It was now twenty minutes before the class would start. Karen had finished setting up, making sure the lighting and seating was both comfortable and welcoming. She knew Paula would arrive shortly, which was good. They needed time for a word of prayer and Karen wanted to fill Paula in on a woman, Alice, who had called late Friday.

With Karen's prompting Alice had agreed to come to this Bible study rather than to wait several months before the next one started. Karen wouldn't have pushed her if she hadn't seen God already at work clearing a way for Alice to attend. Her husband, who couldn't fully understand why something in the past could continue to bother her, wanted Alice to get help... both out of love and frustration. With three active kids, this was the only day Alice didn't have "shuttling" obligations, or women's group, or aerobics. She had just finished a cooking class that had been held weekly on Mondays. Every aspect of Alice's life that required reorganizing to accommodate time for a Bible study was already in place. Alice only had to show up.

Karen was reflecting on her conversation with Alice when she heard the soft, sweet voice of her friend, "Anybody home?"

"I'm back here getting the coffee supplies," Karen responded as she heard Paula's footsteps making their way toward the kitchen.

They greeted each other with a hug and after the brief, *how-has-your-morning-been* interchange they focused on the work ahead.

Karen began, "I spoke to a gal last Friday that's going to join the group."

"Good, I talked to Kalli, today."

Karen sensed that Paula, who usually acquiesced to Karen's lead, must have a concern to have brought up Kalli before hearing Karen give the background on Alice. "You have some concerns about her?'

"She's pregnant and living with her boyfriend," Paula stated bluntly. Karen could hear the fundamentalist in Paula's tone. Karen all too readily heard similar voices from her first few years as a new believer attending Bible studies. If somebody was actively participating in sin, they were not welcome to the Bible studies. She remembered how stunned she was the first time a member of the congregation stood up at the pulpit to publicly confess their sin and asked God and their fellow believers to forgive them. Karen had felt mortified for that person. How cruel, demeaning... how harsh. Was this really necessary?

As she had grown in her faith, Karen began to grasp the power of confession, but the confession between herself and her Lord, or the confession to a friend. Although she still squirmed at the thought of public confession, she had come to understand that as a body of believers everyone was family.

What public confession to your family was meant to do was release the offending person completely from the bondage of sin since the bondage was perpetuated by the need to hide it from others. It also was a reminder to the fellowship of believers that we all have sinned and come short of the glory of God. We are truly redeemed and can repent and be restored. That restoration is made even fuller when done publicly because afterwards the family of believers can rally around with support and encouragement for the cleansed brother or sister. Even understanding all of that, Karen shuddered anytime someone came forward.

Actually, Karen didn't come across that in the church she attended now. Several years ago – gosh, it was seven years ago – how time flies, her husband had been promoted and the family had moved closer to his office to reduce the drive time since his new responsibilities meant later hours. After two months of settling in, unpacking and finally finding all her kitchen utensils, Karen yearned to get connected with a church. They had visited three or four churches, each at least three times and Karen was feeling anxious. The unmet need to connect was disquieting to her spirit. The first time they visited Christ Our Savior Church the entire family left knowing they had found their new church home.

Funny, it was so different from the church they had previously attended, which had been more fundamental, even being somewhat pedantic at times. But it was that church which Karen credits with such tremendous Biblical teaching and rich fellowship that she established a solid understanding of her Savior and God's truths as laid forth in His word. She would not trade those years for anything.

Yet their new church, Christ Our Savior, was almost at the opposite end of the spectrum. Not fully charismatic, but there was a sense of being led by the Spirit that felt right. Karen admonished herself not to base her judgment on feelings. Yet, on the other hand, she trusted God's leading. Her first year at Christ Our Savior was spent always keeping vigil on what was said, taught and exhibited to assure herself that this was truly a Christ-centered body.

Beyond being very mature about choosing a new church, there was one aspect that had convinced the entire family that this was the church for them. The one aspect, not just heard in words but seen in the actions of its members, was their heart to reach out to the community. Karen had heard many churches talk about outreach then watched as everything they did was within the safety of the church walls.

Internally, Karen would scream...*"What is everyone so afraid of!!!"* Then she would try to balance out her piqued feelings by reminding herself that not everyone is called or suited for outreach work. Of course, then she'd counter that rationale with the great commission, God's call to go out to those in need of the saving knowledge of Christ.

It was an internal debate that Karen finally let go of, knowing she was only accountable for herself and what God asked of her. That's how she had ended up at the pregnancy center, first to volunteer, then later to become its director. She heard God's voice and followed. *"Obviously, God was saying something different to other people. No, stop,"* she would remind herself, before the cycle began again.

She looked at Paula knowing that Paula's church was more conservative than her own. That in the structure of Paula's church, Kalli would be admonished to end her live-in situation before being permitted to attend a Bible study. Sure, they would be there to help her accomplish that goal, but her lifestyle definitely would be a factor if Kalli wanted to continue fellowship within Paula's church.

Karen believed that turning from sin and giving over to God your behavior was essential. But something inside of her told her not to move too quickly to draw a line and make Kalli step over it. "Are you wondering if we should talk to Kalli and ask her to leave her boyfriend before she can join the class?"

Paula nodded yes while her eyes bespoke disappointment at possibly having to turn Kalli away.

Karen quietly lifted her heart to the Lord, not knowing if what she was about to suggest was His will. "Let's see what happens today, then decide what we should do about Kalli's live-in situation."

Paula, whose heart was torn between wanting to give Kalli the chance to heal and the teachings of her church, was relieved with Karen's suggestions. "Are you sure you're okay with Kalli being in the class...I mean, if you want me to talk to her I will." Paula was ready to do what Karen wanted, but needed a bit more reassurance.

As they walked to the room set aside for the Bible study, Karen placed the last of the coffee paraphernalia on the serving table and said, "It's okay, we'll wait and see what God is up to. Before everyone starts arriving I want to fill you in on this last gal, Alice...then spend a few minutes in prayer."

Paula chose a seat, sat down and waited for Karen to continue. Karen chose a seat separated from Paula, so as not to give the feeling of a classroom and to allow them to have a more natural view of the women participating. This let them observe facial expressions and reaction without making the women feel like they were being studied.

"Alice is in her mid 30s. She has three kids. One of them, her daughter, is on the brink of womanhood and displaying actions that remind Alice of her teen years, when, during a time of rebellion, she became pregnant and had an abortion. Her husband, they've been married fourteen years, sounds like a wonderful, loving husband but he just can't understand why her abortion, which is in the past just can't stay in the past. I explained to Alice how men and women reacted differently to problems. How we, as women, tend to not let go or compartmentalize past experience?'

"Will she be able to explain that to her husband?"

"Yes. And I gave her suggestions on how she can communicate more about the class to her husband. I get the feeling she has come close to seeking help in the past but pulled back using his "keep it in the past" philosophy as her rationale."

"So you think she'll come?"

"You know, when I was talking to her it became very clear that God was definitely prompting her, so I was a bit stronger in urging her to attend. At one point she started to tread backwards. That's when I listed straight out how I perceived God's hand was on her life, pushing her toward this class. She saw it too. But she's scared...really scared."

"What about her faith?"

"The perfect Christian woman. Heck, she was the perfect Christian daughter...until the pregnancy. But then submitted to perfection again by getting the abortion her parents requested. They all went back to their tidy lives..."

"Except for poor Alice..."

"Except for poor Alice. I bet her parents have struggled with their consciences over the years. What concerns me most is her daughter.

It's like Alice has laid the groundwork for history to repeat itself...even if just subconsciously. I don't think her fears at what she is seeing in her daughter are overrated. I also don't think she can avert a similar tragedy in her daughter's life until she faces and deals with her own stuff."

"I never thought about that. That would kill me. Did you tell her that?"

"I told her that as a mom and a wife she needs to set time aside for herself to get healing so that she can be a whole, healthy person for both herself and her family. She agreed, but still threw in the excuses of having to take care of them in all the ways moms do. Putting herself last. I even tried to give her a word picture comparing her aerobics, being physically healthy, and this Bible study...a workout towards emotional and spiritually health."

"So, what do you think?" Paula knew how many women came right to the brink of joining the class, some even coming to a class or two... only to pull back, never to be heard from again. They would begin dodging calls and not responding to notes of encouragement.

"I truly don't know. Let's pray before the women start arriving." Quieting their heart and minds, Karen and Paula held hands, bowed their heads and lifted their cares and concerns up to their Heavenly Father.

As the first woman entered, the bell, set off by the opening of the front door, alerted Paula and Karen. They went out to the waiting room to greet each person as they arrived and escort them back to the "living room" where the Bible study was held. There was no getting around how awkward the women would feel. Just like there would be no avoiding the personal pain each woman would have to experience as she journeyed toward wholeness. Paula and Karen accepted this, but nonetheless, the fear and hurt in the eyes of those they welcomed pierced their hearts.

Chapter Seven:
Where Do You Need Healing

Karen introduced herself and shared a little about her position as director of the center. She led the group in prayer, then slowly went through the guidelines for the class, explaining to them how to get the most from participating, "So to summarize the most important guidelines for this class, remember to keep what you hear here confidential. Feel free to share with your husband or a friend about your own story, but not about what others in the class share.

"Be good to yourselves. This has been a long time in coming and you will be taking the lid off the past and looking right at it. That means feeling the pain. Give yourself breathing room, especially right after class, to let what you will learn sink in. Don't over commit or get so busy after class that you stuff down what God is trying to show you.

"We want everyone to have a chance to share. Paula and I will help to assure that everything flows properly. You just have to be careful not to rescue and you will want to. You know how we, as women, do that. We want to comfort, make everything 'all better.' Unfortunately, with feelings that have been stuffed down, it doesn't get better until you walk through them. We want God to be the rescuer, the healer, which He will be. But, that means you each have to own your feelings. We won't jump in and rescue you."

Karen let that concept penetrate the group. She saw the reluctance to embrace this guideline which was the typical reaction. Many women were innately nurturing, relational. Part and parcel with that attribute was to rescue those in need. Even more unnerving, this guideline meant they had to walk through their pain. Karen and Paula knew that this walk was a critical one. These were the steps each woman would take and in doing so she would learn to cling desperately to Christ for His provision and healing.

"Don't rush the process and this *is* a process. Each one of you is at a different place. God is meeting you right where you are and will show you what you personally need to know to heal. It is individual and it takes time. God will never take you where you are not ready to go and He leads in a gentle loving manner. You don't have to force it, just don't be afraid to follow Him."

As heads nodded in understanding, Karen turned the next segment over to Paula.

Paula shared why she volunteered to help lead the class, empathized with them about the courage it took to come, then said, "To get us used to talking in a group, I want to ask each person to share how they feel about being here tonight."

"It's a bit disquieting but my intent is the long term gain," Renee started. "My abortion was years ago, but there've been residual effects. I don't like that...or having to be here. I did an article, a while ago, after observing a support group. The people undeniably benefitted. I suppose that experience makes it easier to attend this group." Renee's blend of trepidation along with the well-spoken confident demeanor of a professional woman created nods of agreement from the other women, but dead silence thereafter.

This was Paula's toughest role, allowing the silence. Oh how she wanted to jump in and fill that void with reassuring words. Make it easier, but she knew that was not the right response if she truly wanted to help these women. Her hand began to lightly tap her pen against her leg but she caught herself before the rhythm became intrusive.

Finally, Jill spoke, "I'm scared too, but I've kept too much of my life hidden for too long. I don't want the pain anymore."

"I guess I'm scared but not really," began Kalli, "Maybe 'cause I know I don't want to have this hangin' over me forever. I want to deal with this!" she ended almost boldly.

Gail's timid voice was barely audible, "I'm scared. I feel so ashamed...I don't know how I'm going to do this."

The only person who didn't speak was Alice. That was because Alice was not there. Karen was inaudibly praying for God to remove any barriers to Alice arriving at the Center. She prayed that by His strength Alice would walk through the door. She prayed against the prince of darkness and his schemes to hold people captive. She prayed and prayed and prayed some more, envisioning Alice driving...Alice's thoughts, her fears...praying that Alice's faith in God would overcome all that would be running through her mind to deter her.

She stopped praying when she heard Gail finish speaking. That was her cue to take over, "Talking in a group, sharing, will become easier with time. It's an important part of the healing process. So, now I want you to each share briefly about your abortion."

Fear registered on every woman's face. They knew it would come but had irrationally convinced themselves, "maybe not the first night." Gail and Renee's expressions went blank as fear shut down any further reactions. Jill's eyes welled up with tears and Kalli, who had just stated she wanted to deal with her abortion, turned to stone.

Gently, but factually – because it was going to need to happen – Karen continued, "Who would like to start?" After saying this both she and Paula did not look at the women, giving them time, unobserved, to wrestle through the onslaught of memories.

The silence lingered but not for very long. Karen was surprised to hear a voice to her left begin. It was Gail, whose timid voice resounded with a dose of fatalism.

"I had my first at sixteen." She wanted it said before giving in to her sense of doom. Her reoccurring nightmare flashed across her mind; alone, repelling down a mountain-face, her rope frayed, ready to give out. Her entire body, her life, would be shattered by the sheer reaction at what she had done. Avoiding eye contact, she continued her story.

"My mother played the biggest part in it. After the first abortion, well I guess I didn't expect how awful I would feel. I guess I convinced myself it was the best thing... or let my mother convince me. It wasn't. Nothing has ever hurt so badly in my whole life. It still hurts. After that, nothing mattered."

She paused to screw up her courage, knowing that her life was now destroyed. All the effort to hold herself together through these years was unraveling, like the frayed rope, as she spoke – confessed – to complete strangers the pitiful truth of who she really was. Not the funny, upbeat mother of four kids and a sundry of neighborhood kids, wife to a kind and loving man, daughter of a brutally cruel lunatic. She was more despicable than her mother's most cold-blooded verbal attacks. After all, Gail thought, she had not done verbal injustice to her children. She had physically ripped them from her womb, four of them.

"I had three other abortions after that." Losing all composure, Gail broke into wracking tears. Barely discernible over her sobs, she added,

"What kind of person am I?"

No one moved.

Nothing stirred.

All breathing stopped.

Silence.

Stillness other than Gail's quiet sobs.

No words of condemnation.

No gasps of disbelief.

No recriminating looks.

Or shakes of heads in disgust.

Gail's tears grew softer, then diminished. Her eyes glanced over her clenched fists, which held a wad of tissues to cover her shame. She found herself looking into the eyes of Jesus in the faces of women whom, moments ago, where strangers but now openly shared her pain. Their eyes wet with compassion, their heads nodding in agreement, bespeaking the collective destruction they were all living.

Gail had plummeted down the mountain-face knowing her life would be shattered. Instead her pain was shattered and peace flooded her soul. These would not be the last tears she cried, but these were the first tears she cried that were the tears of healing. One day she would cry tears of joy.

Renee, not fully comprehending what had transpired but moved powerfully just the same, began to share almost apologetically. "My life was so different. I had it all. I was studying abroad, in England. I had this sophisticated older man that I just adored. I was pretty street smart and knew how to take care of myself. You know birth control and the like. When I found out I was pregnant I was shocked. This wasn't in my grand plan, but a part of me was excited, which surprised me, since I was never really very maternal. The "excitement" lasted until Alex – that was the guy – until Alex nixed the whole idea. Of course it turned out the bum was married! I felt completely humiliated.

"Abortions have been legal in England longer than in the states. It was no big deal. Nobody protests, there's no controversy, no battles, none of what goes on here. So, I had an abortion and went on with my life. Eventually I returned home to the states.

"A few weeks ago I was working on a story and out of nowhere all these emotions..." Renee stopped, mid-sentence, remembering back, trying to find words to explain what had happened.

"I can't believe this...I'm a writer and I have no words." Heads nodded in agreement as Renee labored to express what had occurred, "It all came back, the abortion and all this pain. So, I'm here. I think I need to be here but I don't completely know why. I just know I'm not who I thought I was. I need to know who I am."

The room again became quiet. Jill opened up with, "I know why I'm here. I am so tired of the pain. I have a wonderful husband. I go to church, have a catering business, and I can't get pregnant."

Renee was confused and asked, "You mean you're trying not to get pregnant?"

"No. I mean I can't, I'm unable to. I'm barren."

A communal, sorrowful "oh no" escaped from the lips of the others in the room.

Jill went on, "I drink. Even my husband doesn't know how much. I drink to numb the pain. It doesn't help. I just want the pain to stop."

Bringing Jill back to the original question, Karen asked, "How old were you when you had your abortion?"

"Oh yeah... the abortion. We were high school seniors. It was my husband's but we weren't married then. He had a scholarship and...well... we had our futures. A friend of his told him about a clinic so we went there, together. They seemed so understanding and agreed it would be foolish not to have an abortion. They showed us a picture of this glob of tissue and said it was a simple procedure. Simple, sure. I bled for a week. I became anemic and fainted in school. We went back to the clinic. This time they weren't so friendly. They ushered me into a room, a doctor came in, asked a few questions, then did what felt like another abortion all over again. They sent me off with a ton of antibiotics and a womb that would never again hold a baby."

Kalli shifted uncomfortably as her hand went to her stomach gently rubbing her pregnant belly.

Gail had come in broken, ashamed and needy, thinking nothing could be worse than what she had endured. Jill's experience was worse. Gail was overwhelmed with thankfulness that she had her four children. How could you live with not being able to have children? Because her heart went out to Jill she was able to set aside her own pain and reach out to Jill. Lightly touching her hand she asked, "How does your husband deal with this?"

"He thinks it's his fault. Half the time I think it is too, and torture him. The other half of the time I just torture myself or drink. I think he stays with me because he feels obligated. Well and we don't believe in divorce. Our marriage is a joyless hell. I don't know why he puts up with me."

Karen and Paula observed the other women's reactions to Jill's description of her marriage. Relationships, whether with children, men or God often suffered after an abortion. Many women can no longer trust men, some go to the extreme of hating men while desperately needing them, moving from one unfulfilling relationship to the next. Others become over dependent, viewing the man in their life as flawless while they themselves are of little worth.

Noting the time, Karen glanced at Kalli, who was waiting for a chance to speak. Kalli felt she had to address a possible problem, "I'm pregnant."

Her statement was greeted by knowing smiles. Even Jill managed to nod, having already figured out that much by the way Kalli carried herself.

"Yeah, well I guess you knew. But..." Kalli looked at Jill, "is this gonna be hard for you...me being pregnant?"

"No, I'll be okay," Jill answered.

Karen listened for a martyr tone in Jill's voice but only heard resolve. "I want to be here. And I guess I am trusting that God brought us all together. Usually this is where I would leave. But, no, I'll be okay."

Kalli relaxed the hold on her stomach and began, "I feel maybe I shouldn't be here. All of you have gone through years of dealing with this. My abortion was just 3 years ago when I was a freshman at the U.

"Eric... that was my boyfriend at the time...was a jock. Gosh I was so in love with him. I mean being in college, away from home, on my own, new friends and then dating Eric. It was exactly what I thought college life would be.

"We got into going to parties after the games. I learned how to drink, tried smoking but couldn't handle it. I mean we weren't like the druggie-loser types. It was, like, just one big social thing. Making love was a natural part of it all. We used protection, condoms. So it wasn't like I was being irresponsible or anything.

"Just before spring break things started getting tense between us. I still don't know why. I had a ticket to go visit my dad and stepmom in California, at their expense, so I couldn't get out of it. Eric made such a big deal about it, like I was going off to this big beach party while he was stuck on campus, working. When I left, it was after a big argument.

"Two weeks later, when I got back, he was still angry and was doing really stupid; no rotten things. Saying he wanted to get together...even setting a time... then not showing. Or not calling for days. I was ready to say, 'forget it.' Maybe I even did a few times. Then I found out I was pregnant.

"Eric was right back at my side – to take me for the abortion. I mean I never got a thought in. From the minute I told him, he took over. I don't know, that's probably what I would have done anyway. And I guess it was easier letting him handle it all. I think a part of me figured we'd get back together. Ya know, after going through something like that together.

"But our relationship was history the minute he dropped me at my place. I mean he didn't even walk me into the apartment, make sure I was okay. I wasn't. It was so scary...well you guys know. I have three roommates but none of them were there when Eric dropped me off. In a way I was glad, but being all alone that was the worst. I just laid on my bed and cried until I cried myself to sleep.

"After that I wrote in my journal a lot. That was the one safe place I could say everything I was feeling. I wanted Eric back so bad. I would call or go by his place looking for him. Or be at the mall when he got off work. But he was so mean, wouldn't even talk to me. Things got bad. I guess for a long time my life never got better. I was just goin' to classes, goin' home for the summers, my mom lives in Minville, then coming back here.

"This year things are finally lookin' good. I chose my major, it took awhile, art history. Oh, and Sean...that's my boyfriend now. When he found out I was pregnant he didn't ditch me or even mention abortion."

Then proudly Kalli concluded, "I even became a Christian. You know saying the sinner's prayer and turning my life over to God. That's been the best. Sean and I pray together and go to church. Through

63

Sean's love I am learning about how much Jesus loves me. I used to hear that from kids on campus. You know, handing out little booklets and saying 'Jesus loves you.' I kinda always wanted that but felt it was for other people, people better than me. But, Jesus loves me. So does Sean and soon we'll have this baby to love."

Kalli finished with a smile having turned her thoughts to Sean and her pregnancy. Paula figured there'd be questions and she was nervous about how to deal with things if Kalli's living arrangements became part of the discussion. She was relieved that Karen was there, she'd have an answer. But nobody asked any questions.

"One of the things I've learned," Karen began, "is that, like in your situation Kalli, by getting help early on, you will prevent all the stuffed-down feelings from hurting you for many, many years. My age group, like the other gals here, spent so much time taking care of everyone else; our family, kids, husbands, whoever and we put ourselves last...or never. Which means we can carry around all that garbage for far too many years. You won't have to go through that if you let God truly work in your life as we go through these next weeks together."

This was a point Karen mentioned often when trying to give women the courage to take the class and during the first few gatherings. She had seen all too often, how women used the "taking care of others" as a reason to avoid taking care of themselves. Quite often, they didn't even know they were doing that. It was more of a habit, what life demanded of them. Karen felt it was important for them to see that so they would be more able to counter that reaction when it came up and it would come up for most of them.

She slowly looked to each of the other women, "But, do not be dismayed. Even after all these years and all your suffering God is ready to work in your lives as well. So let's get started." Karen looked to Paula to lead the next segment.

"Why don't you take your workbooks and turn to page four where there are a list of questions to help identify what areas of your life have been affected by your abortion." Paula gave everyone time to find their place then gave further instructions "We are going to give you time right now to go through the questions. Remember that much of your abortion experience has been stuffed down for years. The answers to the questions may not come quickly. Try not to answer with just a 'yes' or a 'no.' Let the questions settle in, think it over and see what God brings forward in showing where you need healing."

Paula saw their preference to write instead of talk as they pulled out pens from purses and backpacks, then started the lesson.

While Karen and Paula quietly left the room Renee was already struck by one of the first questions: *Do you find yourself struggling to turn off the feelings connected to your abortions(s)? Do you repeatedly tell yourself it's in the past, forget about it?*

Pen in hand she began to write "no" thinking that she was pretty open about her inner self, but a pervasive heavy feeling crept over her. She remembered a conversation several months ago with Felecia whose sister had had an abortion. Renee remembered the anxiety that she had felt back then. She had past it off as a reaction to Felecia being upset about her sister. Now Renee saw that Felecia's emotional reaction had triggered memories within herself and she had fought to shut them off by minimizing Felecia's reaction. Several other similar incidents also came back to her.

Whoa, she was good, really good, at keeping her emotions in check. But hey, look at the work she did, the ruthless business she was in. She had to know how to put emotions aside. Renee wrote "yes" in her book and thought, *"I sure learned my lessons well!"* She shuddered at the irony of this career woman, with it all together, who couldn't even get past the first few questions without finding a character flaw. This was going to be an interesting few weeks.

Gail was once again in tears as she answered yes with long flowing explanations to almost every question. She was torn between extreme depression, as she look at how messed up her life was from her abortions, and exhilaration at reading the questions knowing they represented the hurts of other women just like herself. She wasn't alone in this. Other women had screwed up their lives. Even Karen and Paula and God had healed them. Her heart ached to be healed, to be whole, to be fully alive.

Kalli was young and the experience of many years living under the shadow of her past wasn't part of her story. So the fact that she was easily going through the questions with minimal inner disruption didn't surprise her. Well, until she got to a question near the end about certain times of the year causing a reaction, the anniversary syndrome. This baby that she carried so joyously inside of her was due the same time her aborted baby would have been born.

"How could that be?" she thought, *"It wasn't like I planned this."* She began to remember the empty hollowness that she felt. Like having her womb in distress wanting to carry life. She knew that at certain times they had been careless about using protection. One lone teardrop found its way over her lower lid, gradually progressed, unhampered, down the side of her nose then dropped off onto the opened page.

Kalli stared down at the wet spot mesmerized by all that it symbolized; the slow deliberate disintegration of her young life, the empty well deplete of emotions yet desperately crying out...deep seated needs echoing up from the damp walls of her heart. She shuddered asking, *"God will I ever be warm? Can Sean's love warm me?"*

Feeling the damp walls of her heart crowding in on her again, the incessant nightmare flashed before her of her uncle touching her when she was a child... his sweaty body smashing onto hers... the putrid smell of his heaving breath.

More tears. But these were dry. They did not exit her eyes and run down her cheeks. They remained inside holding off the nightmare. Kalli shivered as she fought to regain composure. To run away from these haunting memories she went back to the first question and started making up answer, rewriting her history once again.

The more questions Jill answered the angrier she got. *Yes, there're reminders... everything reminds me of what I've done. Every time I get my period I am reminded! There aren't certain times of the year I get depressed. When am I NOT depressed!!!*

I resent my husband for being involved in the abortion. For not being man enough to let me have the baby, my only baby!! No need to rationalize being better off without a child...I am not.

The drugs, alcohol, suicide, unusual reactions, hiding the fact that I had an abortion, all of it is me. I deserved to stop growing emotionally. I deserve living in this hell of a life.

She looked up from her book, her face depicting the anger that raged within her. Right across from her was pregnant Kalli. Their eyes met, and Jill saw the pain of all the dry tears that never crossed Kalli's delicate face. For a fleeting moment Jill's anger abated. She was overcome by a tender desire to embrace Kalli, to comfort her, to rock her gently and whisper soothing words to her.

The door slowly opened. Karen and Paula made their way silently back to their chairs as the women looked up from their workbooks, glad for the distraction, except for Renee.

After the initial questions had revealed thoughts she had kept hidden even from herself, Renee was on a mission to ferret out any other mysteries surrounding her abortion. It became a challenge; she was not going to let this thing, this past, hold onto her any longer.

Without exception, the questions became scholarly promptings to examine her inner workings, dredging out from the dark corners of her subconscious the hideous skeletons that had rattled within her for a prolonged period. Without even knowing it she said, out loud, "I'm almost done. Just give me a minute."

Paula assured her and the others that there was no rush. When Renee had stopped writing and looked up from her book Paula led with, "I remember doing those questions and being amazed at how many parts of my life had been affected. For me, my hot and cold relationship with my husband really hit home. Would anyone like to start by sharing what struck you the most?"

Jill had already fallen back into the anger that defined her life and vented, "I'm angry. I can't believe how angry I am. Everyone of these damn questions made me even angrier. What do I do with all this anger?" she pleaded.

Paula, always acutely sensitive to others' emotions, was stunned and a bit frightened by the intensity emanating from Jill. Karen sat quietly, giving Paula time to regroup and respond.

"Women really struggle with how to be angry or show anger. You know how everyone tells us to smile or be sweet. Almost from our first days, we weren't allowed to show anger. But it is real." Paula saw the grimace she expected as the women recognized themselves. "There's a whole lesson on anger, it's one of the most helpful chapters. So until then...uh...um...well, smile," she said, which lightened the women's apprehensions.

Jill felt reassured and some relief at the thought that this could be an area where God would work. *What would it be like not to feel angry? What would she feel instead?* That was a bit unsettling. Jill had gotten so used to her anger, living with it, fighting with it, wearing it as her excuse for not responding to life. Who would she be if she wasn't "angry Jill," hurting, pitiful Jill? Well, she was ready to find out, mostly.

Renee jumped in to impart her latest self-discoveries. Renee's "observer" tone mixed with honest introspection was gratifying to Karen's soul, knowing God was at work.

"I can't wrap my mind around this," she said, thinking about the question that asked if she shut down any of her feelings connected with her abortion. "I always thought I was so honest with myself...analytical, not afraid to look inside. I sure missed it with my abortion. I had this isolated place inside of me...a vault, where I locked away anything that came close to upsetting my emotional constancy and compelling me look at what I had done. The question asked; *"Did the mention of abortion, like in movies, articles etc., affect you?"* "Nope! Never! Quicker than a bank president at 5 o'clock, I locked away any reaction in that vault of mine. It's difficult to fathom these behavior patterns within myself."

She wasn't done. With two fingers extended, she ran her hand down the page scanning for the question about trying to fill the loss by getting pregnant again.

"Then this replacement-baby concept. I was obsessed with getting pregnant again. Although I didn't search out a man to bed down for the sheer purpose of procreation. I had lots of lovers. I was always on the pill. But when I ended up pregnant, I was resolved to give birth, with no concern to reaction. That's my son Jay. He's my life."

Karen asked, "Then how did you answer number 12 about the bonding process, or lack of it, with your child?"

"Over bonded," Renee said transparently, "I spoil him. He's my world. I'm beginning to recognize how that's not fully to Jay's advantage. More exactly, this question about trying to make a success of my life to prove the abortion was worth it, the right choice.

"That's right on target. I can't believe how driven I have been all these years. Super career woman, super mom. All to prove, no, to make amends for the life I ended."

"At least you have a life," Kalli whispered. "I've been pretending for so long I don't know what having a life means."

Paula prompted Kalli to continue, "But Kalli you've chosen your major, your GPA is the best ever, you've got Sean. What do you mean?"

"Well, my life wasn't real good when I was growing up. I mean I love my mom...and I guess my dad, but I don't know him very well. No, that's not it. It was my uncle and he..." Kalli looked down. A tear made its way down her cheek. She caught it with the back of her hand.

Jill started to reach for the tissue box but remembered they weren't supposed to rescue. Oh, how she wanted to rescue this child. A phone rang in the distance, traffic noise filled the silence but no one stirred. Karen was silently praying. Paula was fighting to keep from speaking.

"I...he raped me."

Jill, instantly infuriated and ready to take action on Kalli's behalf, a legitimate outlet for her own anger, asked, "When?"

"When I was 8 or 9. He finally stopped when I was 12...right after I got my period. I think he went to my younger cousin." It was a matter-of-fact statement spoken without intonation. "I used to pretend I was somewhere else while it was happening. I guess I still do that." Coming back to the present Kalli became more animated.

"I've always had this dream about what love would be like or having a boyfriend. I never really knew Eric. He was just someone I made up in my imagination. So when he did real life things, like dump me, I was lost. I had no identity. I was bummed for awhile...until the next guy and the next. Now I have Sean and the baby that's coming. But I'm scared. What if this is all make believe again?"

Paula encouraged Kalli. "It sounds like what you want to ask God is for help in finding out who you really are. He will surely know, since He created you. Kalli, He made you unique...with gifts and talents...a personality...that only you have. And the best part is, there's a plan in all of this...His plan for your life. Keep praying for God to show you yourself and His plan."

It's a curious thing, that no matter how many times someone explains that a loving God has a plan, the effect seems to ripple throughout all that are within hearing range. Karen watched Gail and Jill, both fairly mature Christians, beam as this basic truth touched their hearts. She watched Renee's analytical mind dissect this concept and conclude that it was one worth serious consideration.

Kalli's taut features gave into it – to God's love – and her eyes sparkled with hope and expectation.

"I had my last abortion when I was 27," Gail, knowing she couldn't hold back what she had learned, began. "Mandi, she's my sixteen year old, was just a toddler. I guess I should have seen that my marriage was in trouble. Neither of us had any respect for life or each other. Booze, drugs, some really creepy friends. We worked on and off. Stiffed a few landlords on rent. I hate remembering all this.

"It wasn't a year later and I was pregnant, again. By then Richard, my husband then, was more or less gone, off on another get-rich-quick scheme. He'd crash at the apartment every few weeks or so. I didn't tell him I was pregnant until I was 13 weeks along; that way I knew I wouldn't be able to get an abortion, at least not where we lived.

"Yet, on some nights, I would lay in bed, high on pot, and focus all my thoughts on the life growing inside of me, willing myself to miscarry. What a contradiction. Part of me waited before I told my husband. The other part of me was wishing the baby would die.

"All my concentrated effort didn't work. I gave birth to Patrick, my healthiest child. He is the sweetest, kindest boy you could ever meet. Yet, I have to force myself to make sure I hug him!

"I'm the mother of the entire neighborhood. The home where all stray kids are welcome. Yet, I can't bond with my own child. Until today, I never realized that was because of my abortions."

It had been a long class. Karen knew how exhausting this kind of deep work could be. Not wanting to end with everyone's vulnerable insides exposed she began to lead the women back to the cross...to Jesus.

"On page eight there's a question. Why don't we all turn there." She paused, then went on, "In closing take a minute to answer the question that says; *I would like to seek God's healing for...*"

A few minutes later, as pens came to rest, Karen said, "Why don't we let the answer to this question be your closing prayer. We can go around the room with Paula starting the prayer. If you're not comfortable praying out loud, just do so silently. After a while I will close." She bowed her head and the others followed suit.

"Dear Father in Heaven," Paula intoned, "who looks down on us with love, who is always near at hand to hear us when we talk to you, hear us now Father. Fill us with a sense of your love and caring as we give up to you those areas of our life that have given us grievous pain for many years."

Renee, having only had brief exposure as a child to church and not having established a belief system of her own was intrigued by prayer, ready to give it a try: "God, I don't recall if I ever prayed to you before. Probably the most you've heard from me is when I swore. I apologize for those times. I think you know it wasn't personal. I acknowledge that something different occurred here today. Is that because of you, all that I learned about myself? I'm so used to being self-reliant, but I think, no, I know, I desire your intervention. This superwoman pretext no longer fits. I am pleased that you listen. I'll attempt to do this on a more recurrent basis...pray that is."

"Abba Father," Jill began, "I know I can call out to you and at the same time be filled with anger...even anger at you. Take this anger from me. I'm scared at what will be left. But I implore you to work in my life."

"Oh Jesus, mighty God, comforter...I exalt you." Gail's words poured out from her soul, "I lift your name above all names. Lift me Father, by the blood of Christ, your son, out of this pool of death that I created. I want to love Patrick as easily as I love all children. Your wisdom is infinite, your grace and mercy are abundant. Pour out to me...to each of us the healing touch we need."

"Thank you Jesus that you love me. Thank you for Sean and this baby. Help me to heal from the past so I can know who I really am."

Karen was blessed to hear everyone pray without hesitation. She knew that corporate prayer was music to the Lord and brought renewal and replenishment to the soul.

"Gracious Lord, we so humbly bow before you and say thank you, for listening, for caring, for showing us what we needed to see today. I thank you that your way is the path of righteousness and you will lead us there when we let you. Father, we give ourselves over to you and ask that you guide us. Be ever so close to each woman here as they prepare to leave. Bring them safely home. I know you will walk closely as they seek your illumination in the week ahead. Oh Father it has been a privilege to spend time together in your presence. We lift up our hearts and prayers to you in the name of your son Jesus. Amen."

"Amen."

As the women began putting things away and preparing to leave Karen gave a quick instruction, "For next week you will be working on the 'God' chapter. It's a long one, so we do it over two weeks. When you get to page twenty-six, question three, stop there. Remember start early and give yourself time for God to speak to you."

Paula added, "I'll be calling you, but if you want to talk just call Karen or I, you have our numbers. We're here for you."

The women walked toward the door, Paula stood watching them leave and Karen began to get things in order knowing that the day's volunteers would soon be arriving.

"It went well, don't you think?" she commented.

"Man, Jill's so angry, not that I blame her. But I didn't know what to say."

"I think what you said was just what she needed to hear."

"You could have said it better. You always seem to have the right words."

"I may have the right words, but you have the right voice. I'm more the teacher, you're the nurturer. It doesn't matter what you say, your gentle tone says so much more. Come on you know better than to compare our styles. We make a good team," Karen reassured Paula and gave her a hug. "Remember this is a lot for those women to face and we feel it too, so we have to keep leaning on Christ. He's who is at work here. It's my teaching, your kind tone and Christ. What more do we need?"

Paula smiled, accepting Karen's words of encouragement. "I've gotta pick up Holly from school. Can I call you later so we can review today?"

"Sounds good to me. Hey... don't let this get to you. God's at work, you know."

"You're right and yes, I know. Talk to ya later."

The journey had begun for four more women who were reaching for God's outstretched hand of healing.

Chapter Eight:
Karen

Just as the journey had begun for the women in the study, so too for Karen and Paula as they waited on the Lord for what He would do. How He would use them to help these women. Karen was drained but very pleased at how well everything had progressed. She began reviewing what had gone well. The group had meshed well. They had been open to what God was showing them. They seemed ready to be honest with themselves. Jill's hostility, lashing out at those in her life, even God, had shaken Karen who abhors violence. But in a few short weeks the chapter on anger would give Jill an arsenal of weapons to fight her angry demons.

Leading the class, seeing wounds laid bare before you, being susceptible to their hurts, took its toll. Paula's tendency was to be overtaken by a sense of inadequacy. On the other hand, Karen concentrated on the positive occurrences.

Deep down she recognized she could feel as inadequate as Paula did, she just fought it differently. To those around her, she came across as strong and self-assured. Not many people saw the times when the weight of all she saw (and felt) left her battered and bruised.

Was it just yesterday, Sunday, after church that Lisa, her daughter, the bride-to-be, and her fiancé left after cleaning up the lunch mess to buy more supplies for making wedding favors. Wes, her husband, had gone into his workshop to putter and she had been listening to music while she doled out birdseed onto mesh doilies then tied bows to secure them in preparation for Lisa's wedding. "One hundred twenty three..." she counted out loud to signify triumph over the mundane. "Some birdies are going to be happy little fellas..."

The next second she was crying. She was crying for Alice who was so skittish, who may not come to the class and if she didn't, what would happen to her daughter? Would she one day be a client at the pregnancy center facing an unplanned pregnancy? Would she, like her mother, have an abortion?

She was crying for the volunteer who had met with her first strongly abortion minded client. She knew the volunteer, moved by the young woman's plight, had gently given her the truth about what laid ahead if she chose abortion then had heard the hardened determination in the client's voice, or the resignation. The volunteer had seen the young woman hear the truth then dismiss it. She left in denial of the truth determined to reclaim her life by aborting her unborn child. The young woman was, temporarily, protected from the reality. But the volunteer knew... Karen knew...a precious little life was about to end and her mom's heart and soul would be shattered. Tears flowed.

Karen always remembered how hard it was to face that first hardened client who was set on aborting. She knew that there were no words to ease the turmoil, the questions, the self doubt that the volunteer would be thrown into for days, the sense that she was somehow responsible for that baby's life not being saved. The feeling of wanting to shake some sense into her client while hugging her and assuring her that having a baby was not the end of her life, but quite the contrary, holding a newborn was holding a piece of the future. Not an event to dread, but something to celebrate.

It was too much. There seemed to be more losses than victories, of late. At church she had held a tiny newborn, marveling at the sure grip of her delicate fingers when Karen had offered her pinkie. Too many babies are dying, too many lives are disintegrating, too many lies are penetrating fragile persons. When will the truth ever be heard?

In the background, Karen's CD player moved to the next Twila Paris song...her voice soothing Karen's sorrowful spirit... the words reminding her of how people see her... look to her for wisdom, guidance...

"Lately I've been winning battles left and right but even winners can get wounded in the fight. People say I'm amazing, strong beyond my years. But they don't seen inside of me, I'm hiding all my tears."

Karen's tears fell as she thought of bills sitting on her desk waiting for enough donations to cover paying them. She cried for the board of directors whose ranks were more depleted than usual, yet there was so much work to do.

Then her thoughts went to her friend Sandi, secretary of the board, who just lost her father. Being a shoulder for the volunteers, being able to encourage them and to help them see God at work was one of the aspects she loved about her job. She had the board to turn to for affirmation. Until now when she felt they had enough hardship of their own to carry.

"They don't know that I go running home when I fall down. They don't know who picks me up when no one else is around. I drop my sword and cry for a while... 'cause deep inside this armor the warrior is a child.

"Unafraid because His armor in the best, but even soldiers need a quiet place to rest. People say that I'm amazing, never face retreat. But they don't see the enemies that lay me at His feet."

It felt too big, too much, she couldn't do it anymore. Hadn't she done enough already?

"They don't know that I go running home when I fall down..."

As the chorus started to repeat, Karen knew exactly what she had to do. All the burden from these past few weeks held within her tears began to pour forth as prayers. She was running home to her Heavenly Father, giving Him all that weighted so heavily on her heart and mind.

Wes had taken a break from the shop and sought out Karen for her opinion on the color of stain he should use for the shelves he was making. The music led him to the den where he saw Karen, from the back, bent over what he thought was the birdseed project. Then he heard her exhale and shudder a faint lament.

Weary. She was weary. He had seen it on her face even while she praised God during worship that morning. He remembered the first time he had seen her depleted and in tears. His reaction had been to suggest that she step back from her work at the pregnancy center. She had agreed. In fact she was thankful that he had actually said the words she had wanted to say but was afraid to express.

How many others had she seen come, give their all, then leave. Some stayed a mere few months, others close to a year. Not too many made it beyond two years. The lost lives, the hurting teens, the broken families that were about to break further, the financial strain when donation were low... it was tough...really tough work. She agreed with Wes...being strong didn't hold up against tough...it was time to step back.

The next morning she had kissed Wes good-bye as he left for the office then went to the kitchen to share a bagel with Lisa. "Mom, ya know the paper I did for my speech class?"

"Yes about post abortion syndrome and how abortion doesn't help women it hurts them. Did you get the paper back yet?"

Lisa handed her mother the paper with a clear, bold red "A" across the top and a B+ just below it. "Right here. I did the persuasive speech last Friday... that's the B+. Wait 'til you read the prof's comments."

Once again Karen was astounded by how inadequate people's knowledge was when it came to abortion. They had ingested upward of 27 years of rhetoric, sound bites, but few had examined the issue beyond what was fed to them. The professor was yet another person who had lacked a comprehensive knowledge of abortion or its subsequent aftermath. From her comments Karen saw that a new awareness had been created as a result of the truth's she had been exposed to through Lisa's assignment. This woman's view of abortion had been transformed by Lisa's well-expressed and passionate conviction.

What Lisa had written had effected the teacher deeply. The veil of deception had been pulled back and the professor had seen beyond the marketing lies that are plastered within headlines whenever abortion is the current issue.

She smiled at her daughter, "You did good Leese."

"The grade is good... so are the prof's comments... but here's the best part." Lisa handed her mother a note scribbled on the torn-off corner of loose-leaf paper, with no signature. The note simply read, "My best friend is pregnant. I thought I should tell her to get an abortion. What you said today changed my mind. Thanks."

Lisa and Karen sat silently for a moment taking in all that a homework assignment, a talk in a speech class, could reap. How God uses our efforts. Too many times we don't see His handiwork. This morning they had the joy of seeing truth make a difference.

"One heart at a time, right mom?! Gotta go. I'm glad you're out there trying to stop abortions. " She threw her arms around her mom, gave her a peck on the check then was off, "Love ya mom."

"Love ya too Leese."

One person at a time. Funny how the world wants to conquer in big numbers like individuals don't exist. But God asks us to connect person to person, heart to heart, that His spirit might ignite the other person's spirit in hopes that a truth, His truth, would be heard.

Karen was again humbled at how God worked. How He still allowed human beings their own free will. How He never gave up on people. He kept trying. She knew He had the power to do the mass media blitz. But that wasn't His style. He was a personal God...using us to reach that one person He places in our path.

With a sense of reassurance Karen knew that He was not expecting her to resolve the entire abortion dilemma. He only asked that "today when you hear my voice, do not harden your heart, but listen." That's what drew her to the pregnancy center and it should be His voice, not her sense of failure or momentary weariness, that drew her elsewhere.

She reached Wes in his car on the cell phone to share what she was thinking. God had impressed the same conviction on her husband's heart. Once again, Karen and Wes marveled at how God worked.

"You can cry all you want Karen. You do hard work. Even the limited glimpse through God's eyes that you see is extremely painful. So cry anytime you need to... I'll hold you. But, until God tells you it's time to leave the pregnancy center, I won't suggest it. Deal?"

"Deal. Of course you know I *will* cry again."

"I know. I'm buying stock in a tissue company the minute I get to the office."

"You're a brilliant man and I love you!"

"Love you too. Bye babe."

"Bye."

Karen emerged from her reverie as Wes began to tenderly rub her shoulders. He felt her release the last sigh as she gave in to his ministrations. Twila Paris's song pointed her to the One who willingly took on her distresses and now her husband lovingly encouraged her with the touch of his strong hands. She was rebounding, ready to enjoy the rest of the day in preparation for the week ahead. A quiet peace had replaced the previous care-worn condition of her heart. "Thank you Lord," she whispered as she reached for Wes' hand.

Chapter Nine:
Mandi

It was almost two months since her grandmother had left. Mandi realized not only had she not found time to talk to her mother, but things with Kip had changed dramatically. For the past month and a half, Kip and Mandi were always together.

Mandi remembered back to the reactions. Nicole had been 100% for the relationship. But, surprisingly, Ryan was upset about it.

In Sunday school class, the one Mandi helped teach with Ryan's sister Jenni for the 3rd graders, Ryan hung around after dropping off Jenni.

"Uh Mand, can we talk?"

"What's up Ryan?" Just the night before, on the phone, Kip and Mandi had established their relationship as exclusive. So far, they didn't go out on dates, they just hung out at youth group and games together. But they had declared themselves a couple. Mandi had only told Nicole who oozed all kinds of exuberance over the phone. At this point, Mandi didn't think anyone else knew. Not that it mattered, she was just mystified when Ryan sounded so negative.

"Your being with Kip. I don't think he's right for you Mand."

Mandi, caught off guard, couldn't respond. Ryan continued, "You know I only invited him to youth group because he's struggling and I figured getting to know some good kids would help."

"Uh, his friends seem okay." Boy that was a feeble response, but she was still bewildered. Ryan always seemed so buddy-buddy with Kip.

"Yeah, sure they're okay if you like the smoking, chewing, partying types."

"Kip doesn't smoke. I mean, sure he's bummed about his parents splitting. But he isn't like the others."

"Mand...what are ya doing? He's not in your league."

Okay...that's it. He went too far. "What league is that Ryan? The goody-goody snooty Christian league!! Well if that's the league you think I'm in, I just quit! Thanks for your holier-than-thou opinion,

Ryan. I've gotta teach kids about the love of Jesus now!" she said as she turned abruptly to begin class.

By the end of Sunday school class Mandi was really confused. She had just taught a bunch of third graders about how Jesus ate with sinners because that was who needed a savior. We are all sinners saved by grace once we believe, by faith, in Christ as God's son who died on the cross for our sins.

Mandi believed in Jesus with all her heart. She knew she stumbled and sinned yet only had to ask God to forgive her and it was a done deal, wiped clean once more. She knew some of her friends gave lip service to all that living a life of faith meant, but to Mandi it was very real. She fully understood Jesus' example of living a pure and selfless life. She understood about not being yoked with an unbeliever.

But it wasn't like she and Kip were getting married or anything. And, even though she wasn't in this relationship to "save" Kip, if he saw Jesus in her and came to accept Him. Oh wouldn't that be wonderful. And isn't that just what Christ did...ate with sinners. How could God use her if she was afraid to step out beyond her safe little Christian world? Of course, some of her friends would criticize her. After all, people criticized Christ too. Not that she was saying she was Jesus.

She had really needed to talk to her mother that day had even skipped out of the youth rally to be home. Everyone except her mom would be out...her stepdad was doing a guy thing with the boys.

Mandi hitched a ride home with Ryan and Jenni. At least he wasn't giving her the cold shoulder, he was even pretty friendly. This was a good sign, wasn't it? Well no matter what, her mom would help. She felt buoyed by the thought of talking to her mother, uplifted, her worries already lighter.

Gail was in the kitchen cleaning up after the troops, savoring the quiet that was all her own. She sure needed it. Paula and Karen were right, this Bible study was going to be hard. The more she had to face her past the angrier she got. At first it was all at her mother. But these last few days she had to look straight in the mirror, straight at her own life.

She found herself pulling away from John and the kids. John thought she was upset because he was again working late. Gail was too preoccupied with her own self-condemnation to assure him it wasn't anything he did. Harshly, she thought to herself, "Why does he think everything is about him!"

The kids had given her a wide berth except for Mandi who was so busy with her own life it seemed she didn't even know her mother existed. She was at once relieved at not having to consider another person's claim on her life and irritated that Mandi could so abruptly eliminate Gail from her life.

The sound of the side door banging shut made Gail jump which unsettled all the pent up anger. She thought, "Who the *#*@*#*@ was invading her space?" She turned to see Mandi smiling like she hadn't a care in he world.

Mandi's smile, her elevated mood plummeted as she saw her mother's taut appearance. Yet there was something more that emanated from her mother's eyes, something she had only seen, when – that's it. She had seen it in her grandmother's eyes, loathing.

Mandi stepped back mumbling, "Uh...something wrong mom...are you okay?"

Gail, striving to regain composure but wanting more than anything to lash out, to purge this self-detestation by spewing it out, fighting to be able to consider the recipient, stared at the person standing before her. The torrential onslaught of her emotional hurricane was reduced to a severe storm as Gail unleashed a harsh deluge; "Can't I ever have a minute to myself! Doesn't anyone know I'm a person...I have needs. Why can't everyone just leave me alone?"

She threw the last bowl into the dishwasher, twisted the knob to "on," and grabbed her coffee not caring that most of it splashed along the counter, then headed to her room.

Mandi stood stunned. This was not her mother. What was going on? Did her mom and stepdad have a fight? No, they never fought. Something worse. What could be worse?

Gail spared Mandi from further concern by returning to the kitchen, "Sorry Mand...I'm having a really bad day. It's just me...I just need a little time to myself."

Gail gave Mandi a peck on her cheek, turned to head out of the kitchen, saw the coffee mess on the counter, reached for a paper towel and began to clean up after herself. Mandi took the dishrag from the sink and gently nudged her mom away from he counter "I'll get it mom...you go relax."

Returning to the present, Mandi thought, was that only six weeks ago, as she held the phone to her ear hearing it ring for the fourth time. Dang it, Nicole's answering machine would click in after the next ring, *"Be there Nicole...answer the phone,"* she said out loud, willing her friend into action.

"Hi," came her friend's voice.

"Nicole...where were you?"

"Oh, just putting the last coat of polish on my big toe. Purple midnight glitter! Really sexy. You ought to try it. Ya know, keep Kip wanting you!"

"Nicole...be serious."

"Why...you're serious enough for the both of us. How is the Kipster anyway? He sure was all over you last night."

"No he wasn't!" Mandi protested. But then she remembered that this was her best friend, the one she could tell anything to and she relented "Was it that obvious?"

"He's a goner. I mean he's got it bad for you, girl. Just one look and I can tell."

"And you're the expert...right?"

"You got it sister. So how'd the party end anyway? Poor me...I do a little favor...drive Staci home and I get stuck listening to her sad break up story. Did you know Angela went after Josh? That's what ticked Staci off the most, her closest friend honing in on her boyfriend. Low...really low. Hey...you're pretty quiet. Whatzup?"

"So you think it shows...I mean that Kip really likes me?"

"Sure...big time. But you know that. I mean he's the one who told you right? So why the...whoops, what happened last night?"

Mandi couldn't keep this in any longer. Her shame, her fears, her confusion were just too much. "We did it. I mean we didn't mean to...it just happened."

"Mandi...no! Say you didn't."

That wasn't the reaction Mandi expected from her worldly-wise, man crazy friend. She figured Nicole, of all people, would say it was about time. Instead this felt like a stab to the heart. Mandi defensively jabbed back, "Well, if you can...why can't I?"

"Me? No girl...you've got it all wrong. I never have. I mean I've done lots of stuff...maybe gone further than I should. But no way am I doing 'it.' Nope that's not my thing. Truth is...I want to save myself, you know for Mr. Right. I thought you did to. I mean listening to you always helped keep me from going all the way."

Now Mandi felt even worse, if that was possible. "Oh Nicole...you've got to believe me. I didn't want to..."

Nicole jumped in, "He forced you!"

"No...I mean he knew I never wanted to. Sure he pushed sometimes but I just held my ground. He would lighten up and we'd be okay. Well, until last night. I don't know what happened. I just gave in...I don't know, I think part of me wanted to. Oh this is the pits. Nicole, what should I do?"

"Oh Mand...you've gotta talk to him. Don't let him think this is the norm now. Is it?"

"NO! And we did talk...right after. I cried. He felt like a real jerk. He didn't want to bring me home 'til we were okay."

"Are you okay?"

"No. I'm worse. I'm everything I never wanted to be. I did what I never wanted to do. I feel so...so...I'll never be pure again...tainted. And scared. What if I'm pregnant?"

"Chill Mand, that's the least of your worries. You can't get pregnant the first time."

They talked late into the night. Nicole dispensing unfounded wisdom, Mandi soaked it in as if it were fact. She fed on the advice and affirmation generously given by her friend. In a way it was bittersweet. Sure, she told Nicole everything, but this was yet another time she had wished her mom had been more accessible. That's who she really wanted to talk to but her mom seemed so preoccupied lately. Mandi missed the times they shared and felt saddened by this quiet distance creeping in-between them.

Chapter Ten:
Gail

How long ago had it been since her mother had left? Three months. No, not quite. For a week after her mother left Gail tried to keep all those memories shut down, tried to not let the past once again wreak havoc in her life. Finally, she had told John everything.

She had been frightened believing John would leave her when he heard the entire truth. He knew about the one abortion just before they began dating. Now, finally, she had told him about the other three, in detail.

"John, I'm the mother of eight children."

"More like 15 with the way this neighborhood is growing. You're a natural...they all love you."

"No, John, that's not what I meant." She proceeded to tell him, calmly, not wanting to play on his emotions or make him feel sorry for her. When she was done they were still sitting together on the couch. He moved closer, lightly touched her knee and said, "That's a lot to take in Gail. Can you give me some time with this?"

She hadn't known what to expect but had prepared herself for the worst, that he would leave her and rightfully so. He had already far surpassed what a woman should expect from a man. He loved her two children as his own. He knew some of her past yet never threw it up in her face. And he tolerated her mother...no he kept Gail sane when she had to deal with her mother. But to count on his kind heartedness extending to encompass the decay in her soul the root of which was from taking the life of her own children, that was asking too much of any person. Especially a good, kind man like John. She could well imagine the disgust he felt toward her no matter how well he hid it.

Gail waited out the days throwing herself into her classes and work, taking comfort in the needs of others at the nursing home. John's actions toward her were consistently loving and true to his tender care of her and he did not punish her by making her wait long.

Holding her in his arms in bed he said, "Knowing how much you love children...how you never hesitate to give to others...how deeply you hurt when we hurt, I can't even begin to imagine how hard it has been for you to carry this around inside yourself for all these years, never telling anyone.

"Your relationship with your mother...the tension between you. It all makes much more sense now. But, Gail...I don't know how to make the pain go away. You shouldn't have to carry this around...to live with it eating away at you. You're too good a person. There has to be something we can do."

We. She had heard him say we. With that simple word, Gail's heavy heart lightened tremendously. John did not reject her. Instead he took on the yoke she had labored under year after year, always alone. *Could it give her the courage to seek help?*

"There's a support group I heard about. I even called a while back, but was too scared to do anything about it."

"I want you to do it Gail. If it'll make it easier, I'll go with you. Anything. You deserve to have a full life. I want you to have that. Do you want me to call?"

"Well...I think it's just for women."

"Women? Well I guess that makes sense. As long as it isn't all that feminist ranting."

"No...no John. In fact, it's a Bible study."

"Well there then. That's it...a Bible study. Yeah, that would be perfect. Are you sure I can't go with you? You know I would."

"I wish you could. I'd rather have you there with me. I need you."

"I'll be waiting right here for you," he said as he absent mindedly stroked the small of her back, feeling her relax and snuggle closer.

Gail had done it. She had finally made the call, gone to the class, poured out her guts then tried to remember everything the leaders had explained might happen as she dug into her past to allow God to heal her. This better be worth it, she mumbled to herself as she laid out her workbook and opened her Bible to the story of Abraham taking his son, Isaac, up to be sacrificed.

God as provider. Abraham had trusted God to the max. He had bound his son Isaac on the alter then took his knife to slay him. An angel of the Lord appeared and a ram was provided for the sacrifice. (Genesis 22)

Gail wished she could trust God that much. The next question asked how she had seen God provide in her life. The mental picture of that night with John holding her and responding to all she had told him immediately came to mind. Then the faces of her children...one by one...throughout their years...as infants, toddlers, laughing, mischievous...Mandi as young lady.

Gail's heart filled to overflowing. "Oh Father...you do provide. When the only thing I could do with my life was mess it up...you provided. You drew me to Jesus, your son...your sacrifice for my sins...you washed me cleaned, then you provided...John, the kids, nursing school, my job. Even this study. Thank you...thank you so much."

Gail spent another hour searching God's word as it pertained to knowing Him and dealing with her past. There wasn't a lot about the past, it was mostly about who God was. By the end she felt strengthened, nourished, replenished.

Putting her workbook and Bible away, Gail heard Mandi's bedroom door close. She hadn't spent any time with Mandi in quite awhile. She missed their talks. A flutter of guilt brushed against her heart but she pushed it aside not wanting anything to encroach upon her uplifted mood.

She straightened out the comforter on the bed, ran a brush through her hair, grabbed the basket of laundry from the bathroom and headed to load the washer. With that done, she headed to Mandi's room. She knew Mandi had put off doing a paper for school and would be scrambling to get it done. But a break for some girl talk wouldn't hurt. Gail knocked lightly then entered.

She found Mandi sprawled out on her bed, deep in conversation on the phone. When Mandi saw her mom, guilt flooded her face, then alarm. She was on the phone with Kip and he was going on about how their recent sexual playing wasn't the end of the world. In a rush of words he was saying they cared about each other...didn't she want him as much as he wanted her...it wasn't like they were kids...

"Uh, mom...uh hi...did you want something?" she said with her mouth still against the phone hoping Kip might hear her.

Kip didn't clue in, he was still talking. "...it's only natural...foreplay...you know getting to know each other." He expanded, "That's what people do when..."

She clamped her hand over the phone panicked that her mother had overheard Kip's passionate appeals.

Gail saw the culpable expression in Mandi's reaction and although she did not know what was amiss, she responded sharply, "Young lady, aren't you suppose to be working on an overdue paper? I think it's time you hung up that phone."

"Yes mom." Gail waited. Mandi waited. Kip was still talking unaware that he had lost his audience or truer still, had become part of a larger drama.

"Mom," Mandi whined as she looked toward the door. Gail got the hint.

"Okay...I'm leaving. But say good-bye and get back to work."

So much for girl talk. My daughter has time to turn her ear red pressing it against the phone, but she doesn't seem to have much time for me lately. It's probably Nicole...that girl can talk forever. Gail smiled at the thought of her daughter's best friend. Nicole can be a little ditsy at times, but she had a big heart.

She heard the thumping of the washing machine being off balance and ran to rescue her protesting appliance. "Just give me 6 more months..." she implored the metal cube, "...six more months that's all, then you can go to washing machine heaven." Heaven reminded her of God...the God who would provide. All was well in Gail's heart.

Chapter Eleven:
Kalli

Sitting in a remote corner of the campus leaning against one of the renown sculptures, which none of her friends could identify, Kalli was torn between writing in her journal or writing in the Bible study workbook all the thoughts that were swimming through her brain.

Kalli only came to know the Lord when she, wanting to keep Sean interested in her, had agreed to go to church with him. The church was not church as she had imagined. She actually liked it, becoming the impetus for them attending regularly and joining the college group. Jesus became real to her. A safe harbor, solid, never changing with absolutes that didn't spur her to rebel but filled her with a sense of protection. Someone was looking after her and it was Jesus.

Kalli began the lesson and learned that God sees. Sure she knew that. In fact at times that knowledge bothered her. She didn't like Him seeing her. But this was different. This was Hagar, the maidservant of Sarah and Abram. Because Sarah couldn't give Abram the son God had promised him, they had taken things into their own hands.

Sounds like what I would do, thought Kalli. So Hagar, at Sarah's urging, gets pregnant by Abram and Sarah becomes jealous and turns on Hagar treating her like dirt. *"Boy and I thought my life was a mess."*

Pregnant Hagar runs away and is totally alone having fled from the palace of a great man, wandering around with no where to go and no one to turn to. Then an angel of the Lord appeared to her.

Wow can you imagine that! Hagar is to name her son, Ishmael; "God has heard" and He is referred to as "the one who sees."

Kalli thought back to all those times she thought that she was totally alone. She wasn't. God could see and hear her. He sees her now and hears her when she calls out to Him.

There she sat, curled up as far away as possible from all the activity and motion on campus, hiding as it were, behind a granite piece of so-called art, and God sees her. She is never alone, never was, never will be.

Moving on to the next question Kalli read; At the time of your crisis pregnancy, what did God see?

It's all out in the open now, she thought, no need to hold back. Choosing her workbook over her journal the words surged from her pen.

Eric was so upset when I told him. He accused me of lying. Tried to say it was someone else's...all that blame. I couldn't tell my mom and stepdad. I guess I could have told my dad. But he would have done just what Eric did...throw money at the problem. Make it go away.

I almost told Rachel. I think she had an abortion. I don't know what I wanted...for her to talk me out of it or tell me it would be okay. I never did end up telling her. I felt so stupid getting pregnant.

God, the one who sees. Kalli felt His eyes on her. Not harsh or condemning but seeing her. God, the one who sees. She tried to go on to the next section but lost her concentration. Her mind kept envisioning God, the one who sees.

It became disconcerting. She slammed her book shut, shoved it into her backpack. Standing up she saw people across the commons at the student center. Deliberately she grabbed her backpack, put on her upbeat people face and taking long fast strides headed toward the activity. There would surely be someone she knew in the sea of people...she wanted to mingle, get a cup of java...she could finish the lesson later...much later.

God, the one who sees. See God, I'm just fine. I'm doing okay, happy, I can deal with it. Thanks though for seeing, but you can watch over someone else for awhile. I'm fine...just fine.

Kalli could fool those around her...even fool herself. But she sensed she wasn't fooling God although she wasn't ready to admit that just yet.

Chapter Twelve:
Jill

God who is there.

God who is there.

Jill must have read that heading several times before putting her book aside. It was meant to bring comfort. It brought her anger...and fear.

If you were there God...why didn't you stop me. Why did you let this happen to me? We were just kids...goods kids really. And you knew...YOU KNEW it was my only chance to have a baby. Now I have an empty womb, an empty marriage and a life full...FULL of your punishment.

She needed a drink. The pain was too much to endure. Everything up until now had been hard, but she had been okay. The worst it had gotten, right after the first class, she had gone for a 5 mile run. Afterwards she was fine. In fact, Russ had brought home 2 pizzas and a six pack. She ate a few slices of her favorite, chicken garlic pizza, had a few beers with him and then they watched *Law and Order*.

That evening had given her new confidence that she could do this Bible study, make it through and be whole...healed. She realized that she didn't have a drinking problem...she didn't *need* to drink. She could just enjoy a beer or two like anyone else. She only drank too much when the pain got to be all consuming. The Bible study would help solve that problem.

Maybe God was even waiting for her to be healed before he would let her get pregnant? Yeah, that would be just like God. If I prove I can do this Bible study, do all the forgiveness stuff...then he'll make me pregnant.

The pizza, beer and inflated confidence was a mere three days prior. As Jill thought back on that day the taste for a beer cried out greedily. *It's just a beer...not like hard liquor or anything.* She told herself as she headed toward the refrigerator in hopes that Russ hadn't finished off the six pack.

Lately, he had been keeping close tabs on her. Bringing home only enough of whatever, for the evening. One small bottle of wine for a special dinner rather than having several bottles in the pantry. Doling out liquor like it was priceless gold. *Man he pisses me off...I mean who is he anyway, my father!!! He drinks as much as me...but no, it's like I'm the one with the problem. He's Mr. Nice-guy. No problem for him. Sure!!*

The refrigerator was empty!

@#**@*#@**! Jill swore, then slammed her fist against the door of the refrigerator. She began to breathe heavily and was sweating as if she had just finished a run.

Well, God...since you're the God who is there...the least you could have done is have one piddly beer left for me.

She stood, gripping the refrigerator door's handle, staring into the beer-void cavern, cool air wafting up onto her face when she heard her doorbell ring.

Slamming the refrigerator door, which rattled the empty cookie jar on top, was the last expression of anger she allowed herself as she made her way to the front door. Jill was an expert, most of the time, when it came to regaining composure...or what appeared to be composure.

As she entered the front hall she was able, through the lace curtains, to make out the profile of a neighborhood friend she often jogged with. Sally was bobbing up and down, which told Jill she was out for a run and keeping pace as she waited for someone to answer the door.

"Sally...Hi. You lookin' for a running partner."

Wiping her brow, Sally gave Jill a warm smile, "Not just any partner...you! I need to be stretched. I've slacked off and you're the best at making me pick up the pace. Can you get away for a while?" Then Sally noticed the dampened hair framing Jill's face, "Oh, unless you just came back from a run?"

A sense of shame...of being caught...struck Jill. To hide any reaction she turned to the hall closet saying, "Let me throw on my runners and I'm ready. The question is...are you!!"

The course they ran was a combination of quiet side streets and trails that were once railroad tracks. There was a terrific straight-away that was perfect for warm up and then gave way to a gentle incline.

Once they reached the first trail marker both women knew the rest of the route was a formidable task albeit one they relished.

At first they chatted a bit, catching up on each other's lives since the last time they had jogged together. But, both women were comfortable with the companionship sans deeper conversation. Basically, it was pretty much impossible once they hit the first marker. Their rewards laid at the end of the route where, after the final leg through a dense wooded area, they exited at the base of Canyon River waterfall.

They both knew it awaited them...could hear the pounding water well before seeing the falls. But the glory was in having pushed their bodies beyond previous limits, feeling thoroughly drained yet fully invigorated, then coming out of the darken woods to the splendor...the magnificence...of the falls cascading with amazing strength right before them. The experience never became old, rather, every time Jill heard the sound of what lie ahead her heart leaped in anticipation. She was never disappointed.

This day was no different. The sound of her pounding heart gave way to the roar of the falls. Jill was overtaken by awe at the sight of rushing waters drenched in sunlight, sparkling with radiant beauty, and spring vibrantly in bloom all around her, all framed by a few old swaying willows. The chorus from a worship song she had sung last Sunday at church played in her head, "For He is good...For He is good...For He is good to me..."

Sweating, panting hard, but buoyed by the visual banquet before her, Jill stepped closer. The sun's reflection threaded through the liquid veil. Fluid jewels caught and cast sunbeams of profuse light. One gleaming gem burst forth, momentarily blinding Jill. In that moment her soul was wholly illuminated by a truth...

He made the blind to see. In her heart she was able to see. In her heart Jill saw God...who is there.

She took another step toward God and was washed in the misty spray of His presence, inhaled the rich, loamy texture of His love. God...who is here.

Chapter Thirteen:
Renee

"Okay young man, the video is just about over. Then it's time to set out your clothes for tomorrow," Renee said, lightly touching Jay's shoulder to assure that she had his attention. She didn't let him watch very much television and instead preferred videos she had reviewed. Even though she scrutinized what he did watch, Jay became transfixed, oblivious to the world around him when he sat in front of the television. Renee had seen many times when she had dropped a pot, banged into the coffee table or stepped on the cat's tail...all of which created loud, sudden noises yet Jay didn't flinch. His eyes (the window to his soul) remained glued to the 27" screen.

Just what was being absorbed into his soul as he was transported into the realm of unreality? Renee, with her hand resting on Jay's shoulder, stood and watched the video trying to see as a 5-year-old would see.

She was a big fan of Sesame Street. Bert and Ernie had an endearing place in her memory. One peek into Jay's bedroom revealed fuzzy red everywhere. He loved anything Elmo. Tonight the Count was teaching how to tell time. When she tucked him into bed later Renee would discuss what Jay had learned.

Of course the one thing you couldn't avoid when the TV was on, no matter how limited the time, were the commercials. It floored Renee that consumerism was propagated with such abject intensity to young children. They bombarded little malleable minds with raw greed dressed up to look "every day"...no dressed to the hilt while stating "you were less" if you didn't own such-and-such. Yes, that was the feeling. Like walking into an evening event wearing your most comfortable pair of jeans and favorite blouse only to have people in tuxedos and formal wear snub you as if you didn't measure up, you were unattractive, undesirable.

My God, Renee thought, it starts so young. Too many of today's grown ups were yesterday's believers in what commercials proclaimed.

In the end the person with the most toys wins. What a sad commentary. But sadder still were the number of people who bought into that, many of whom didn't even know they had been bought!

Renee caught herself beginning to tighten her grip on Jay's shoulder and wanting to yank the plug from the socket with visions of smashing the TV to pieces in protest of all things wrong with America that began in the bowels of free enterprise.

Wait a minute, she told herself, you make your living at a paper that depends on advertisers. Get a grip, she exhorted herself. There are responsible advertisers, not all TV is bad just like not all reporters are sensationalist.

The video's theme song began to play as the cast was saying good night to all their viewers...their special friends. She had released her grip on Jay and ran her fingers down his spine where he was ticklish while saying, "I'll run your bath water, Jay. By the time you're done setting out your clothes your bath will be ready."

"Can I have another snack, Mom?"

"Another snack!" Renee exclaimed in mock horror. "One more cookie and you won't fit into the tub."

Jay got up puffing out his stomach, scooping out his arms, trying to imitate the movements of a larger person. His skinny body gave him the appearance of a stick figure who only lost mass by having its arms and legs extended while looking malnourished with his belly protruding.

"On second thought...maybe you should have two cookies!!"

Jay's eyes lit up. He released his pose and ran to the kitchen to claim his reward before his mom could come to her senses. Two cookies...she never let him have two cookies. This was a good day!

Renee cherished the few hours of time that was all her own after Jay was sound asleep and before she began to fade. This evening she had made herself a decaf latte, recalling how Jim had called decaf "why bother." But, coffee at this hour would wind her back up again. What she wanted was the warmth and flavor without the buzz. Jim craved the buzz!

This was her time. The house was quiet except for the Cole Porter CD playing softly in the background. Renee picked up her Bible study and turned to where she had left off; God as all-powerful, all-knowing, protector, never changing.

She remembered when, in her youthful naiveté she thought a man could be that. Boy was she wrong...dead wrong. But could God be all those things...is God all of that? Could it be that the perfect image of what she had dearly desired from a man could be found in God?

The discarded desires of her unsullied youthful heart resurfaced. With eager anticipation, Renee opened her Bible and began the study. Awkwardly at first, Renee fumbled to find the Scriptures referenced in her workbook. She was thankful she had purchased a Bible with tabs on the outside edge. That gave a small sense of competence.

Again, she thought of how little she knew about God. This was actually the first Bible she had ever owned and the first time she was studying it. Images of fanatical, Bible thumping people swam through her mind. But, Renee caught herself with a laugh. Guess where those images came from...TV! Let's see, Renee, she asked herself, do we believe all...or any...of what is portrayed in the media?

Nope, she answered herself with conviction, not unless it's an article I wrote!! She smiled to herself then began to read the scripture verse her finger underlined.

Jeremiah 32:17: "Ah Lord God! Behold, Thou has made the heavens and the earth by Thy great power and by Thine outstretched arm! Nothing is too difficult for Thee."

Renee thought of the walk she had taken with Jay just that morning at the park. It was no big hike or outing. Just a little time alone with Jay, bonding time. He was full of questions and curiosity when it came to nature. Renee loved to explain even the limited amount she knew about trees, plants, bugs and whatever else came up during their walks. Jay's comment as they exited the park was astute, "Mom, there are so many different kinds of trees and bugs and animals. Somebody had to be pretty smart to make all these things."

I'll have to reread this verse to Jay, Renee thought. I have to teach him about God. Renee reread the passage and became curious as to what prompted Jeremiah to make that statement. She went back to the beginning of the chapter and started to read.

It was well past ten when the ringing phone brought her back to the present. Not ready to switch modes she decided to let her voice mail get it. Her search into Jeremiah's motivations had led to searching out most of the other verses that were in her workbook.

She perused what she had written highlighting the verses that had spoken the most to her. She carefully dragged her yellow marker over Psalm 18: 2-5, 16-19 where she had to choose the words that implied David felt God's protection. All the words she had written bespoke such strength: rock, fortress, deliverer, refuge, shield, salvation, stronghold, rescuer. Yes, that was truly a section that deserved to be highlighted.

For "all-knowing" Renee had been struck by 1 Corinthians 4: 4-5: "I am conscious of nothing against myself, yet I am not by this acquitted; but the one who examines me is the Lord. Therefore do not go on passing judgment before the time, but wait until the Lord comes who will both bring to light the things hidden in the darkness and disclose the motives of men's hearts; and then each man's praise will come to him from God."

That was humbling. Renee had prided herself on being well versed and knowledgeable on just about any subject that could come up in conversation. She exhibited a prowess because of her refined ability to converse comfortably on anything from the arts to social issues to even sports and cars (her least liked topics but two that were important in a man's world so she had educated herself to be fluent in all things male).

She chuckled at herself for the way she had often, in times passed, discussed religion. Sad to say, the TV stereotype was the impression she held of Christians. Talk about motives of her heart. What a better way to avoid God than to hold fast to loose ideas. Renee had just spent over 3 hours alone with God, getting to know Him which quickly eradicated her former shallow perceptions of God and yes, of Christians.

He is not a crutch, God is a stronghold. We do not know it all, our knowledge is minuscule when compared to God's. How bloated I was to walk around with such a superficial view and pontificate so adroitly about religion when I hadn't even opened a Bible.

Liz, the friendly nurse at Jay's school, came to mind. That's right, she's a Christian...a real Christian. Not this perfect person by any means. But genuine, transparent, never hesitant to say she was wrong. Liz wasn't a doormat that groveled at the heathenistic world around her. She was smack in the middle of it but unlike Renee, Liz was always trying to find ways to help others. Sure, Renee talked a good game when it came to community service, but Liz lived it! Just with Jay alone, she went out of her way to fill the gap for Renee when work pulled her away from mothering.

I bet the motives of Liz's heart are closer to being in tune with God's than mine are. Renee vowed to build on the friendship with Liz and see if she could broaden her opinion and understanding of God and Christians. Lord, she prayed, sorry for all the erroneous perceptions I had and verbalized about people who love you. That's what I want to be like. Please help me.

As the prayer left her silent lips she read the next question; *What is one way you can respond to your belief that God knows everything?*

Gee, God, I barely get the prayer out of my heart and your answer is there...in my own handwriting besides!! This is eerie. Taking the cap off her highlighted, Renee again began marking her book.

In Psalm 46:10 she learned that she should be still, cease striving and exalt God.

That is such a contradiction to my entire life, she thought. Isn't that what I learned at the first class...I put much of my energy into striving to prove the choice I made was right!! Instead God wants the complete opposite...to be still and exalt Him.

In Psalm 32:5 it showed Renee how to begin, by acknowledging her sin and confessing it...do not cover up iniquity.

At first it bothered her that word confession...it provoked thoughts of burn-them-at-the-stake zealots. Besides, Renee thought, if God knew everything, even our hearts, why confess? But now she saw the damage, felt the damage, had lived the damage done by covering up iniquity. Again, she thought of Liz and how quickly she was to come clean...that's confession. Liz's way of keeping things right out in the open, not covering up her failings, Renee admired that about her. Now she too understood the tremendous value in God's truth. All-knowing...that's for sure.

The phone rang again. Renee looked at the clock, saw that it was after eleven then remembered she had promised to call Jim. He usually got very possessive when she neglected him. She bet that if she accessed her voice mail it would be him who had called earlier. Why did he feel such a need to invade her space?

"Hello," she answered, her voice close to professional, definitely projecting to the caller to distance themselves from her.

"Renee...Hi...good, you're home. I just wanted to catch you before I turn off the lights. I have to be up at four to head for the airport," Jim said, totally oblivious to her signals. He spoke in a friendly, unassuming voice.

Then Renee remembered the reason she was suppose to call him. She had wanted him to go to the paper's employee dinner on Friday. He, obliging as always, was going to try to rearrange his schedule to get back from his trip in time.

Renee was about to recounter with an abrupt remark placing the onus on Jim but instead said, "Sorry, I got drawn into something I was doing here and didn't even think to call."

"Oh..." Jim said not quite believing his ears at hearing her apologetic tone, "...no problem. As it turns out things don't look promising for Friday. There's a lot of money riding on this presentation. Jack told me to leave my schedule wide open in case we have to do a little schmoozing."

Jim was just a date to make life easier when socializing at work got boring or heated. He did his part well and she was never without an excuse to change the topic, retreat from a group, or leave early if the event was a dud. Her obligations to work only went so far, Jim was her escape route, her excuse to make her departure.

She was annoyed because this dinner was an evening of listening to too many people stand up and self applaud their work. Renee was disappointed that Jim wasn't going to be there for purely selfish reasons!

Again, before making a chiding remark, Renee caught herself and said, "I know how that goes. But you've been working to bring this account on board for a good nine months now. It'll be big and worth giving up a Friday night with your closest friends at the Daily Journal."

"Aaah, the people you work with aren't so bad," he said, meaning it. "More importantly, I like being with you...that's what I'll miss."

Jim must say things like that hundreds of times a week. Renee just never listened, never heard his words of caring. This time she heard and it unsettled her. He likes my company...being with me.

97

Not knowing how to react to old news that was new news to her, Renee responded with, "It's late. I'm tired just thinking about you getting up at four. Get some rest...and have a good trip."

Jim heard gentleness in her voice. He had only heard that when she interacted with Jay...never when she spoke to him. But, he wasn't about to question it. "I'll call you tomorrow night. Sleep well Renee."

They hung up but Renee hung on to his simple statement, "I'll call you tomorrow night." Her skin use to crawl when he would make possessive, space-invading declarations like that. Yet, this time it felt like the first sip of hot chocolate on a cold wintry night as the swallow languidly entered her body permeating her entire chest with a gentle flowing radiance that continued down finally reaching her stomach enfolding her in a warmth that felt like love.

Love? No, not Jim...not love. But whatever, it felt nice. She'd leave it at that. She put her Bible and workbook in the end table drawer, reached over to turn off the light, then curled up in bed, thinking, "What does God know about tomorrow that I don't know?

Chapter Fourteen:
Paula

Paula was tiny. One of those women you see and know that she is at the mercy of any strong wind. She had soft white skin, a lilting sing-song voice and quiet blue eyes. Every motion was expansive as if to made up for her size and being labeled the runt of the litter. Paula was from an unusually large family – both in number and size – with seven siblings, a total of nine aunts and uncles most of whom were married with a minimum of four kids each. Her list of cousins, second cousins and once removed family could fill a county. Basically, as dairy farmers, their name was synonymous with Highland County. They were a hardy, *tall* family of mainly Dutch heritage. None of the women, with the exception of Paula and one aunt, were under five eight, hence the label "runt."

Growing up with so many relatives right in her own backyard...the barn, the corn fields, the pastures, Paula's identity was not singular. Everyone knew everyone else's business, which was in fact their business as well, or an offshoot of the family's farming business. More often than not the interaction was healthy with boundaries respectfully recognized. But, there were those occasions when the lines got blurred, a toe got stepped on or feathers got rustled.

Planting season was usually one of those times when tensions were heightened and strong words were spoken. They had a short window of opportunity to get the fields plowed and readied for planting before the rain made maneuvering the equipment too dangerous and would wash away any seed that hadn't begun to take root.

Paula's father, the oldest in his line, called the shots but not without the wisdom offered by Uncle Al. It was Uncle Al's idea, years and years ago, to maximize the efficiency of operating a farm by growing their own feed. That was the one larger outside cost that had put many dairy farmers under. With foresight, Uncle Al had initiated that change which had proven itself worthwhile through many of the lean years.

But it did mean facing planting season every year. Paula's father was the planner, organizer, the man of order, details and checklists. Uncle Al was the research man. He kept abreast of trends, advances and new technology that would assist them in bringing in a better feed crop.

Paula, her husband Vince and their two children lived in a small ranch house on the south side of the newest pasture about ten miles from the main farm. Basically, they were all within 20 miles of each other. None of the women worked outside the home, since the demands of farming and making a living at it, required everyone's involvement. Raising up future farmers was one of the responsibilities the women took on and home schooling was their way of combining exposure to farming with solid, values-based teaching for their children.

This was another area where Paula fell short, as she would say, waiting for someone to get the pun. She didn't home school her kids. In fact, she once worked outside the home at a bank, loving every minute of it. Vince was happy to let her continue but, when she worked, her days were so darn busy she felt like she was neglecting her kids. She was. Even though she felt more contented, fulfilled, and accomplished, she was tired at the end of the day, short with the kids, less responsive to Vince and they ate soup and grilled cheese more often than she liked to remember.

When Paula was at work she could see the results of a hard day at the office and have a sense of accomplishment. The rewards of raising a family came in quick, almost-to-be-missed spurts; a loving hug from her daughter; a wise word from her young son that showed he had heard something she had been saying; or the quick peck on the cheek and murmur of gratitude from Vince at least once a year! At work she felt like she was using her brain and by doing so keeping it growing, active...alive! At home she was using her nurturing skills on children which seemed to make her brain feel atrophied. Oh to have a problem to solve requiring more brain cells than first grade spelling required. But in her heart Paula believes in the long term, in the future and the future, without a doubt, was about her kids...her family. For right now that meant some sacrifices.

She had hated quitting especially since she had just received a raise and knew of an upcoming position opening that she had coveted. She liked her boss and the people she worked with. She like the muffled sound of work in progress as oppose to the endless rumble of cows in distress wanting to be milked.

In the bank things were clean, stayed clean, smelled clean, crackled with cleanliness. At home you could never escape dirt, mud, tracks through the entry way, dust, grime, and the ever present odor of manure.

Paula wasn't built like a Dutch farming woman nor was she drawn to the earth. But she had quit, for her family. Which didn't mean she became the canning queen of Highland County. Nor did she take that opportunity to remove her precious ones from the school and instruct them at home as others pointed out that she should do.

The kids stayed in school and Paula kept busy with endeavors that took her off the farm; den mother, brownie leader, volunteer school aid, and volunteering at the pregnancy center whenever Karen needed her. Once a week she went in to do the books; pay the bills, enter information onto the computer, and run reports. Whenever a group of women were ready to participate in the post-abortion bible study, she either co-led with Karen or led it on her own if Karen's schedule conflicted with the best day for the women to meet.

She liked working with Karen which kept her motivated to do that which was difficult for her to do...lead the Bible study. Without fail, when a new class began she was bombarded with feelings of inadequacy. Subtle constant harassment from Satan. It took a while for her to see Satan at work. Things would start getting tense at home between she and Vince. The kids would be edgy, mouthy, on the verge of rebellion. The family would be engulfed in another feathers-ruffled situation. Keep in mind, Dutch feather ruffling is not like the booming, in-your-face venting Vince's Italian family voiced...all in love!

With Vince's family, Paula shrunk down as small as her tiny frame would allow. Vince had assured her time and time again, not to take what was said seriously. They were only venting...very expressively, but venting just the same. They all knew it, and no one held onto a grudge. Once it was out, no matter how distorted by the explosive verbalizing of impassioned feelings, it was over, in the past, time to move on, no big deal.

What amazed her most was that is exactly what happened. She wondered at how people could do that. Her family counted every word as sacred, thought before they spoke, used intonations that were a decibel above monotone and maintained a facial expression that was neutral...never angry or excited, or bored, just neutral...placid.

Paula, ever sensitive to what amounted to ruffled feathers within her family, reacted by wanting to make everyone around her happy. If you had asked her she would have told you she knows she can't make everyone happy. But, she tried...the mini peace-keeper trying to soothe, brush down, smooth over, bring calm to the silent storm.

This morning's storm, after the argument with Vince and fighting to get the kids to stop bickering Italian style which, in Paula's opinion, was anything said antagonistically before 8 a.m. or her second cup of coffee, was the call from her sister-in-law outraged because her husband, Paula's older brother, had to operate equipment that had not been properly serviced, which was Brad, the youngest brother's responsibility.

Neutral, "Paula, I'd like to mention a concern that maybe you could advise me on what is the best way to address a potential problem."

Peacemaker Paula, "You know I'll help anyway I can." Putting her hand over the mouth piece, "Deanna leave your bother's toast alone. Eat your cereal."

Neutral, "My concern involves Tom (her husband, Paula's older bother) and the risk he faces by using the farm equipment when the maintenance hasn't been completed. I mentioned to Tom that he might want to bring it up to Brad (pause) again."

Peacemaker, "That sounds like the right move." Hand over mouth piece, "If you kids don't settle down, I'm taking the snacks out of your lunch pails!" That threat seemed to get their attention. "What did Tom say?" Paula continued knowing her sister-in-law had her own ideas of what Tom should think, say or do and was forever trying to guide him toward her expectations.

Neutral, "Oh you know Tom, always the big brother. He doesn't seem concerned." She was feeling out Paula, "You're his sister, how do you ever get him to do what he should do...as I see it?"

Peacemaker, "Well, maybe he's right." Paula had learned not to tread within another's marriage, even if it did involved her brother, who she would have to agree with her sister-in-law, could use some guidance! " Maybe it's not as bad as you think. I'm sure if it were, Tom would take care of it." She opened her son's lunch pail and removed the baggie with double fudge cookies inside dangling them in front of the kids, daring them to push her further. They sat bolt upright, then quickly finished their breakfasts. Paula slowly placed the cookies back in the lunch pail as if to say, *I can still get to them.*

Neutral, "I could give Melody a call." She was Brad's wife who could win a cat fight before you knew there was another cat in the room. Sweet girl but defended Brad to the end.

Peacemaker, "Why don't you talk to Tom when he comes in for lunch...ya know, see how the equipment is running?" Crisis averted?? Only time would tell. But Paula felt on edge, not from the conversation that occurred on the surface, but because of all that was unsaid.

After they hung up, Paula had walked the kids out to the end of her driveway where the bus stopped. On the days she was going in the opposite direction, like today, she would let them take the bus...an adventure they considered as good as fast-food burgers.

Wouldn't you know it, Melody was driving by just as they reached the road. She pulled into Paula's driveway to chat.

"Hi, Mel," Paula said, thinking this was the last person she wanted to see. Oh, Lord, couldn't I just have a few peaceful moments???

"Auntie Mel...Auntie Mel," The kids cried out simultaneously, running to the car door to greet her.

"Hi kids. Are you headed to school?" They both nodded with happy faces...hey they were about to ride on the bus.

The two women saw the kids off then leaned against the car chatting amiably. Paula wrestled with mentioning the equipment problem, knowing Mel knew. Brad was an excellent mechanic but terribly unorganized. Maybe if Paula suggested to Mel ways for Brad to set up schedules to service the equipment that would diffuse the tension.

It usually began with Tom's wife, then her sister had a few words to add, since she had to purchase supplies and would get asked to buy parts and have them sent overnight express to make up for poor planning. Her uncle would start talking about the way they used to run things in the old days. But Brad came back with, *How many parts did a plow horse need back in those days Uncle Bud?*

Uncle Bud would grin, ever so slightly, and come back with, "Just remember son, I can still beat you one-on-one on the court." That truth always leveled the playing field for the men. Hoops, farming and fishing...those were their passions. Although they might add God and family, the women, in good fun, would tease them otherwise.

Her dad's answer to rising tensions would be to call a family meeting. Nobody said a word in response to his talk. Then five minutes later her dad would say a prayer for the farm, they would nod, shake hands and leave agreeing on how well the meeting had gone. Maybe what they needed was a few of Vince's family to stir things up, show them how real communication was handled. Paula chuckled to herself at that thought. She loved her family, just as they were...no matter how frustrating at times. And this was definitely one of those times!

Mel left and Paula was proud that she hadn't said something she shouldn't have, then she became upset because she hadn't said something she probably should have. This stoic, keeping your own counsel stuff didn't play out well with her. But, wasn't it better than a knock down, drag out fight?

Why couldn't interpersonal communication be like what she saw at the pregnancy center's Bible study. People taking turns talking, sharing openly, from their heart, praying for God's direction, revelation, and help. What is it about people that makes what is most important to relationships, communication, the most illusive?

Paula had several hours before she had to be downtown to help stuff bulletins at her church. Surveying her morning she felt she was in a slump. It had been like this for the past few days. No, more like a week. Then it dawned on her. It had been like this since the Bible study began. And she had neglected her time alone with God because she had been letting life's circumstances, once again, dictate to her.

"Can't I ever get this right?" she scolded herself. She turned the volume down on her message machine, Vince was into screening calls, picked up her Bible, went into the living room and got comfortable on the couch. Draping the chenille throw across her bare feet, she opened God's Word and began to read. Her quiet time with God reading and praying was her best defense against Satan. Then she would call the women in the Bible study to encourage them and see how their week was going.

Chapter Fifteen:
God Never Fails

Karen was glad the class was in the morning. As each hour passed, in her day, the urgency of life heightened. By early afternoon the Center would be buzzing with activity, needs, phone calls, walk-in clients and an assortment of minor emergencies. Oh how she cherished the mornings when only one phone line rang at a time, young women were still in school or classes and Karen could chip away at the stacks of paperwork nagging at her. Her pace, although diligent, allowed for reflection, thinking through a situation rather than the immediate response that would be required of her later on in the day.

Knowing the class was today, Karen didn't dive into a paperwork project but rather wrote notes of thanks, encouragement, or "I prayed for you today," answered simple inquiries, and reviewed the lesson they would focus on in today's class. She loved the God chapter, as she called it. The women would get to fully experience God before having to walk through the pain of their past.

"Hi Karen...Oops, did I interrupt you?"

"Paula, no...Hi. I didn't hear the door. How are you?"

"Sorry I didn't call out." Karen waved the apology off knowing Paula thought Karen expected more from her than Karen did. It often left Karen in a quandary, not knowing how to get Paula to understand that Karen appreciate her exactly as she was...is. Karen changed the subject, "Hey, I was out in your area over the weekend...smelled that wonderful aroma of dung! I couldn't close my windows fast enough, but that didn't help. It must be planting time?"

"You got it."

"So...are tempers flaring?" Karen said with a smile. She and Paula had often spoken of each of their respective families and the little peculiarities that defined the generations.

"You bet. Uncle Al actually raise his left eyebrow a smidgen!" They both laughed as Karen got up from her chair, walked around her desk and gave Paula a hug. "Glad you're here. This will be a good class."

"Yeh. I was wondering..." Paula began but was interrupted by the phone. Karen leaned across her desk to answer it as Paula stopped talking and indicated she would go await the women.

One, two, three... "Mid City Pregnancy Center, may I help you."

"Karen?" The voice asked.

"Yes."

"Oh, hi...uh, this is Kalli...I uh...well I don't think I can make it. Um, I have a test today...well later, but I need to study...you know. So..." her voice trailed off.

Karen's heart sank. This is how it started, one excuse, one class missed, then another. Funny how there always seemed to be something else more pressing. Karen didn't want to lose Kalli. This kid needed to continue with the class. Karen felt it was up to her to fight for the women until they gained enough strength to fight for themselves. She understood the powers of darkness, how Satan rallied to prevent women from healing. Often the women themselves didn't know that a battle raged for their souls. His weapons were those of chaos, confusion, and disruption, using the everyday occurrences in people's lives but tweaking them just enough to cause discomfort therefore goading the target into altering their course.

"Kalli, I'm glad you called. You're probably right about giving more time to study for your test."

"Yeh, that's what I was thinking. So you thinks it's okay?" She wasn't as much asking permission as she was seeking affirmation. Karen knew there were times you didn't go into battle against the prince of darkness straight on, because then the actual human could end up being wounded by both sides. Kalli was fragile. Karen would rather let her go than hurt her further. But she wasn't ready to give up just yet.

"Well, I guess what I think from getting to know you is that you know what's important in your life. Let's face it Kalli, it takes courage and determination to come to a post-abortion Bible study. So...if you think you need to miss something which is that important to you...then I can accept that."

"It is important to me. Oh, I don't know...I mean this test and all. It's my easiest class. Well, it's just that...well I want to come but I didn't do all the homework. I mean you said doing the lessons were important."

Thank you Lord, Karen thought. "Oh Kalli, don't worry about not having finished the chapter...just come to the class. You'll still get a lot from it. It's such a good chapter...the foundation for all the others." Karen made herself stop speaking. She didn't want to sound like an infomercial.

"You sure it's okay?"

"I'm sure." Then Karen added, in a friendly yet authoritative voice to overcome any hesitation Kalli may be wrestling with, "Get your stuff and head on over. We'll wait for you."

They said good bye and Karen went to join Paula.

"I wanted to ask...did you ever hear from that lady who was suppose to come to the class but didn't show last week? What was her name...Linda."

"Oh you mean Alice. I talked to her that same day. Can you believe she was actually here. Well, she drove down the street and found the Center but didn't see lights on so thought we weren't open." Paula had a questioning look on her face.

"Yeh, I know. But then she couldn't find a parking place to check and see if we were open. So she drove around the block and prayed that if God really wanted her to come to the class he would make a parking place available."

"Didn't you tell her about the parking lot right behind us?'

"Yes." Paula nodded starting to get the picture. "Sure enough there was a parking spot but she panicked and kept going. Then, she got up enough courage to come around again." Paula knew what that meant...not just the emotional courage to walk into the unknown, but just driving downtown with all its one way streets took a certain degree of courage...or insanity. She avoided downtown unless absolutely necessary. Or to go to Le Creme de Creme ice cream parlor. She would drive backwards up a winding cliff side road blind folded for a scoop of pralines and cream at Le Creme!!

"Sure enough, she got back on our street, the spot was still open but she kept on going. The thought of walking up to the door and finding it open terrified her."

Paula shook her head, her heart saddened by how real that scenario was in numerous women's lives. They didn't want to find the door to healing open. How ironic. They spend years in pain, the pressure of it always pushing in on their lives, always haunting them, pricking, wounding, not wide gaping wounds, just a few droplets from their soul, but precious drops everyone.

Because the pressure is constant, even for those who are adept at stuffing, the pain seems to loom larger than it truly is. But, women don't know that. They have been lulled into believing that the amount of pressure, the years of insidious pressure, from the pain signifies roots of pain that if they tried to pry it out would rip them apart.

Instead when the raw root of pain becomes visible they throw on more dirt and try to bury it again. What they don't know...what Paula and Karen do know...what the women who have come to the Bible study also know...is how shallow those roots of pain really are in comparison to how great God's love is and his healing touch on our lives.

Yes, the pain is real but it does not loom as large...as volcanic as women perceive. They mistake the amount of energy it takes to hold back the pain as the indicator to how great the pain will be if they let it out.

Alice was there...right there...and fled.

"What did you say to her?"

"Not much. I just listened. She kept saying, 'I can't go through that door.' I didn't know what to say, she was gripped with fear. She talked...I listened. In the end she had worked herself up more. Then I got scared. I mean, I didn't want someone going off the deep end all alone somewhere out in the county."

"Man...that must have been horrible."

"You bet...worse for her. Finally I calmly started consoling her, sharing how it was okay...that God was there for her even if she couldn't get here. He was there. I prayed with her that she would have a sense of God's presence, that she would let His love cast out her fear."

"How was she then?"

"Better. She even asked if she could call me in a few days."

"Did she call?"

"On Friday. I didn't expect her to. So I thought I'd try again, carefully feel her out, see if she was ready to come to the class."

"Was she? Is she coming?"

"At first she was skittish. But towards the end of the conversation she agreed to come. She didn't have the book and wasn't coming into town. So I said I'd drop it by her place after work. She asked if that would be before school let out."

"Didn't want her family to know?"

"Yeh. I felt the walls were starting to go back up, so I said I'd come right then. I hopped in my car and drove to her place. I think meeting face to face really helped. We chatted for awhile. I took her through the table of contents explaining what would go on...how God could work. When I left, she was buoyed...ready to get into the God chapter and get caught up to the rest of the group."

"Oh good. So she'll be here today?"

"Sure looks like it. I was going to call her yesterday but never got the chance. But, I'm expecting her. Wait 'til she sees what God will do in her life."

As the women started to arrive, Karen waited with anticipation for the arrival of their new participant, Alice, and the delayed arrival of Kalli, who should get downtown and to the class about 5 minutes after the class was due to start. Since they were starting to get to know each other it wasn't quite as awkward as the first week and the gals quietly talked among themselves. Karen let the conversation meander while giving Kalli time to arrive.

It was Paula that took the lead in getting everyone ready to begin, "Hi ladies." Sentences were finished as nods acknowledge Paula, "We're waiting for Kalli who should be here any minute now...and Alice, who was suppose to be here last week but didn't make it. After today, we will not allow any new women to join the group. It's tough enough getting used to talking about this without having to get used to new people every week." The women agreed. "And, as we mentioned last week, every chapter builds on the previous one. Should we open in prayer?"

When they said "amen" and raised their heads Kalli was seated to Karen's left. Alice had still not appeared. Karen brushed off her feelings of apprehension by beginning the Bible study. She knew they had connected when she had gone to Alice's house and expected her to walk through the door momentarily.

"What struck you about God as you did this lesson?"

As the women shared they began to relax even further. Karen led them into deeper waters by asking them to pray out loud the written prayer from their workbook. "Why don't we take a moment to pray using what you learned about God as summarized on page twenty-six. Again, if you are not comfortable praying, pray silently."

As they bowed their heads Renee spoke up, "I left that section blank."

"That's okay. As we pray if there is something now that you would like to pray, you can do so."

"Lord, I thank you for your comfort. Please help me deal with all this anger and to accept your unconditional forgiveness. Show me how to forgive myself and those involved in my abortion." As Jill's voice trailed off Gail prayed, "Dear Jesus, thank you for suffering for me that I might be healed. O Lord, show me what I need to do to allow you to heal the scars on my soul from my bitter life experiences. Lord, I want you to have dominion and authority over every area of my life, not just the parts that are visible. Lord, help me behold you, for you alone are my perfect and all-sufficient Savior. I am longing to know you, love you and worship you more with all my mind, heart and soul that I may experience your fullness."

Renee was reminded of that day, so many years ago now, when she had caught a glimpse of herself in the mirror hanging in her parent's hallway. She was dejected, at the lowest point of her life, not wanting to go on, yet she had gone on. Was that God? If He could get her back on her feet, cleaned up and working again, could He also clean up what remained inside of her? Could He heal her? She found herself praying, "God...Lord...you have so many names, I don't know which one to use. Father...yes, that's it, Father...what I learned about you being all-knowing and all-powerful enlarged my understanding of you. It gave me reverence for you, which can equate to distance. But you are not detached, are you? With all that you are, you also care and want to be part of my life...to transform my life by healing me. I want that Father. I want the pain that came flooding forward to recede...but not to be a perpetual ebb and flow of pain...but taken in its entirety. That's what healing is when you do it...and that's what I am asking of you, Father. That's my prayer."

She thought she should add more but didn't know what that should be. The room was quiet. Renee's descriptive words and the other's fluent prayers intimidated Kalli. With her head bowed she was reading what she wrote, yet felt too timid to read what she now felt was a childish prayer. Since she hadn't completed the lesson and that was the small part she had done, she felt she had to share it.

Kalli swallowed and began to read. "Thank..."

Paula, uneasy by the long silence, started to pray at the same time. Both women halted in deference to the other. Another awkward silence ensued broken by Kalli, "Thank you Jesus. I love you and I need you. I don't like that you see me, but since you do, please see into the part the hurts so bad and make it better. Amen."

"Amen" the unison voices of women softly sang.

Karen led them into the day's lesson, "Your prayers show how you are starting to view God in relationship to your abortion experience. God is always there for us and wants us to turn to Him, call on Him. Sometimes that is hindered by our image of "father" or authority due to our parents...those people in our life that were given the authority over our lives. Part of this lesson was to help us separate the human fallibility of our parents from the infallibility of God. To view our parents as they truly are...human and imperfect just like us...so that we can view God as He truly is...perfect.

"Let's turn to page 15 and take a look at some of those parental traits that are similar to God's and talk about the imperfect way they may have affected your life.

"The verses that best describe perfect love are in 1 Corinthians 13:4-8. You were asked to rewrite that scripture, inserting 'my Heavenly Father' for the word love. Would someone like to read their version?"

Gail looked at Karen, who nodded for her to go ahead. "My Heavenly Father is patient, my Heavenly Father is kind and is not jealous, my Heavenly Father does not brag and is not arrogant, does not act unbecomingly, He does not seek His own, is not provoked, does not take into account a wrong suffered, He does not rejoice in unrighteousness, but rejoices with the truth, bears all things, hopes all things, endures all things. My Heavenly Father never fails."

Gail, her eyes moist, looked back up to Karen who sat quietly giving the words time to penetrate.

Renee was the first to speak, "When I read that, I remembered in

111

college that was a poster everyone had – the 'love' poster. I had it hanging above my desk. I never knew it was from the Bible until I read it this past week. Back then it's what we aspired to, perfect love. Of course we didn't quite make it. Even my parents, and they are the most wonderful parents a person could ask for...even they can't attain to all of this." In awe, she finished, "But, God can."

Gail found her voice, "He does not rejoice in unrighteousness but rejoices with the truth. God doesn't like what we did, but rejoices when we face the truth of it and then He does not take into account a wrong suffered."

"How does that happen?" Karen asked.

"What the rejoicing?"

Karen clarified for Gail and the others, "No, how does God not take into account a wrong suffered?"

"Because He loves us?" Kalli offered. Karen waited.

"Jesus already paid the price for our sins," Gail added.

"But, we still have to confess, right?" Renee asked.

"Put that all together and you've got it," Karen said. She glanced at Jill who had, so far, been fairly quiet but held back from directing a question at her to prompt interaction. Jill was probably processing something that struck her during the conversation.

Paula picked up the next segment, "God's discipline was hard for me to grasp at first. My father is a quiet man but was incredibly strict when it came to discipline. Anyone else have trouble with this section?" Karen was pleased that Paula opened the topic up in a way that allowed the women to struggle through the issue of God's discipline rather than give the expected answers.

Gail immediately connected with Paula's statement, "My father was an alcoholic. Discipline to me was him, dead drunk, flying off at whoever was closest for stupid, little things. Then there was my mother, whose mouth was her weapon. She was either mealy mouthed, apologetic, when my father was in a tirade, or she was vicious, blaming me for all the wrongs in our life.

"I guess I never thought much about God's discipline. For a long time I kept waiting for the boom to drop...that He would one day thunder down from heaven and give me everything I deserved! Finally, I started telling myself He was a loving God...and He forgave me. So it wasn't as bad. Yet I never really could shake that fear of Him striking me down."

"I never gave much acknowledgment to God...no acknowledgment really. So I wasn't afraid of Him punishing me," Renee said.

"Is it punishment?" Paula asked.

Renee corrected herself, "Not according to the verses in Hebrews 12:5-11."

"Why don't we look at some of the verse s in this section," Paula said which prompted the women to open their Bibles. "Who does God discipline?"

Kalli had that answer and proudly spoke up, "Those whom He loves!"

"Right Kalli...anything else?" Paula asked the women.

"He disciplines us because He loves us...for our good...to train us," Gail offered from her workbook.

"What is the goal in all of this discipline that God gives to those He loves?" Karen asked wanting to remind them that God's discipline wasn't just random or vengeful as some may have experienced from their parents.

"For the long term," Gail said.

"Good. Anything else?" Karen asked.

"To rid us of our iniquity...our sin?" Gail added.

"That's part of it." Karen knew that most post-abortive women had spent years in self-punishment which also equated into seeing God as punishing. They were giving the right answers but had only half of the picture. She prodded them to look further, "What else?"

The silence indicated they were not yet able to see the complete picture. "Jill, would you read Hebrews 12:10-11." Karen decided it was time to draw Jill into the discussion indirectly.

"For they discipline us for a short time as seemed best to them..."

"Meaning our parents," Karen interjected then nodded for Jill to continue.

"...but He disciplines us for our good, that we may share in His holiness. All discipline for the moment seems not to be joyful; yet to those who have been trained by it, afterwards it yields the peaceful fruit of righteousness."

Kalli jumped right in, "My Bible says discipline is painful."

113

Jill finally gave an opinion, "That's for sure."

Paula saw the frustration in Karen's eyes. They had both been here before. They had both read these verses themselves at one time seeing only the punishment...the pain of discipline. She gave Karen a knowing nod and they both waited.

"Holiness?" Renee questioned almost to herself. "He disciplines us for our good, that we may share in His holiness?"

Her revelation caused the other women, in a state of disbelief, to search what was just read to see where the word holiness appeared. Paula's eyes smiled at Karen whose face showed relief and joy. They were getting it.

Renee's thoughts poured out, "Punishment...or discipline isn't to hurt us...or for revenge or even because we deserve it. God wants to make us holy. Can you believe that, holy?"

"Look at the last part of verse eleven," Gail said, "Look what happens after the pain." She read, "'afterwards, it yields the peaceful fruit of righteousness.' And all these years I've been stuck in the pain part. I've been missing the peaceful fruit of righteousness."

"Wow, God really does love us," Kalli added.

Karen was waiting for Jill to respond. Something was going on that Karen wanted to bring out into the open yet she was concerned she might come across as too direct and make things worse. She was thankful when Paula spoke up, "Jill are you still struggling with these verses?"

"Not these. I can see what it's saying, but you're forgetting God's judgment, His wrath. I'm afraid of His wrath like it talks about in Romans 2:5."

Paula regretted opening her mouth. The word judgment conjured up images of her own father. His silent, stoic presence, while never verbally condemning, seemed to shout judgment; after all he was a pillar in the church. If anyone could pass judgment, her nearly perfect father could. She ached for him to just once say what was really on his mind, whether it was, 'I love you.' or 'I'm disappointed in you.' or even 'I wish you were more like your sister.' Paula always had to fill in his silences. It was the worst when she had to tell him something that wasn't good news. That's probably what drew her to Vince. She never had any doubt what he was thinking. His words were out of his mouth

114

before his thoughts even finished being formed.

She nodded in understanding then started to direct Jill to the full meaning of Romans. "Back up to the verse before that and begin reading."

"'Or do you think lightly of the riches of His kindness and forbearance and patience, not knowing that the kindness of God leads to repentance?'" Jill read.

Paula continued, "'But because of your stubbornness and unrepentant heart *you* are storing up wrath for yourself in the day of wrath and revelation of the righteous judgment of God, who will render to every man according to his deeds.'

"Let's not miss God's grace. How are we exempt from that wrath, that final judgment?" Paula asked.

Kalli's face lit up with understanding but, before she could speak, Paula motioned with her hand for Kalli to hold back and waited for Jill to reply.

"Repentance?" she said not fully believing.

"Repentance," Paula confirmed.

Karen felt an avalanche of anger welling up in Jill. Paula had pricked the surface, but there was more going on inside of Jill. She was angry with God and that would take some time to work through. Seeing that they were coming to the end of their time together Karen wanted to end by reiterating the revelation they had experienced during their time together. But before she could speak, Kalli got antsy, a sign to Karen that something was about to spill out from her lips, "I need to repent," she said bluntly catching everyone off guard.

"I lied. My life is a lie. I mean...well...don't take this personally or anything. I didn't come in here to lie to anyone, but I did. Eric wasn't the father. He was right. When I went to California to visit my dad, I was hanging out after a party in this guys hottub and...well...we, made love. It was stupid I know. I felt so embarrassed afterwards. I didn't even see him again before I left. But, well I know that's when I got pregnant. Eric was always so jealous and he was cold...acting mean and...well, I guess that's not an excuse for sleeping with some one I didn't even know. I just couldn't face that about myself so pretended it never happened. But it did."

Kalli caught her breath, then finished with, "You're the only people who know the truth. Well, you and God."

As a means to strengthen Kalli's faith Paula asked, "Would you like to say a prayer of repentance?" As Kalli bowed her head, everyone followed suit. "I'm sorry God for my life being a lie...and especially about Eric being the father of the baby...which he wasn't. I'm sorry for lying to everyone here also. Please forgive me."

She looked up at Paula who said, "That's it...God has forgotten the lie...and all the lies that went with it." Kalli smiled.

Karen picked up where they had left off, "Before we close in prayer, let's take a quick look at 1 Corinthians 4:4-5. Would you read that for us Gail?"

"'I am conscious of nothing against myself, yet I am not by this acquitted; but the one who examines me is the Lord. Therefore do not go on passing judgment before the time, but wait until the Lord comes who will both bring to light the things hidden in darkness and disclose the motives of men's hearts; and then each man's praise will come to him from God.'"

"How many years have you spent condemning yourself...judging yourself? How many times have you jumped in and punished yourself...helping God out, trying to do His job for Him?"

Heads hung low as Karen continued, "What we learn from this verse is that we are not suppose to judge ourselves...because we don't fully know the motives of our heart. It's God that is at work in us to do His will in our lives. We do have a part...our part is to come humbly before Him, listen for His voice, be open and when He reveals a wicked way in us, repent. When we sin, repent...don't beat yourself up or inflict punishment...repent. Why?"

Gail jumped in, "Because, then our hearts aren't stubborn and God can make us holy like He is holy."

"He's training us to be holy and to have the peaceful fruit of righteousness," Renee added.

"Because of your past abortion God's Word filtered through your own self condemnation. Your interpretation of God's truths were mostly head knowledge. I believe today, maybe for the first time, He spoke to your heart." The nods confirmed Karen's thoughts. "As you go through these next weeks, let God work through your mind...your soul...and your heart. Don't read the scripture verses and give answers

116

as if you were taking a test. Let God speak to you through His Word."

Karen glanced a Paula, who then closed the class in prayer.

As the women proceeded to leave, Paula walked with them toward the front door but didn't leave. She had put time aside to talk with Karen. Meanwhile Karen went into the outer office to greet the volunteers, look at the appointment book of clients who called in for a free pregnancy test and checked her messages.

She noticed that one of the volunteers was with a walk-in client and the other was praying quietly in preparation for a client scheduled to come in shortly. Karen sat down next to her and joined in the praying. They greeted each others afterwards then Paula announced the arrival of the client. The volunteer went into action as Karen and Paula headed back into Karen's office.

"I have a message from Lisa. Let me give her a quick call before we talk."

"Sure. I'll just clean up the coffee cups and things," Paula said as she left Karen's office.

"Eckard, Jones and Willowby Financial Planners." Karen recognized Lisa's voice and wondered why the receptionist hadn't answered.

"Can you help with finances for the poor family of a bride-to-be?"

"Hi Mom! You got my message."

"No...I need your services!"

"Too late...you're in too deep. Nothing can help you now!"

"Well, then I guess I'll drown myself in wedding cake!"

"How'd you know that's why I called."

"What's up?"

"First the caterers. The only time they could meet with me, if I didn't want to wait a month, was today. Can you come with me?"

Digging out her calendar from under several file folders, Karen flipped to today's date, "What time are you looking at?"

"Two-ish."

"I can do that. How long do you think we'll be there?"

"Well...as long as you're getting out of the office, could we run by Rosewood Manor to give them the deposit and look over the layout again?"

Karen smiled knowing there was more, "What else?"

"The pastry chef from Le Creme supports the Center. She gets your newsletter. When she heard my name and connected it to yours, she said she would love to do the cake. I just want to stop in quickly...you know say hello. Do you have time?"

"Well, I don't know. If I don't earn a living how can I pay for this wedding?"

"A second job after the wedding? Come on...you probably need to get out of the office for a little while anyway."

"Can we keep it to an hour and a half?"

"Sure, except that doesn't give me time to buy you a Le Crème Supreme."

"I'll pick you up at one forty five."

"Deal. Thanks Mom."

"Bye."

Karen entered the time on her calendar. If it didn't get buried by this afternoon it would remind her to leave the office in time to pick up Lisa. As a fail safe to pandemonium, Karen wrote 'Lisa 1:45p <u>today</u>' on a neon orange sticky-note and stuck it on her phone, which was used too often to get buried. Then she went in search of Paula and a fresh cup of coffee.

"Paula let's get some coffee and talk."

Paula saluted with her cup saying, "Ready whenever you are boss." And they both headed back to Karen's office. Karen had no sooner walked through her office door when she stopped suddenly, turned to face Paula and stated, "Alice never showed." Her face screwed up with consternation as the full impact of what her statement revealed. Anger welled up in her along with a feeling of helplessness and loss.

Shaking her head she said, "She was so close. I really thought she'd be here."

Paula placed a loving hand on her friend's shoulder, "Maybe you could call her?"

"No. That would be going too far. She was ready, I know she was." She took a deep breath, exhaled slowly then walked to the comfortable tub-chair usually occupied by guests and sat down. Paula, closing the door, joined Karen in the other tub-chair saying, "Jill's a pretty angry woman, even without words it's right there."

"Yes she is. But God's dealing with her."

"She barely said two sentences today."

"I know, but it looked like the wheels were turning."

"Should I try to get her to talk when I touch base with her this week?'

"Well, see what happens but I'd say try to avoid being her private counselor. If anything comes up, listen then point her back to God and this week's lesson," Karen advised.

"Sounds good. Isn't Kalli sweet...just like a child seeing this for the first time."

"It always amazes me at the genuineness of new believers. God seems to be hitting Gail pretty hard also, breaking down walls and letting her see who He truly is."

"When she first prayed I thought she was such a Godly woman. Her faith seemed so real. It's unsettling when I hear her struggling with things like God punishing her," Paula said, somewhat bewildered.

"It's like the trauma from abortion puts a ceiling on your relationship with God. Maybe it's more like wearing glasses that the prescription is so old that you think you're seeing clearly but, although you can make out the basic image, the reality is distorted."

"Well, this Bible study will grind out a new prescription for her."

"Every week her vision gets clearer. This upcoming week is Relief and Denial. Remember all the mechanisms we subconsciously put into place to avoid looking at the truth of our abortion?"

"Drinking...going through boyfriends like flies on a cow."

"Every time the pain started to surface you took a drink. I simply built another wall to separate my current life from the past that was trying to suck me into this vast vacuum. I always thought I was so in control being able to compartmentalize the different aspects of my life. I was so good at it, I could shut down an emotion like flipping off a light switch. I was in control!!!" Karen stated mockingly.

"I was outta control. Booze and flight. The fact that I am alive today baffles me. Not to mentioned, married with two great kids."

"Did the judgment thing get to you this time?"

"There was this little prick of sadness. But, my dad's not gonna change. He's a good man, but definitely old world when it comes to showing emotions."

"Speaking of emotions, Kalli's an open book. Maybe too open. I think this next lesson will help her get to know herself better. I think letting her take part in this Bible study, even knowing her living situation, was the right move. The world seems to pull her all over the place. She's so busy responding and trying to be accepted that she doesn't even know who she really is. I can surely understand why...oh to see her come out from under being at the whim of others and seeing herself as God sees her should help her make better choices."

"Yes, I agree, I can see that. Renee's a pretty smart person. What do you think of her?"

Paula's tone perked up Karen's antennae, "Does that bother you at all?"

"Oh," Paula said then quietly examined her heart. "A little bit. In one sense she's the career woman I dreamed of being. I guess there's envy?" She thought a little more, "She's so educated...traveled abroad...you know me, I'm always waiting for the one question I can't answer. It'll probably come from Renee then I'll feel doubly stupid." Paula smiled weakly and shrugged as if to say, it's old ground, I'll deal with it.

"You know what I say to that?"

"We don't have to have all the answers...God has them."

"You've been brainwashed well my dear!!! You get a star for the right answer. Joking aside, do you see God at work in this group?"

"Yeh, I do. And He's working in me as well...like usual."

"Speaking of work...I'd better get a few things done. I have to pick Lisa up before two...we're doing the wedding prep rounds today, squeezing in 3 appointments back to back." As Karen stood up, Paula did as well. They both headed for the door.

"I don't envy you."

"Yes you do," Karen said with a Cheshire grin, "Lisa promised me a Le Creme sundae afterwards."

Paula gave Karen a big hug, then headed out. Just before reaching the front door she triumphantly said, "I'm serving fruit cup to a million second graders. If I'm lucky they'll be an extra one for me."

"I'll pray for you," Karen responded and they both shifted their thoughts to the day ahead.

Chapter Sixteen:
Mandi

Her period was late.

Nicole, in all her wisdom, had told Mandi it was because of guilt. "All that being upset with yourself is messing up your whole body. Just chill. Like, you can't get pregnant that easily. Quit stressing. Your period will start any day now."

Any-day-now turned into two weeks. Still nothing. What made it worse was Kip. He started every conversation with, "Did you get it?" Then ended everything with, "Call me, no matter when...promise?"

At home her little brothers were all getting on her nerves, her dad was blaming her, not them, for everything and her mother was...well who knew what was up with her mother lately? One day she was just like she'd always been, then the next day she'd be all teary, crying over nothing.

At school her math teacher was upset with her because she didn't sign up for competition this year. Boy, you weren't even allowed to have a life!! And suddenly she didn't like teaching Sunday school either. It wasn't the kids as much as it was all the preparation time. It took away from her time with Kip. Well, she'd finish out this year then that would be it. Too bad Kip never picked up on all her hinds for him to help her teach. That would have been fun.

But lately, nothing was much fun. She has sex and her whole world starts to fall apart.

By the time her period was over two weeks late she had gotten out the phone book and flipped through the yellow pages. She didn't know what she was looking for – answers probably – that neither Nicole nor Kip could give her. She didn't even consider her mother as a person to turn to, as she would have in the past. The past few months had shown her, time and time again, that her mom was preoccupied with her own life and, obviously, Mandi wasn't important to her anymore. Well, what the hay, she had Kip, he was always there for her – well most of the time.

121

She stopped in the yellow pages under "B" for baby, but only found listings for baby clothes, toys and furniture stores. After allowing herself a split second to daydream, she pulled herself quickly back from entertaining fantasies about babies.

Under "C" she found many listings for childcare – no she wouldn't need that. Mandi was getting irritated. How can you find something in the yellow pages when you don't even know what category to look under? Think Mandi – think.

She mentally ran down the alphabet playing word association with letters. "D" for doctor; no I'm not ready to face my doctor. "E" for emergency – yes, I need help fast – but more like a genie who would grant me even one wish to make this all go away. "M" – maternity, or medical; no, I don't even know if I'm really pregnant. Oh, that's it "P" for pregnant.

Mandi flipped to the "P" section, found pregnant and felt very uneasy that she had found what she was looking for, struck with the realization she didn't really want to find it. Instinctively she placed her hand over the page covering the ads shouting out their services.

"Oh Lord, I can't be pregnant. Please make it so… please. I beg you. I'll do anything – I'll teach Sunday school for the rest of my life, even without Kip, if you could make this not true."

Half convinced her pleading would produce the results she wanted, Mandi slowly removed her hand from the page. The advertisements seemed to be jumping off the page to get her to call them. She pulled back feeling scared and ashamed, like the people behind the ad already knew what she had done and that now she was considering their services. Like hawkers at a carnival they called out to her and even though she was repulsed by their aggressive manner she was mesmerized by the lure of an easy fix… a quick win.

"Step right up young lady and you can be a winner. Yes you, little lady. For just a bit of coin you can take a chance on a new, fun filled, free and easy life. The choice is yours – everyone is a winner. There are no losers here. Come on, don't be shy. Step up to the line and try your luck – it's all right here waiting for you. Leave your worries behind and take home the thrills that can be yours."

Down in the right hand corner was a small advertisement Mandi almost overlooked. She was just about to turn the page when the word "free" caught her eye. It was a simple ad offering free pregnancy tests and stating that all services were confidential. "Free" definitely fit her pocketbook and confidential wrapped her in a sigh of relief – her parents would not have to know.

Of course, getting through to the number listed was another situation in and of itself. Not that the agency offering their services didn't have an adequate amount of telephone lines, but Mandi's fingers couldn't seem to get through all seven digits required to complete the call. After fifteen minutes of partial dialing attempts, Mandi slammed the phone book closed. "I don't need this. What am I doing. I'm not pregnant. I can't be pregnant."

But, the next day after school Mandi headed over to HHS where she corralled Nicole and led her over to the most remote public phone. She opened up the yellow pages, pointed to the number and said, "Will you call for me. Just see how they sound when they answer."

"Mandi, really? Do you think…. Nah you can't be."

"I know, but just call for me, please?"

"Well sure – no problemo girl. I gotcha covered." Nicole was geared up for the unknown, the act, and her role.

"Good afternoon, Mid City Pregnancy Center. This is Leslie, can I help you?"

"Well yes," Nicole said in her most confidant, mature voice. "Do you give free pregnancy tests?"

"Yes we do, would you like to make and appointment?" Leslie was a bit curious by the detached way the question had been asked.

Nicole was surprised that Leslie had gotten to the point so quickly. She had not prepared what to say next. "Pregnancy test? Well, uh, no I mean…" She caught herself sounding unsure and recapture her earlier character, "I mean, could you tell me a little about what you do?" Phew, got out of that okay. Mandi, nodding in affirmation, clutched Nicole's free hand.

"Sure, I'd be glad to. We offer the free pregnancy test because we know how upsetting wondering if you are pregnant can be. This way you can know for sure. Also, we are here to help you, if you are pregnant, to decide what to do next." Leslie wondered why the young woman might be apprehensive so again asked, "Would you like to come in for a test?"

"Well actually, it's not for me." Mandi tugged at Nicole's hand to get her attention. When Nicole looked over, Mandi was frowning and shaking her head "no."

Leslie was speaking, but Nicole had missed what she was saying and cut her off by announcing, "Uh thank you for answering my questions." Then hung up.

Mandi collapse on the curb by the phone. "Oh, God. Oh God. Do you think she knew who we were?"

"Mand – get a grip. How could she?" At that moment Mandi was envisioning hidden cameras that had zoomed in on her with neon words flashing above an arrow pointed straight at her – not Nicole – screaming; "She's the one!"

Mandi was brought out of her fear of exposure by the brigade of students jogging past with their team uniforms on, equipment in hand. "I've gotta go. I've got 5 minutes to get back to the Hill for my newspaper staff meeting!" she exclaimed.

Nicole groaned, "Ugh – and I have to go to the dentist! Yuk. Poke, prod and drill – my adored after-school activities," she said while rolling her eyes. "My dad thinks I need braces. Metal mouth – can you picture it!"

Mandi smiled at her friend's depiction thinking at least she had the school paper and Mr. Van Pellar waiting…her favorite after school activity led by her favorite teacher. Anything to distract her from the reality of her life.

"Hey, Nicole, uh, thanks…really. You're the best."

"You got it girl – anytime. That's what best friends are for. Later," she said as she headed off to her appointment with Dr. Drill.

Best friends. The words warmed Mandi's heart as she turned to hurry back to school. It would be more than two weeks later that Mandi could not postpone taking action. She had, by then, missed two periods and hiding behind her fears wasn't working any longer.

The weeks slowly passed. By the end of the day, the not-knowing would be over. Kip was meeting her after practice and they were going downtown to the place that gave free pregnancy tests. God, how embarrassing. But she had to know.

Glancing up at the clock in the locker room she knew Kip was probably outside right now. She had lingered behind the other girls hoping Angela would be around. Mandi had heard that Angela had gotten pregnant last fall. She wasn't pregnant now, so Mandi wanted to see if Angela would open up and talk to her.

But Mandi had missed her opportunity. Just as she had been ready to approach Angela, Coach Francine came in to check on things. Angela left before the coach did and that ended that.

Now there was just Kip and that place downtown. She headed out through the gymnasium doors knowing Kip would be leaning against the playing field fence. Even at a distance she knew his stance, the way he leaned and cocked his head in thought when no one was around.

Her heart pumped faster. Oh how she loved him. Everything would be alright. How could they not be with Kip by her side?

"Hey baby," he said when she was a few yards off. He came up and put his strong arm around her waist pulling Mandi to him and kissing her long and hard on her lips.

"Kip," she pulled away, "not here is plain sight of everyone."

She liked when he kissed her, except that all too often it led to him wanting more and then an argument. So, when he kissed her in public, she felt safer knowing that he couldn't go much further. Except if "public" meant right in front of her school and the eyes of her teachers and peers.

"Hey baby...love ya don't ya know?" he said, flipping his hair back from over his eyes.

"Yes, I know. Guess I'm jumpy that's all." She reached up to brush back an errant cluster of Kip's hair.

Taking her hand and holding it to his lips he kissed her quickly and let her hand dangle in his as they began to walk, "Yeah, I know, me too. Let's get this over with."

After not being able to find a parking space, Kip let Mandi out in front of the building whose sign stated "free pregnancy tests" and told her he'd park and be right in. "Don't get pregnant without me," he joked.

Mandi rolled her eyes. "Please God let this just be your way of warning me. Let me not be pregnant. I promise not to have sex ever again until I'm old and married." She knew that "old" meant her life would be just about over – at 25 – but if that promise would prompt a miracle by God, it was worth it.

Even that prayer pricked her conscience as she remembered just four days ago when once again, she found herself undressed with Kip and unable to stop. Guilt. Big time. How did it happen again?

She was so ashamed she never told Nicole. She didn't even react when Kip asked her if she was okay. "Sure fine," she said in her best pretend voice. How could she make a big deal out of her morals when she couldn't keep the standards she had set for herself?

How could she ask God to forgive her – and now pray that He would not make her pregnant? What a jerk she was. She sat in the waiting room not even noticing the welcoming surroundings, the fresh lemonade, or the small framed scripture verse that would have told her God was there with her.

"Hi, may I help you?" a lady greeted her at the reception area.

"I'm here for a pregnancy test," she said not able to look at the woman, then added, "Mandi."

"Ah, yes, Mandi. Here we go," the woman said after consulting the appointment book on the desk just below the reception window framed by a lace valance. "Darlene will be with you in just a moment. Help yourself to some lemonade and cookies," she said, pointing to the left where the goodies awaited partakers.

A moment later Kip walked in, smiled at Mandi and headed straight for the food. "Want any?" he asked. Mandi shook her head no and wondered how he could eat at a time like this.

The door that separated the waiting room from whatever laid beyond it, opened and a casually dressed lady, who looked like she was younger than Mandi's mother, walked toward her, a warm, gentle smile on her face. "Mandi, I'm Darlene." She nodded at Kip, then turned and continued to address Mandi, "Why don't you follow me and we'll get started."

Darlene looked at Kip and said, "We'll come get you in a few minutes." Having just taken a bite of a cookie, Kip was only able to nod in response but was relieved he did not have to be *that* involved. Coming to this place was hard enough.

Actually these last weeks – no over a month now – had been a nightmare. He thought Mandi loved him and wanted to be with him. Then she'd pull back every time things got really going in the right direction. He did appreciate that she was different – better – than the other girls he dated. He liked that she had standards but they loved each other. It wasn't like a one-night stand or a party-girl thing.

Sure there were other girls in the past, but they were different. Even Susie who he had dated for most of last year. He liked her and all, a lot, but he knew the score with her. There was no future with them – as a couple – they just were together until whenever. Whenever came when his parents told him they were getting a divorce.

Kip was devastated. Never saw it coming. Everything had seemed just fine at home, then one day his dad ups and leaves. Kip's reaction was anger. He partied harder, drove faster, took riskier chances and lashed out at the world. That's when Susie decided she preferred Eddie – a real nerd – over Kip, which fueled his anger and risky behavior even more.

Somewhere buried inside of himself he must have known he was on the fast track to self-destruction because when Ryan invited him to a church youth group he accepted. Let's face it, religion wasn't cool in Kip's book, but he had to pull out of this crash and burn attitude. Ryan was a nice enough guy, great at b-ball, so why not?

Kip didn't fully get the God connection; even though going to youth group brought a calming effect into his life. And it brought Mandi into his life. Man, he loved her. If there really was a God, he sure hoped – prayed – he would help them out of this one.

None of the other girls he had sex with ever got pregnant. He knew how to handle himself. Why now? Why Mandi? This was so different – she was special – too good to end up pregnant. It was the least he could do to sit and squirm in the waiting room. Every time someone walked through the reception area his raw nerves became more evident as he waited for the door to open and that lady – what was her name – to take him in to where Mandi was. He chugged down the lemonade and went to refill his glass. Anything to distract himself.

On the other side of the waiting room door life-changing decisions were being made. Darlene, a single mother, who worked evenings as the overnight caseworker at a home for troubled teens, had been a volunteer at the Center for just over a year. She remembered the first time she had escorted a young girl and her boyfriend to do the test together. The girl was so concerned with and aware of her boyfriend that Darlene never connected with her. Since then, she always gave the

127

young woman a chance to talk alone before inviting the boyfriend into the room, if he even came along to the appointment in the first place.

The two women entered a small but homey room and Darlene began to explain the paperwork to Mandi that needed to be completed and signed. Then she handed Mandi a plastic cup and explained what she needed and where the ladies room was located. She left Mandi alone to read the welcome letter that explained who they were, the services they provided and why they did so. After reading everything Mandi signed the paperwork.

When Mandi came back from the bathroom, Darlene was already back in the room. Mandi set the plastic cup on the counter and sat down. Her foot wiggled uncontrollably and she clutched her small purse so hard the pen inside stabbed her palm, although she didn't even feel it.

Twenty minutes later Mandi heard herself laugh. Her tight short breaths were becoming more relaxed and she felt that Darlene was one of the kindest people she had ever met.

"Now the young man out in the waiting room, is he your boyfriend?"

"Yes, Kip."

How long have you two been going out?"

"Since the end of February."

"I want to tell you Mandi, I've been doing this for a while now and it is not often that the boyfriend comes in with his girlfriend. You have a pretty special guy out there."

Mandi beamed.

"Does Kip go to Chapel Hill also?"

"No, he's a junior at Highland."

"A junior, neat. How did you meet...at church?"

"Yes. Well no. I mean, he comes to youth group, but he doesn't go to my church."

Darlene had noticed that on the intake form Mandi had filled out the faith section indicated that Mandi regularly attended a church. Mandi had even written the name of her church, which Darlene recognized as a solid church with an excellent reputation for its youth program.

During her time of trying to make Mandi feel at ease, Darlene had learned about how involved Mandi was with her church and that her faith was based on a personal relationship with Christ and important to her. Darlene did sense some inner turmoil but didn't probe deeper. She waited on the guidance of the Holy Spirit. Darlene knew, without even a trace of uncertainty, that the young women that came into the center, a ministry dedicated to God, were led there by the Lord.

Every day, before the volunteers began seeing young women, they quieted their hearts before God and prayed for His wisdom and guidance. They all desired to keep their focus on God and what He would show them as they spent time with a client. Each young woman was drawn to the Center for a purpose which, if patient, God would reveal during the volunteer's time with her.

Darlene did not feel anxious or have a need to push beyond where God led. With a peaceful heart, she knew that she only had to love this frightened young lady sitting across from her, God would do the rest.

"I see," she said, kindly acknowledging Mandi's answer. "It sounds to me like you may be closer to Jesus than Kip is." Mandi nodded affirmatively, so Darlene continued, "How is that for you – has it been hard or caused problems?" Right after the words left her mouth, Darlene heard her closed-ended question, which usually resulted in a yes or no answer stifling conversation.

Because Mandi felt comfortable with Darlene and was worn down from carrying the burden of all her inner turmoil for so long, she did not hesitate or hold back.

With the candor of desperation, of one craving redemption, Mandi opened her soul to the woman sitting serenely in that little room, "It isn't what I thought it would be. I don't even remember what I thought at first. Maybe that Kip would accept Jesus, but he never has. But he always treated me like I was super special.

"Truthfully, the guys at church – I mean they're nice guys and all – but they are always so serious. And, even though I never dated, until Kip, some of the guys at church could be so mean – like women are below them. That's not what it's like with Kip. Never."

Darlene felt the sincerity in what Mandi said. This young lady was not making excuses or justifying her attraction to Kip, it was truly what she had encountered and responded to being young and lacking the wisdom or hindsight of past experiences. Sure, some young Christian men may come across more serious, but that's primarily because many were taught self control, moderation, discipline – they were made aware of the temptations that the world held and what it took for a young person to try to withstand them.

Strong Biblically based churches exposed young people, on a more regular basis, to moral standards and the responsibility of upholding those standards. Darlene knew this was not to say that kids outside of a church setting were morally void. But on the whole, she could see what 30-plus years of "no values" teaching in the schools and the disintegration of the family had reaped. It was an anything goes world where what was right or wrong was relative giving each person the ability to be their own god and exempting a standard outside one's self. This was said to produce respect of individual rights. What it truly produces was self-centeredness and disrespect of others. *My rights* meant me... me... me. Oh how quickly they take care of number one not even realizing the harmful effects on those around them.

Just a walk through the halls of her son's middle school convinced her how off course things have gotten and how dreadfully harmful it was for children. Middle school, not high school, where little girls who were just beginning to blossom into womanhood were entangled in the clutches of boys not old enough to hold down a paper route. The teens kissed, petted, swore, and expended a great deal of energy posturing as mature adults.

Once Darlene had invited three neighborhood girls over to her house to help bake cookies. One of their moms had just had a baby, and Darlene wanted to give the mom a break while providing some womanly attention to the girls. Baking soon gave way to playing dress up. Darlene dragged out older outfits from the back bedroom closet along with gaudy costume jewelry and make-up relegated to the discard drawer in her bathroom.

What a fun time they had. There they were, three little eight years olds dressed and made up as sophisticated women – their version at any rate. They walked around Darlene's living room and through the kitchen with exaggerated moves replicating what they thought was womanhood. Soon, that was not enough. It was time to show their stuff to the world. With Darlene's permission and their own daring of each other, they went outside and proceeded to walk – swagger – up to the corner and back again. They collapsed in giggles, tripping on their too-big high heals and losing all their womanly sophistication as they crossed Darlene's foyer.

That's what it felt like walking through the halls of her son's middle school. The only difference – sad to say – was that these kids didn't know they were only pretending – they were trying hard to convince themselves they were for real which gave way to them going further in acting out adult behavior that ultimately had unhealthy consequences.

What have we done Lord? Darlene thought. Our precious children, not even fully developed, not mature enough to take on adult responsibilities or make adult decision are playing at adulthood headed straight for collapse. But they won't fall giggling into the safe home of a neighbor. They won't be able to wash off the make up, kick off the too-big shoes and get back into their jeans and their young lives. Their collapse could radically change their tender young lives.

In contrast to this, within the perimeters of Godly living, many of the young Christian adults she encountered knew how to have a good time – rip-roaring laughter and all – but good, clean fun – without enmeshing themselves in drinking, swearing, sex, and disrespect for authority, that the world offered.

Darlene had never laughed more then when she chaperoned one of her son's youth group campouts. There was freedom within boundaries that Darlene knew many kids yearned for but in not having them filled the void with other enticements. Unfortunately, those experiences usually brought more negative outcomes and fewer positive building blocks in a young person's life.

Not that churched kids were exempt from these enticements – from bad choices and wrong decisions. Volunteering at the center shattered that illusion really quick. Darlene had been startled out of her false impression that keeping her son sheathed in everything Christ-focused would protect him from the harsh realities of the world.

How naive she had been. Even Jesus knew that we were all sinners – all fallen. That's why Jesus came in the first place. Her son would fall, stumble in life just as she had and all mankind before her and after her. The thing was that when you fell, if you reached out to Jesus, He would pick you up and point you back in the right direction.

Having finally come to accept that her son would have to face some struggles on his own, she began looking for opportunities to show him

Jesus' ready hand of redemption and restoration. She stopped treating the Bible as if it were a rulebook and instead absorbs God's Words as they were meant to be. That's when Darlene began to undergo personal encounters with the Almighty sovereign creator who sought to connect with her to demonstrate His abundant love for her and to guide her through life on a path He has chosen specifically for her.

She rested in the truth that God had a plan for her son – and for this young lady sitting across from her.

Darlene wanted to help Mandi get back on course, pointed back at Jesus and felt His prompting to ask the hard questions, "What about having sex? It sounds to me like that may not have been what you had originally wanted for yourself?"

"It wasn't." Mandi stopped as tears welled up in her eyes. She hadn't meant to cry – had never cried about having sex with Kip since she got over the shock of that first time. What was going on? Why was she having all these confusing feelings?

Darlene waited.

"I love Kip and I know he loves me. I mean, you're right I didn't plan for this to happen – it just did. But, shouldn't it be okay if you really love someone? It feels like it should."

"Isn't that the way most temptation draws us in?" Darlene asked.

"Oh God," Mandi groaned, "Temptation wouldn't be temptation if it wasn't tempting," she said quoting what Pastor Dale often said during Bible study. "Oh what have I done. I really do love Kip – but I love God too. What a mess I've made of it all." The tears of a confessing heart came unchecked as Mandi felt the impact of having strayed from what she held in her heart as the truth. She glanced upward then lowered her face to the tissue she had taken from the nearby dispenser.

Darlene was surprised by how brutally honest Mandi was with herself. This girl's faith went deep. Darlene felt, even more strongly, God's prompting to turn her back to Him.

After a few moments Darlene asked, "What do you need to do now Mandi."

"Repent – ask God to forgive me."

"Turn to God not away from Him because He wants to help you. Would it help if we brought Kip in and talked about how to build a

132

relationship without having sex a part of it?"

At the mentioned of Kip's name, Mandi was reminded why she was even in the room with this woman. "Oh. What about the test," she asked turning toward the lidded cup that held her urine.

Whoops, Darlene thought, she's not ready to go there. "Sure, why don't we get that going. It'll take a few minutes, so we can finish talking as it's processing."

After administering a dropper full of urine onto the pregnancy test they sat back down. Darlene felt some distance between herself and Mandi so tried to ease back into conversation.

"You said Kip's big into sports and you met him playing basketball. Do you play any sports?"

"Yes. I was captain of our girls' basketball team at school. And we placed third at state."

"That's my son's favorite sport. He's got the build for it, tall. I love watching his games. Do your parents go to your games?"

"Yea they do. At least one of them and usually my brothers too."

"And how about Kip?"

"Sure – if he doesn't have a game."

"So your parents have met Kip," Darlene assumed, "How do they like him?"

Mandi grimaced and became fascinated with a piece of lint on the floor.

"They don't know about Kip?' Darlene offered.

"Kinda," Mandi told the piece of lint.

Darlene waited – how long could a piece of lint hold a teenager's attention? Mandi expected another question and was preparing answers in her mind when the silence hit her. She shifted in her chair, while doing so tried to get a glimpse of Darlene's face. But Darlene was not paying attention; She was calmly writing on the intake form.

"I'm not suppose to be dating – just group stuff. My parents have met Kip but they think he's just one of the group. Besides my mom's been off in her own world for awhile now. I mean we used to talk a lot, but now it seems we never do. My dad is always protecting her or something saying, 'Don't bother your mother right now, she's having a tough time.' What does that mean? And why can't I talk to my own mother!"

Darlene heard the pain in Mandi's question. "If you are pregnant, how do you think your parents would react?'

"My parents?" Mandi said in horror, "I could never tell my parents!"

Darlene had least expected that reaction from Mandi. Connect the dots. How do you not tell your parents you are pregnant? By not being pregnant. Good Lord, was Mandi contemplating abortion!?

Gathering all the calm she didn't feel, Darlene asked the question for which she didn't want to hear the answer, "Well then Mandi," she said as gently as possible, "what would you do if you are pregnant?"

Mandi, who up until a few moments ago was still convincing herself that she wasn't pregnant, who was holding pregnancy at arms length, not letting it clamor in on her, was now forced to finally examine that possibility. In doing so, she also had to connected the dots. If her parents were never to know, then the pregnancy could never be.

No questions remained in Mandi's mind. With full resolve her eyes met Darlene's as she stated, point blank, "I would have an abortion."

The finality in Mandi's words – the finality of such a decision – cut sharply to Darlene's heart. Her response was unchecked, "What do you mean – you can't really mean…" She caught herself mid-sentence and stopped speaking.

Mandi held her eyes. Darlene, visibly shaken, slowly took a few unnoticeable deep breaths, relaxed her tense posture, loosened her grip on the pen she held and tried again, "Mandi, I'm sorry I reacted. You threw me. I guess hearing about your faith and your heartfelt sorrow over having sex with Kip – I just figured that abortion wouldn't be an option for you."

Mandi neither responded nor turned away from Darlene. "Since abortion is something you are considering, can we talk about abortion – the procedure and some of the emotional effects?"

Mandi said, "No." At this point Darlene perceived that Mandi was pulling back.

As much as she tried, Darlene had lost her connection with Mandi and could not draw her back into open conversation. The test was positive. Mandi didn't so much as blink. Just sat back down, picked her purse up off the floor and looked at Darlene as if to say, "Is there anything else?"

"Would you like me to invite Kip in so we can all talk about what's next?"

"No," was all Mandi said, then as an after thought added, "But thanks. You've been kind."

Darlene guided Mandi through the paperwork that needed signatures and the exit form that gave clients the opportunity to evaluate the service provided to them. She lightly touched Mandi's upper arm and said, "I'll wait outside while you finish the exit form."

It was over. Nice as Darlene was, Mandi was glad to be alone in the room. She used the act of completing the paperwork as a reassurance that she was just fine, in control. Kip was just a few yards down the hall. He would be there to comfort her, make her feel better, help put this in the right perspective. But she didn't rush. With great care and deliberation she answered every question thoroughly on the exit form proof that she could handle this…. this ….

No, just write. She told herself. Don't think about it. Wait until I'm with Kip.

She left the room, headed down the hall, saw Darlene in conversation with another woman, felt thankful that she could probably walk past her unnoticed, then saw Darlene look her way. Ugh! She's smiling and walking toward me!

Mandi tried to smile but her lower lip wavered and collapsed. Darlene slowly approached, giving Mandi space, but not wanting her to leave without a final connection.

"Mandi, thank you for coming in. I know this hasn't been good news for you. I just want you to know, I am here for you, anytime."

"Thanks," Mandi replied looking away from Darlene as she continued heading toward the waiting room door.

Darlene again gently touched Mandi's shoulder, which caused Mandi to stop and look into Darlene's eyes as the older woman said, "I will be praying for you, every day."

Mandi saw in Darlene's eyes that she meant it and that it was said in kindness not judgement. Her heart was jolted by the love she felt. Not knowing how to respond she just nodded, turned and opened the door to the waiting room where Kip sat clutching a cup of cold coffee.

The look on Mandi's face told Kip what he wanted to know. Leaving the coffee on the table by the chair he had occupied, Kip rose and walked toward Mandi. They took each other's hand and without speaking walked back out into the day.

Traffic passed, people with places to be hurried by, horns beep, parking meters expired, a group of pre-school children corralled by their care-givers where being led on an outing, a dog barked, life kept on going. How could that be? Mandi thought. My life is ending. Don't these people know that? How can everyone else be laughing, smiling, going about their day's work like everything is normal when it's not normal.

She was overwhelmed with a desire to shake people out of their foolishness; their pretending that life was just fine. Life was a joke. A big, horrible joke that God plays on us.

Kip led Mandi to the far end of a greenbelt where a gazebo nestled among a few trees offered privacy and shelter from a sunny, humid day. Mandi neither felt the cooler air provided by the gazebo, nor did she allow the cool breeze to refresh her. She just sat, starring, contemplating the unfairness of life.

Kip sat quietly beside her. It was not that he was in tune with her needs, he too, was overwhelmed, baffled at a complete loss of what to say, how to help. In the waiting room he had come to terms with being a father. He knew that Mandi's beliefs meant if she was pregnant he would be a father.

Father. What an alien thought. Father's were old. Fathers had jobs, good paying jobs. Father's had it all together, understood life, were able to solve life's problems. Well, except his father, who bailed. Some example! So, how could he be a father? How could that word become an adjective describing him? And, yet it had.

He sat on the bench thinking about fatherhood. Where do I start? I obviously started it all backwards. So now what do I do? How do I make it right?

Feeling a tremor as Mandi leaned against him, he looked over to see she was crying. He removed his hand from hers and placed his free arm tightly around her saying, "It'll be okay Mand. We'll be okay. I can do this. I promise to be the best dad ever to this baby."

Mandi cried harder which prompted Kip to pour out more reassurances; "I'll be with you through everything; when you tell your parents... all of it."

136

"No! Kip, you don't understand! I can't tell my parents. There won't be an *everything*."

He stared at Mandi. She was right. He didn't understand. What was she saying? "Well Mand, you have to tell them. I mean, don't you think they'd figure it out... they'll see for themselves. I mean this isn't something you can hide."

"I can't do this. I can't. I have to have an abortion." Kip was stunned beyond words. Not that he could have spoken. Mandi had, at last, let down her guard as the full impact of her situation struck home. "My mom couldn't handle it now. It's the wrong time. She's...we've...Oh I don't know. It's all wrong. Everything is wrong. I mean, my God, I teach Sunday school. How can I stand in front of a class of kids and... And youth group... me an example for my peers. Sure this is some example. I'd probably be kicked out of school. Oh God! Oh God! My life would be over. No one would understand. It'd hurt too many people. I can't, Kip. I just can't."

They sat, huddled within the shelter of the gazebo built there as a peaceful oasis in the midst of downtown. Yet they felt totally exposed to the harsh elements of life. The late afternoon crept into the evening. As people went home to those they loved, to meals that needed preparing or whatever awaited them as the work day ended, Mandi and Kip remained transfixed, anchored on the bench, the last bastion of unreality, knowing that to leave would be to step fully into the impending calamity. Neither desired to take that step. And so they sat, holding tightly to each other against a life that had turned on them.

Chapter Seventeen:
Gail

Finding quiet time to work on her Bible study lesson seemed to be just out of Gail's reach all day. She knew that it was now or never. Once the kids started arriving home from school the house would take on a life of it's own in which Gail would only be a player.

Adding milk to her fresh cup of coffee, she ignored the ringing phone, proud of herself for not letting something else disrupt her time with the Lord. To distract herself from the insistent tug of the ringing she reflected back on the previous week's class about denial. She liked the way Karen had explained the process of denial and at what point it became unhealthy and harmful to a person.

As a teen it did seem like life swooped down and engulfed her in a nightmare after which her only means of survival was to go into denial. She doesn't remember even consciously choosing to do so, it just happened.

The Bible study for that week had made her look at the part she played in allowing the abortion or in her case the four abortions, to occur. Sure she was only a kid, but she did play at part in the abortion. Gail knew she had given in to her mother, partly, in a perverse way, to please her. She can see now how she had chosen to believe she was doing it for Rick so as not to ruin his life and his dreams for them.

She had convinced herself her mother was right. That was a first, but it helped to take the onus of the decision off of her. It would keep peace at home. It would prevent Rick's life from being wrecked. But why weren't those the sentiments she felt while she laid on that cold table knowing that all the nurses were probably talking about her, whispering about what a slut she was to be pregnant at 16.

Even feeling embarrassed didn't overshadow the connection she had made with the tiny life inside her. The life she and Rick had created. Torn between humiliation, what awaited her at home and the tenderness of blooming motherhood, Gail had laid sullen on the table as the abortion was performed. The pain she endured was due her, and more. Why should she suffer any less than her baby did whose life she felt incapable of saving.

The pain threatened to devour her and so she hid within the sanctuary of denial. Her relationship with Rick could not survive the secret she held, the secret she didn't deliberately keep from him so much as she couldn't face it herself. He had come back from boot camp a new man. An adult moving forward to build a life. In contrast, she had taken a life, the act of which, in turn, had stolen hers as well.

Gail had seen and faced the stark differences between she and Rick within minutes of greeting him at the bus station. That weekend, at a party, she once again threw caution out with her dreams as she drank, smoked her first cigarette and had sex with some guy she didn't even know...or want to know for that matter. But, she told herself, she accepted that she was no better than the rest of the losers at the party. She knew the score; why pretend she was anything different or better than her own family. Yup, she knew her score...a big zero!

Rick wasn't at that party. He was baffled by the changes he had seen in Gail. On the other hand, his dad and stepmom, with open welcoming arms, were trying hard to make him feel included in their lives. He found he was able to confide in his dad about the changes in Gail.

"Son, people aren't always as they seem. I know you loved her, but you were going through a tough time. This Gail just happened to be there, available. It doesn't mean that she was the one for you to build your life with, as you see now. Be thankful for her help. But also be thankful that you see her true colors."

Rick didn't want to give up on Gail, but he couldn't cross back to where he was before his life started to turn around. Nor could he join her where she was, hangin' with the dredges of the school. How could they have been so close to only be so far apart now? It was because of Gail that he had been inspired to make changes in his life.

In the end, Rick couldn't go backward and Gail couldn't move forward so their lives went in opposite directions.

As Gail thought about that period in her life, about the initial hopes and dreams; marrying Rick, building a life together...the whole, 'til-death-do-us-part dream the irony of the truth struck home.

'Til death do us part. Yeah, not my death, or Rick's, but our baby's. The ending of that life dashed many hopes on the cliffs of destruction.

She had never understood how something so unendurable could be done again and again.

That was the greatest burden, the mammoth guilt, and a weight that never let up. How could she have had another abortion and another until she had taken the lives of four babies? The verses from Jeremiah 8:4-6 so aptly described how denying her first abortion had produced subsequent abortions. *"And you shall say to them, 'Thus says the Lord, "Do men fall and not get up again? Does one turn away and not repent? Why then has this people, Jerusalem, turned away in continual apostasy? They hold fast to deceit, they refuse to return. I have listened and heard, they have spoken what is not right; no man repented of his wickedness, saying, 'What have I done?' Every one turned to his course, like a horse charging into battle."*

That was Gail – a horse with blinders on just charging headlong into more and more sin. When John had sought to console her by coming to her defense, "You were just a kid Gail. Give yourself a break. I mean where were your parents. They weren't there helping you to make a good, healthy choice. No, they were so wrapped up in their warped lives that they could only drag you in with them."

"I know John. But come on, you were 16 once too. How often did you defy your parents? I could have gotten on a bus and gone to the base where Rick was. I don't heap all the blame on me, but I was part of it. My parents never knew about the other abortions. Those were 100% mine. I didn't get off that first table and say 'never again.' I'm not seeking to excuse my actions. I just want to understand them. This verse showed me with such clarity where I was back then."

"I guess I can see that," John admitted, "I just don't want you beating yourself up about what's in the past. Sometimes I think I gave out the wrong advice, encouraging you to take this Bible study. It seems to have stirred up some painful things in your life. You're always so down. It's like I lost my wife." There, he had finally said it.

Gail heard it, finally putting together his distance over the last few weeks, his remarks that were suppose to be concern but more often hurt her. *"Ya know Gail, there's more to life – our family – than that Bible study."* Lately, "Bible study" has been a bad word. Didn't John know how much she needed this? Couldn't he see the miraculous changes God was making in her heart? Why did she always feel like she had to

140

defend herself. Was she missing something? Was she denying the effect this was having on her family?

Then she had remembered something Paula had said during the first class, "I want you to be aware that your closest friend, even your husband may not fully understand or be able to identify with you and what God shows you as you go through this study. That does not mean that they do not care or that they don't love you. It is not rejection."

Gail needed John. She was afraid that he may one-day look at her as not good enough for him. She had been so glad when he had supported her in going to the Bible study. She would do anything to please him, keep him happy, keep their family together and not end up like her life before John seemed to dictate. He meant too much to her. It was because of him that her life had a second chance. She didn't want to spoil a good thing; a very good thing.

Her inner turmoil became a fierce cyclone within her, twisting and building up speed with each week. Gail was torn between pleasing John, being there for her family and continuing to participate in a Bible study that was working deeply within her. The cyclone of divergent feelings produced a vortex that was sucking everything out of her. Gail felt constantly on the verge of screaming.

She couldn't explain to John how much this group meant to her. Yet, on the other hand, she also could not face Karen and tell her she was dropping out. In resignation she told herself to give it one more week. She opened her book to this week's lesson on anger thinking to herself, "This ought to be a hoot!"

An hour or so later Gail heard the postman drop mail through the slot in their front door. She knew that meant it was close to two-thirty and the kids would come streaming through the door in half an hour. She had made it through the section on God's anger – and His wrath, then Jesus' anger – so much more gentle, not a wrathful as God's anger. Even having to give consideration to how she got angry and the effect it had on her family was more educational than inspirational.

She had reached the bottom of page 38 when the mail dropped through the door. There were only a few questions left so Gail decided to finish up the lesson. The question asked her to give an example of her anger and the way she sins when angry. She began writing, "Just being pushed to the boiling point – living with squabbling children, a

141

messy house, no time for me to do fun stuff, no family to help with the burden, John working too many hours, a grumpy teenager. I get angry because nobody will cooperate with me. I screamed. I kicked a pile of books across the livingroom floor the other night.

"I get jealous that others have life better than I do. I have outbursts, am unloving, greedy – me – me – me! I become filled with malice – wanting to strike back – justify my own sorry state as the fault of others – say hurtful things I wouldn't otherwise say – eat more – gossip – slander."

Gail reviewed the appraisal of herself. Added a few more angry actions then moved on in hopes of finding a better way of dealing with her anger. Although she answered all the other questions, the revelation she hungered for was not apparent. She was just about to write her closing prayer when she heard the door open. Glancing at the clock she knew it was too early to be the kids. Just then John came into the living room.

"Hi sweetheart. I'm heading out of town tomorrow, so I left the office early to give us a little time together."

Gail, remembering what she just bemoaned in her lesson about John's long hours smiled, both to welcome him and to acknowledge God's admonition which seemed to say, "You don't always see clearly."

John saw the workbook on Gail's lap and the open Bible next to her, "Oh, did I interrupt your lesson."

Gail was grateful that his statement was not derogatory. "I was just finishing up – on anger. Which, of course, we both know I do not have a problem in that area!" she added with a conspirator's smile.

"Absolutely not. You can get angry with the best of them."

"The very best of them! Would you like some coffee?"

"Sure, why don't we drink it in the back yard. It's a bit muggy but I'm sure the old maple will afford us some shade."

They spent a glorious 15 minutes totally alone, a snatch of intimacy in the midst of daily life. They heard the voices of the twins, the slamming down of lunch boxes, squabbling for the pudding and the take-charge tone of older brother Patrick as he entered the kitchen.

Taking Gail's hand, John stood and began to walk toward the house. "John, I wanted to ask you…"

Hearing her more serious tone, John paused to listen. "Do you think everything's okay with Mandi? I feel so bad, like I've been in my own world lately. Maybe I'm neglecting her – all the kids."

"Well, I do have to admit, since you brought it up, that I've felt a bit neglected lately. I try to cover with the kids, but you know the hours I work. Maybe this isn't the right time do be doing this group study."

Group study. Didn't he hear me? I asked about Mandi and he's whining about being neglected. Gail saw John watching her so she responded in the only way she knew how. First she had to suppress her feelings, then she had to smile sweetly. Then she had to tell him what he wanted to hear, "I'm sorry John – really I am. I didn't know this would cause so much trouble. Maybe I should just quit."

"Dad! Dad! What are you doing home," came Pauly's excited voice from the back door. John's eyes brightened at the sight of his son, then both his sons as Brian came bounding out of the back door like a playful puppy ready to engage with it's beloved master. "Dad, wow this is great. Wanna ride bikes with us?"

John gave their mother a quick peck on the cheek, released her hand and ran to scoop up both boys in his arms, "You bet."

Gail shook her head – intimacy lost – how fleeting. Remembering her books laid out in the living room for anyone to see, she hurried to gather them up and put them in a safe, hidden place.

It wasn't until the next evening when Gail was able to answer the last question in her lesson. John was out of town, the twins were in bed, Patrick was watching a game on TV and Mandi was – where was Mandi anyway, youth group? Gail didn't quite know – how could you ever keep track of a teenager.

She plumped her pillows, got comfortable in her bed, opened her book, reached for her pen and began to read; *Quiet your heart and ask God to show you any unresolved areas of bitterness..."*

After reading the paragraph Gail closed her eyes and tried to empty her mind of all distracting thoughts. Then she beseeched God to reveal any residue of anger, bitterness, hate or hurt that remained from her abortions. In the back of her mind she figured that how she felt about her mother would be what God would address but she did not force that forward. Instead she began to write the prayer prompted by partial sentences in her workbook.

Dear God,

I am angry with myself for always wanting to please everyone. I hurt because I continue to punish myself for my abortions, for my lifestyle back then by not letting you – or others – love me. All this junk buried inside of me causes me to stuff things down rather than to deal with them – until it's too late and I reach my boiling point. Then I explode like a volcano and everyone in my path gets strewn with my garbage.

I want to learn how to deal with my anger better. How to acknowledge it then express it in a more positive way. I've had anger for a long time towards my husband John because he didn't treat me any differently than any of those other men.

I want to learn to forgive my husband."

Gail was aghast when she saw what came out of her. Angry with John? But she had no sooner stopped writing than the dam broke and anger flooded her being.

He was a solid, mature Christian man yet he couldn't wait to get her in bed just like everyone else. She didn't have the strength to fight him. What did she know? She was a new believer, a baby. He took advantage of that, just like all the other men she had dated.

She finally understood this dance they did. When she felt the lowliest, after a volcanic eruption of her anger, she was her most sensual. But, any other time there was always a distance between them when it came to physical intimacy. Basically she didn't like sex, she just endured it to be a good wife – to keep John.

How could she feel so much anger towards him and yet be afraid of losing him? How could she be anxious every minute he was away yet put him off when he was near?

This push-pull dance began when he said, during their wedding vows, that he would honor and cherish her. But that vow held no security within it because it laid upon the truth of John's actions; he did not honor her timid requests not to have sex before marriage. After which Gail could not honor sexual intimacy within marriage.

"Stupid. Stupid. Jerk!" She was ranting, throwing pillows, and punching the bed. When that didn't relieve her fury she knocked over the family picture, with John's irritating smile, from the nightstand. The crash and sound of shattering glass had a cathartic effect and spurred Gail on to more demolition. Later she would refer to it as *redecorating her soul from the bedroom on out!*

From the bedside lamp to the lose change on John's dresser, to the cosmetics on her make-up table and even the satin nightgown hanging from the peg on the door, Gail swung and smashed, careened and threw, stomped on and ripped up settling old scores, leveling the playing field, bringing her life to ground zero – since it had never gone beyond that to begin with, had it?

At 11:15 p.m. Gail was sitting on the floor with her back against the foot of the bed staring intently at nothing when the phone rang somewhere far away in another galaxy. The sound disappeared only to return minutes later.

Mandi, who had come home just after her 10 p.m. curfew, was in the kitchen snacking. Having finally removed her headphones, she had heard the second round of ringing and answered. After chatting with her dad for a few minutes she walked down the hall to get her mother. She must be sound asleep to not have heard the phone ringing, Mandi thought. So she opened her mother's bedroom door slowly and gasped at the sight before her.

"Mom, Mom…are you alright? What's the matter?"

"I'm fine Mand. What did you want?" Gail droned.

It was all too much for Mandi to take in. Her mother's room represented Mandi's life. Her father was on the phone upset that he hadn't gotten through on his first try. Was the whole family falling apart?

With an abrupt announcement, "Dad's on the line." She turned and went back into the kitchen to hang up the extension. It was taking awhile for her mother to come on the line so Mandi finally spoke up, "Dad?"

"Yes Mandi, what is it?"

"Mom doesn't seem too good. Talk to her."

"Sure Mandi. What seems to be the problem? Did the boys get to her?"

Just then Gail picked up the other phone, "Hi John. How was your flight?" she said warmly.

"Good sweetheart," he said a bit puzzled. Then remembering Mandi said, "Bye Mandi – sleep well."

"Bye Dad."

"Gail, is everything alright at home. Mandi sounded worried."

"It's never been better," Gail said with such calm resolve that she surprised John. "I've just been doing the Bible study. You know the one you wanted me to take part in but, ever since have been taking pot shots at me. I guess you would call that kicking someone when they're down."

John was so stunned he couldn't respond. Gail wasn't screaming, lashing out or running off at the mouth as she usually did when she was upset. He had never heard her sound this calm while discussing an issue that caused her distress.

"Well, John you should know what I learned tonight while finishing this week's lesson."

"What did you learn?" he asked curiously.

"I don't like having sex with you," Gail announced.

"You don't like – you what?"

"Yeah, doesn't that just throw you. It's not what I meant to do. I was a little thrown myself. Would you like to know why – what God showed me?"

It was late. He was tired. But John was not about to end this conversation, "Yes, I would like to know."

For probably the first time in Gail's life, she told all; she opened her heart and did not hold back. She did not try to please, to sooth, to cajole, to change the subject or to deny the painful truths. She just talked, explained, clarified and shared everything that she had come to acknowledge. After all, she was at ground zero, the only way to go now, with God's help, was up. But this time she wasn't taking all that baggage!

They talked past midnight, then past one. John too was able to open up and share his fears, insecurities, failures and disappointments. No resolution was reached, no actions defined or promises made that would wipe away the past. They had gone into the garden of their lives and methodically tug, yanked and wrenched out weeds, over-growth and vines that had been choking off the potential for beauty.

It was hard, backbreaking work. It ached and each felt an inner soreness. But the ground was cleared, ready to replant because they had been willing to tear out much of what had hindered growth, by honestly revealing what had taken root in their lives, separately and corporately.

Stripped of every defense, elevated by the brutal honesty John and Gail found themselves in stitches laughing over the redecorating that had taken place in their bedroom.

"It needed a new look sweetheart. I guess so does our relationship. I promise you I will make this up to you. Can we start again?"

Gail was touched by his words, but did not try to please him with her response, "I'm willing to try John, but I don't know if there's anything left."

"There is Gail... there is. And we'll find it. Now you'd better get to sleep. We both have busy days tomorrow."

"You mean, today don't you?"

John prayed with Gail – long distance – but the connection was as clear as still waters. He had some reparative work to do, but only with God's help could he even hope to recapture what he had helped to tear asunder.

Lying in bed, as he was about to drift off to sleep, it became clear what his next step should be – to woo back his wife. John would court Gail like he should have done years ago. He would honor her with chastity, put her before himself, respect her, and edify her heart, mind and soul. Without fully understanding how his actions ten years ago had brought about these results, without even needing to understand, John knew it was important to rebuild, to start again with the first brick, the cornerstone for the years to come.

Fifteen hundred miles away, Gail washed her face, brushed her teeth then made the rounds into each of her children's bedrooms to kiss them lightly. Something had changed. A drain had been unclogged. A wall had crumbled. A dead branch had fallen. A seed buried below the hard winter's ground had found its way beyond the packed earth, breaking through into daylight, welcomed by warm sunshine.

The anger was gone. The victim was gone. A person, once non-existent held captive behind the veneer of mother and wife, had emerged.

As Gail began to doze off the verse from Ezekial 36:26 came to her, "I will give you a new heart and put a new spirit in you. I will remove from you your heart of stone and give you a heart of flesh."

Tenderly – softly – peacefully Gail fell asleep.

147

Chapter Eighteen:
Renee

"Mom, really, I won't be too late. Haggerty set up this last minute meeting and well, you know him. Gosh, sometimes I feel like I'm a kid being called down to the principal's office. He sounded so serious. Not that he ever lightens up.

"Well, I don't want to carry on, just give Jay a big hug from me. Tell him I'm bringing home ice cream sundaes for dessert."

"That's fine dear. He's out back with the two little neighbor boys. They're absorb in war…you know all those little green army men your Dad bought him."

"Mom. Wasn't I against war?"

"No dear, you were off writing in Europe while your former classmates spoke out against injustices."

"Oh, right. But if someone had asked I would have said I was a pacifist."

"That's nice dear, just remember your dad fought and served his country with pride. A few little green men does not an aggressor make."

"Nicely stated mom. Have you ever considered journalism?"

"No, dear but I will consider hot fudge on my sundae."

"You've got it. I'll top dad's with an American flag!"

"You'd do him proud Renee. Whoops, a small battle has begun and it's not the little green men. See you later darling."

"Bye mom." Renee hung up the phone with a smile on her face. Talking to her mom had a way of lifting her spirits, even if she had to go to the principal's office. It must be a big game with Haggerty to sound as sour as possible when interacting with staff. If he gave an inch, showed that he was human, the paper would probably collapse. Other than the staff's daily meeting with Haggerty (come fully prepared, be on time, be concise and be brief), most of her job could be done beyond his reach.

Mike walked through the pressroom. "Hey Renee, I hear you've been called upstairs." The bad news was already spreading.

Not to be seen as caught off guard, which she was, Renee replied, "Yes, I have, and this may be your great photo-op. Are you coming?"

"I'll pass on this one. But, good luck," he said as he headed into the sales office. Was that concern she heard in his voice?

As Renee waited for the elevator she wondered, what does Mike know that I don't know? Probably nothing, but she wanted to be prepared for the worst and not taken aback by Haggerty.

Haggerty's office took up the entire west wing of the top floor. The elevator door opened into his executive secretary's office. Nobody got past Elaine, not even Haggerty's wife. Elaine, a woman in her early 40's, had a straitlaced professional air about her that came from years of being the keeper of the gate and a spinster. Not a word Renee used often but it suited Elaine. Actually, it went beyond that. Elaine made being a spinster look attractive.

Her life, much like her office and her job was neat, orderly, well structured, properly balanced and fully accessorized. She had many acquaintances but few intimate friends. She was involved with her church and other extracurricular activities yet none were a passion for her. She was well read, equally well traveled but had never lived anywhere but in the small town five miles east of the city, where she was born and raised.

She was a bright, talented woman who greeted you with a smile that never went as far as her eyes. Renee had read some of the kindest words ever written to employees who were grieving or even to those celebrating a milestone in their lives from the pen of Elaine. Elaine remembered birthdays, anniversaries and special holidays with simple but meaningful gifts. Yet, never once had Renee heard Elaine utter a compliment.

Elaine was an enigma. Knowing everything Renee knew about Elaine, she had to like her. But that never flowed easily, it was something Renee told herself to do. After all these years there was no camaraderie, no relationship beyond proper professional etiquette.

Elaine's meticulous smile and manner greeted Renee when the elevator door opened. "Good evening Renee, you are right on time. Please have a seat while I let Mr. Haggerty know you have arrived."

Elaine gracefully slipped her chair away from the desk and walked down the corridor to Haggerty's double mahogany-doored office. After a slight rap of her forefinger, Elaine purposefully yet exactingly opened the right-hand door, slipping inside just beyond Renee's line of vision.

Renee began reviewing the stories she was working on, her most recent achievements and some ideas she had for the upcoming season as a way to bolster her confidence as well as to prepare herself for whatever Haggerty threw at her.

During this mental gymnastics she was reminded of a blunder on a story a week or so ago. Suddenly, it all came together. Yes, it was one of Haggerty's pet projects, handed off to her and she had messed up. That's it, she thought. That's why I'm here.

Renee didn't want to sound wimpy by having excuses ready, but the blunder and its ripple effect weren't all her doing. My God, she thought, the lady she interviewed was pushing 90. Her memory was obviously faulty. She was definitely not the best basis for building facts to support the story.

Oh no, wasn't she a distant relative of Haggerty's? Renee resigned herself to being dragged over the coals. She decided not to offer up any excuses, knowing it would only make the situation worse. Deep in thought she didn't see Elaine return.

Polite, as always, but not one to mince words, Elaine cleared her throat and announced, "You can go in now Renee."

Elaine's voice startled Renee as she was abruptly brought out of her reverie. For a second she felt confused but met Elaine's efficient smile with one of her own, gathered her knapsack, stood up and strode meaningfully into Haggerty's office, ready to take her lumps like a man. No, even better, like a woman. Well, like a woman who doesn't cry when her feelings are hurt, a modern, new millennium woman.

Renee was laughing at herself as images of women passed through her mind. When she entered Haggerty's office she realized she was smirking and quickly looked away from the stern face that greeted her, hoping he hadn't seen her expression.

"Renee. Come in, sit down. Always nice to see your smiling face."

He saw it. But what's with this warm hospitality. Renee took a seat to the left of Haggerty who was seated in the leather high-back chair, one of three by a couch positioned around a marble top coffee table. This casual setting was different, rare. Haggerty always sat behind his desk placing the summoned party uncomfortably across the wide expanse on a rather too upright chair.

Settling into the soft leather, the smell, the feel, Renee thought, I could get used to this. The next time dad suggests redecorating the den in leather and mom objects; I'm siding with dad. This is nice, really nice.

She looked up to see Haggerty watching her. Was that a smile? Almost. "Renee there are some matters we need to address."

Here it comes, she thought, make your face relaxed yet concerned, non-readable yet pensive.

"It's about a story you did."

What's the worst that can happen here? It's not like I'd get fired. Renee thought back on others who had messed up. She couldn't recall anyone getting fired for messing up a story.

She nodded, smiled quietly, but not too bubbly as Haggerty spoke.

"Your piece on the drive-by shooting at the mall and the follow up, the personal interest perspective..."

What's he saying...the mall? That was months ago. It was a good piece. What did I do wrong on that? A questioning look crept onto her face. Haggerty saw it before Renee caught herself.

He interrupted himself mid-sentence. Just stopped talking.

"My mall story. Oh, sorry, I thought... well it doesn't matter. You were saying?"

Haggerty rewound his conversation and began again, with a touch more pomp and circumstance.

Man, he's building this up big time. What the heck did I do wrong? I thought that was one of my best pieces – series even.

"...And I believe it is one of your best pieces. The entire series was of a caliber I have not read in years. It is exciting to me, after all these years at the Daily Journal to come across such talented work."

The tone of respect in Haggerty's voice swept over Renee like dawn gently announcing a new day, a fresh start, the promise of dreams waiting to be fulfilled. Renee sat watching the sunrise with each word Haggerty spoke. She felt the warmth, was drawn into its radiance, was speechless as her world was softly outlined in the blush of a new day. On the horizon of her life the images illuminated, glowed with assurances, with hope for something more.

"…. your horizons are unlimited. You have a unique talent. I've seen it right from the start. But this mall series, that was both hard hitting and tender. You combined the meat of a story with the humanity of it. Never did it become so over-laden with facts to become boring yet never so personalized as to become soppy. And I want to help you realize your full potential, Renee. To get the recognition you should have. The readership that will truly appreciate all that you bring to what you write. I am, well, if you are in agreement, I would like to submit this series to corporate for consideration for the society's award."

Thank you God, Renee thought, as she spoke, "Thank you Mr. Haggerty. Writing to me is like breathing. I have to do it. And who doesn't dream of receiving literary acknowledgment. Oh, yes that would be an honor. Just having your opinion… that you would think ….Would recommend my work for the society's panel to review."

Renee realized she was rambling, almost gushing, but didn't feel the need to stop herself. This was too much. This man, that she had held at a distance, had used as the brunt of her jokes, had imitated mockingly with coworkers…was opening the door to a dream that had eluded her own efforts for years.

"I can't thank you enough. You don't know what this means to me."

"Oh, I think I do. I remember my many years of apprenticeship, when I first started out..."

As he meandered into sharing his story, a habit that irritated everyone during meetings, Renee felt an affinity toward this man. Listening, truly hearing what he was saying was no longer irritating. He became a source of encouragement. He had been where she is and gone further. She could learn from him. If she hadn't scoffed at him all these years, she may have already been learning from him. How foolish she felt. How stupid she had been. How focused on the power of being a woman and the belittling of men – this man, had left her with less.

Yet here he was, opening a door when, on her own, she could never have reached the knob.

Haggerty finished his reminiscent and returned to the business at hand, "Elaine will work with you on what we'll need to get this off to corporate. We have to move quickly, the submission deadline is drawing near. But, it's doable. And with Elaine…" He smiled with the knowledge that all was in the best of hands where his secretary was concerned.

"Yes, I now. She's the best." Renee, too, felt gratefulness for this woman who would assist her in reaching for the brass ring.

"She is isn't she. Well, it's getting late Renee. Come up and see Elaine in the morning."

I'll do that Mr. Haggerty. And thank you. Really, thank you I truly appreciate this."

He held out his hand, which Renee shook and said, "You are welcome Renee. Actually it is a pleasure for me to be able to work with you. Good night then."

"Good night."

Leaving Mr. Haggerty's office Renee noticed that Elaine's desk was at perfect rest after hours as it was during the busiest of workdays. She smiled with the knowledge that this woman's expertise, her exactness would be put to work on Renee's behalf.

Since the elevator had been used for everyone's trip to leave the office, Renee had to wait as it made its slow climb back up from the ground floor to where she stood, trying to contain all the excitement she felt. Once cocooned in the 4x4 enclosure Renee gave out an unrestrained whoop and danced as if she'd score the winning touchdown of a Super Bowl.

Walking into her parent's home, Renee's arms were filled with enough ice cream delights to feed an army, which included an ice cream cake with army men parading about on top of it. She barely got through the door when Renee began running over her own words trying to explain what had just occurred.

Her mom was indulgently listening while trying to extract the softening treats from her daughter's excitable grip. Jay, heightened by his mother's excited state, was jumping all around celebrating ice cream… and little army men on a cake, chattering faster than his mother, "Can we eat it now momma? I ate all my dinner. Didn't I Grammy? I ate everything even the peas I hate. Now momma, please? I have the bowls on the table. Oh look at the army men. Can I eat them momma, can I?"

With winsome authority Renee's father strolled into the commotion, watched the people he loved most in the world then spoke, "How 'bout

153

we move this party into the dining room." Upon which he put arms around the shoulders of his two most favorite women and guided them toward that end. Jay was right under foot, staying as close to his ice creamed army men as adult movement would allow.

The celebration lasted late. Jay was asleep in grandpa's lap when Renee, spent from retelling the story and her every thought, was ready to leave. Her mother had offered to prepare the spare room but Renee wanted to lay in the quiet of her own bedroom alone with her thoughts.

It was in that stillness that she felt overwhelmed with gratitude for more than her good fortune. She had been blessed by the hand of God and saw it. Not three days ago she had trudged through the Bible study lesson on anger, ready to fight, ready to state her defense before God. But, yet again, God had taken her down a different path.

Flipping through the workbook she found the question that for her had become another answer, another piece to her puzzle that simmered with rage.

Is there anything about abortion that you still feel angry about?

She could have said Alex, his lies, his manipulations. She could have said the blasé way that abortion is accepted in England. She could have said her parents' expectations of her that seemed, then, to play a part in her decision. But, upon reading that question the only answer that came to mind was an answer she didn't even know existed until she wrote it.

That in my pride...my self-reliance, I never even bothered to consider a different approach to "my problem."

She wasn't a victim. She was better than everyone else was. She was out to show the world who Renee was. Her writing talents, her fine ways, her world traveling sophisticated nose-in-the-air persona. Alex had called her cheeky. She used to take it as a compliment, now she heard the biting truth in that word.

At the end of the lesson her prayer said it all, *"Dear God, I knew you existed but you didn't fit into my perception of myself. I was the all knowing and no one, not even Alex, was going to direct my life. I am angry with myself for being so prideful. For desperately needing to be in control of my life, when I wasn't in control at all. I only hurt myself for being so focused on my career that I shut everyone else out or pushed aside anything that got in my way.*

"Thank you God, that I didn't do that with Jay. But I did with his father and how many other men.

"I thought so highly of myself. But everything I am you gave me. You created me and in doing so poured into my heart a yearning to write. In my prideful way I claimed it as my own doing and hurt many people in the defense of my fulfilling my zeal to write. Even to taking the life of a child you created. I am so sorry.

"I deserve only that you would take this talent from me. Please don't. No, I know you won't. You are forgiving. And that is what I ask, that you forgive me, again. As many times as it takes."

Sitting in her room, re-reading what she had written, Renee thought, I deserved to be punished for what I have done, for who I have been and yet, God has given me this tremendous blessing. I want to be like the verse from Ephesians 4:32: "And be kind to one another, tenderhearted, forgiving one another just as God, in Christ, has forgiven you."

Tenderhearted. The last thought Renee had before falling off to sleep was; *I want to be tenderhearted.*

Chapter Nineteen:
Kalli

Kalli watched out the large picture window as Sean headed out for his second interview with a geological research firm. His love of rocks and small water creatures baffled her yet when she accompanied him on treks to explore the world from a geological perspective, she fully enjoyed all Sean taught her.

Now it seemed possible that his love of things "earthly" would turn into gainful employment. Since Kalli didn't have any morning classes they had laid in bed sharing, dreaming and planning their future if a job offer occurred.

Getting married was part of their dreams. It comforted Kalli that Sean was the one that pushed to find a job so they could be married. Though Kalli would talk marriage, even have the white-picket-fence image floating through her mind, the thought of facing it as a reality scared her, gave her a sense of suffocating. Not that she felt Sean smothered her. It was a sensation of life closing in on her, trapping her, pinning her down with no way out.

Yet, she chatted amiably with Sean actively taking part in where they would have the wedding, who would be invited, the colors, the food, the honeymoon and their future together afterwards. Getting this job meant the world to Sean. It was his field and the basis for building a future with Kalli.

Sean turned and gave the watching Kalli a thumbs-up signal, ducked into his car and drove off. Kalli stared out the window for a few moments longer wrapped in ambivalent feelings. She remembered her vow to work on her Bible study and not to put it off until the day before class as she had done every week so far. Kalli did not turn from the window and pick up her workbook because she had suddenly gained more self-discipline. The Bible study was a good excuse to escape thinking about the future Sean kept painting for their lives.

Avoidance. Escaping into fantasies. Denial. All techniques Kalli had perfected to help her live out each day. She put off the study wanting to avoid what truths it held. But to hide from Sean's dreams she escaped into the study. The topic was anger. This would be easy since Kalli believed she loved everyone and harbored no anger against others. Anyone could tell that by her easy smile and always-upbeat personality. People constantly commented on her high energy, light-heartedness and fun-filled attitude. Kalli fed on their observations determined to be that person. And why not, that was a good kind of person to be.

Kalli had developed a love-hate relationship with her Bible study. She was starting to see how she hid from the harsher realities in her life. She was thankful that God was gentle when causing her to look at painful incidents. But this scared her. Her defenses, so fine-tuned, didn't work as well anymore. Without these defenses properly in placing and working, how could she deal with life?

She remembered how relieved she felt when a defense was pealed back and God's strength had helped her through. God really was there for her. But to let go completely, to not have places to hide, Kalli still wasn't able to grasp how life would be if that were to occur. Sometimes she fought the change, which was probably what putting off doing the workbook every week was about. Yet, when she did the work and went to the group she was given a glimpse of another Kalli, a Kalli she was beginning to like. If only she could be who she was in the group when she left the group.

Being with those women was safe. She especially liked Paula. Although Karen helped her to look deeper into herself, Paula's words wrapped around her with reassurances. It made it bearable to examine the dark shadow that seemed to emerge out of nowhere and engulf her.

Opening her workbook Kalli began to do the lesson about God's anger. Intense! She didn't like the wrathful God that became apparent. Moving on to Jesus and learning about the way he dealt with anger was much easier to take. She was beginning to understand that even under God's wrath, the people of the Old Testament still didn't get life right. That's why God sent his only son Jesus into the world. He lived as an example to people and when he died on the cross, he took with him all the sins of the world. She paused to recite her favorite salvation verse, John 3:16, out loud. Kalli didn't have to fear God's wrath because the atoning blood of Christ saved her from it.

Kalli equated God's wrath to some of the ferocious storms she had witnessed that had uprooted trees, collapsed hillside houses and caused her favorite river to flood with such driving force that cars were swept away. That was the energy behind God's wrath, yet Jesus' death and resurrection saves us from His wrath.

To Kalli personally, that meant she didn't have to walk around in fear worrying what would happen if she messed up. Yet, sometimes that was hard to grasp. She knew part of her cheerful demeanor was to ward of punishment for all the times she did mess up. She believed, at some level, if she were good enough she would counter-balance her wrong actions. Except that somewhere inside she wasn't fully convinced of her balanced-scales theory and lived in fear, awaiting her just rewards. Kalli knew it was a case of accepting the verdict of life-time condemnation.

As Kalli did the lesson she saw that she still needed to have reverence for God, to respect him but she did not have to be afraid. When she messed up she could turn to Jesus, confess, repent and go on, hopefully learning from her wrongs. The big mallet in the sky was not going to be hammered down on her. It was a freeing thought. Kalli caught her self looking up at the sky lightly dusted with puffs of white thinking that doom no longer hid behind the soft whiteness above. God wasn't mean and vengeful hovering up there ready to render a verdict and exact payment. Kalli's heart brightened. Yet this brightness was not the for-show expression she put on for the world. It emanated from within her, from her heart, the heart God tenderly nurtured.

This fresh sense of freedom made her wonder why Jill didn't know that God wasn't angry at her. Why did she keep expecting God to wreak havoc in her life? Kalli became excited with what she had learned and the thought of sharing it with Jill so she too could be set free.

Kalli continued on and when she came to question eight she paused to consider if there was anything about her abortion for which she still felt angry. *"Nope, not really,"* she thought. But something a gal said on campus pricked her conscience and Kalli began writing, *"People are very vogue about abortion. No one considers the child. All they care about are women's rights and political groups. They've lost sight of the one who gets the worst of it – the child. There is very little good counseling available. Good meaningful, unbiased. A mother and father sometimes don't even know their daughter is pregnant. Some fathers of unborn babies put such negative pressure on the pregnant girlfriend. And too many women treat it like birth control or life-control... to keep control over their lives without thinking about or knowing the real harm it is doing. How would they know anything else, most have never had a baby, held a tiny miracle in their arms. They make, or are pushed to make, a decision about a phenomenal process – giving birth...life...at a time when they don't fully know what that means or how it feels to bring a precious life into the world. All because a law says it's okay! But it's not!"*

Once Kalli began railing against society her defenses relaxed and her feelings became more personal. *"Eric's mom...I thought she was my friend. I liked her. But the minute she found out she did everything she could to save her precious son's future. And I believed her! It was only one encounter, one quick walk in the park but I knew the path before me was already paved with selfish Eric, protective mom and lying Kalli."*

Kalli had convinced herself that she did not harbor any anger. Now she saw differently. She was incensed at the callous treatment she had received. But she was even more enraged knowing it was built on a lie, her lie. The baby wasn't even Eric's.

The next question asked, "What have you done with all this anger?" She squirmed at the question, knowing that God would show her. And he did as a scene from her happy, perfect life with Sean flashed before her. It wasn't exactly as she liked to portray. She was violent, said things to hurt him, called him names and started fights. Most of this was not about anything Sean had done it was all the anger she *"didn't harbor."*

"Oh God," she moaned, *"now what do I do?"* No answers came to her, which made Kalli restless and impatient. *"I need a break."* she thought then caught herself flirting with the need to run, escape, hide. Instead she resolutely opened her Bible to look up the verses about bitterroots.

Half an hour later she turned a page and realized she was at the end of the lesson, the summary. Kalli beamed with pride. She had seen a lesson through from beginning to end. She had tried to put it aside only once, but had made herself keep going. Now she had one page of summarizing and her lesson would be done! Let's see, she thought, what did I learn.

God's anger is just, fair and short lived. Jesus expressed his anger by peaceful explanation, except in the temple when he showed righteous anger. The thing about abortion that makes me angry is that people are so selfish (I'm included). They engage in sex irresponsibly, create a life and because it's not convenient for them they destroy it. I want to respond to my anger by forgiving those involved that were of this opinion.

I sin when I am angry by harboring bad thoughts, using harsh word and violent actions. I will practice self-control of my anger by trying not to strike out but to take time to think through my feelings. I want to learn to forgive as Jesus does!

In the back of her mind Kalli knew that forgiveness was somehow linked with her uncle who had sexually violated her, but as yet, God was not bringing that issue forward for her to examine or walk through with Him. She was neither ready nor strong enough to go there alone. One day, maybe, she would be.

Kalli heard a car door close and glanced out the window. Sean locked the car door and headed up the walk, deep in thought. He did not see Kalli watching him, attempting to read his expression as a clue to the way the interview went. She was also searching for a clue as to what her true feelings were about Sean, this baby and their future together. Did they even have a future together? She didn't want to live in a make-believe world anymore. More and more she wanted to know who she really was and what that meant in her relationship with Sean.

"Funny," she thought, "I'm not afraid to question about our relationship." Kalli felt assured that God would answer her. Even further, she was ready for whatever it was that God had to say to her.

With that she also realized the first thing she had to say to Sean was how sorry she was for the way she had taken out her anger on him when most of the time he did not warrant it. She thought that if she wants to forgive as Jesus does, she would need to know when to ask for forgiveness. Sean is a good place to start.

Coming out of his own preoccupation, Sean looked up toward the apartment he shared with Kalli and a broad grin spread across his face as he saw her at the window. One day they would be married. With this new job that day would come a lot sooner. He lifted his hand to acknowledge Kalli and picked up his pace taking the steps two at a time.

Chapter Twenty:
Jill

Jill was angry.

She was pacing the living room staring at the phone rehashing her conversation with Russ. Doesn't he get it? What doesn't he understand? When will he?

It felt like Russ wanted her to change, to heal and yet he couldn't let go of who she was. The phone call was just one more example of that. The conversation kept running through her mind.

"Jill, I just heard from Frank. He says you're not catering his company's yearly customer appreciation event. You've been doing that for three or four years now. Frank was your first customer. He put you in business. What's going on?"

"Russ, I tried to explain the other night. Franks a good guy. I really like him and I am grateful for what his business meant to me, back when I was starting out. But things have changed. I've changed. Catering Frank's events has very little to do with good food and friendships and more to do with four solid hours of alcohol consumption.

"You know, Russ, how I fight to avoid booze. You know what happens to me. I just can't be part of others drinking to excess. It's not like I left him high and dry – no pun intended – I gave him two other caterers I know who could do a great job for him."

"Jill, I owe him. He's one of my biggest accounts. What will he think about me because my wife's on a non-drinking kick?"

"Can we talk about this later Russ?" Jill could barely contain her reaction long enough to get off the phone.

"Non-drinking kick!" Jill yelled after vehemently placing the receiver down. Thoughts raced through her mind, *His image – what about my life! I'm self-destructing in an ocean of wine, beer and booze right before his eyes and he wants me to wade out deeper but not get wet!!*

Her rage was swift and pointed moving from Russ to God, *"It wasn't enough to let me abort my baby. No it's not good enough for you, my 'loving' God. No then you had to make me barren. I am finally fighting to stop drowning all my pain in this sea of booze and the next wave to hit – a tidal wave – comes from my own husband! It's not fair. Where are you? When does it ever end?"*

Jill found herself on the back patio pacing, crying and muttering when she felt a restrained touch on her shoulder. She must have sense someone approaching because she was not startled, she was calm as she turned to see her jogging friend Sally.

"I rang the bell," she said as she gently led Jill to a bench facing the picturesque rock garden. "It looked like you were home so I thought maybe, since it was such a nice day (Jill snickered) you'd be working in your garden. So I came around back."

Sally didn't feel the need to explain herself. She was merely trying to comfort Jill with soft familiar words. It was only fifteen minutes or so ago while reading her daily devotion that God prompted her to visit Jill. Actually, it was much stronger than a prompting. Sally didn't hesitate. She had already discerned that Jill was in a battle far fiercer than Jill's previous snippets of conversation about her life had revealed in the past. Sally had been praying continuously for this woman, her friend, who never would allow a more intimate relationship.

When God's nudge came, Sally didn't hesitate. Right in the middle of cross-referencing a Bible verse, Sally, nonetheless, closed God's Word in response to His voice. Sitting next to Jill, softly voicing soothing words, Sally continued to pray seeking God's wisdom. Sally reached into the purse still slung over her shoulder and pulling out her miniature Bible opened to Ephesians 5:6 and began to read. *"Let no one deceive you with empty words, for because of these things the wrath of God comes upon the sons of disobedience. Therefore do not be partakers with them; for you were formerly darkness, but now you are light in the Lord; walk as children of the light (for the fruit of the light consists in all goodness and righteousness and truth), trying to learn what is pleasing to the Lord. And do not participate in the unfruitful deeds of darkness, but instead even expose them; for it is disgraceful even to speak of the things which are done by them in secret. But all things become visible when they are exposed by the light, for everything that becomes visible is light."*

They sat quietly for a few moments, Jill's tears subsiding, and an aura of peace calming the turbulent tensions within her heart. Sally eased up from the bench, delicately touching Jill's upper arm, then, in silence, left Jill to the care of the Lord.

Jill didn't stir as her thoughts, which minutes before had been a pounding surf of fury, became a refreshing cascade quenching a deep thirst. She no longer was consumed by the need to punish Russ, to stab at him, twisting the knife in his gut. Nor did she have to fix him. She only had to learn what it is that God would have her do in her own heart and soul.

The battle over not catering an event had more to do with a means to hurt each other than it did with Russ's business or image being in jeopardy. She shook her head wondering how often they had found places in the sand to draw their personal lines of battle, to take a stand and inflict retribution upon each other.

"I will no longer partake of darkness. I am a child of light in the Lord." Jill kneaded that thought into her mind wanting to make it a part of her psyche. As she massaged her thoughts, rooting out the lingering darkness the light fell on her life years ago when she and Russ had first learned Jill was pregnant.

Jill remembered her aunt sitting next to her on a couch. It was at Jill's house. Where was her mother? Oh, that's right, her aunt was visiting from down south to allow her mom to attend a convention with her father. Jill chuckled remembering that her mother had used the word visiting rather than babysitting, so as not to belittle Jill. Jill, in truth, preferred having someone there when her parents were gone, especially her aunt. She always came up with some kooky adventure, whether it was baking an exotic dish or going to the upscale stores and trying on pricey gowns. Jill looked forward expectantly to her aunt's "visits."

But this memory was different. Her aunt's face was serious though kind. She was leaning forward speaking in almost a whisper. *"Jill, you're not alone. I'll be with you every step of the way. I'll help you break the news to your parents. Trust me. They'll come around no matter how they react initially."*

Jill gasped at the memory which, until that moment, had been buried into non-existence. She remembered more of the conversation.

"You know your uncle and I have never been able to have children. If you aren't ready to raise this baby we would welcome it into our home with open, waiting arms."

Jill sat dumb-founded. How had she completely forgotten that talk with her aunt? Mulling over that conversation evoked another memory. Her aunt's response when she lied to her aunt telling her she had miscarried.

She had heard the muffled sounds of crying on the other end of the phone as her aunt tried to find words to comfort Jill. Then her aunt had said something Jill had heard her mother say often, "The women of our family have been cursed with pregnancy limitations. I've been unable to get pregnant. Aunt Sissy lost two pregnancies before having Wyatt. And your mother almost lost you twice during her pregnancy. That was the only time she was pregnant."

God had been there. He had tried to stop her, provide a way out that was life giving. She had even told Russ about it but they had both run headlong into keeping everything swept under the rug of their perfect-couple image.

Where earlier Jill had cried tears of anger flailing at God, at this moment tears of remorse and contrition streamed forth. "You were there, God. You tried to help but I refused you. I am sorry. I am so...so sorry," she cried out to both God and her lost child.

She noticed that Sally had left her pocket-Bible lying next to Jill on the bench. She picked it up and turned to chapter five in Ephesians to reread the verses Sally had shared. Her eyes caught the last few verses of chapter four that began at the top of the page where she had turned. *"And do not grieve the Holy Spirit of God, by whom you were sealed for the day of redemption. Let all bitterness and wrath and anger and clamor and slander be put away from you along with malice. And be kind to one another, tender-hearted, forgiving each other, just as God in Christ also has forgiven you."*

Jill marveled at how astute God's Word was. If those verses didn't describe Jill, nothing did. Yet, she did not feel condemned because God had also provided instruction as to how she was to change. More powerfully was that God had already – past tense – forgiven her through Christ's death on the cross.

Jill closed the little Bible and hugged it to her heart as she walked toward the house. *"If I shower and freshen up I can make it to Russ's office before noon and take him to lunch. But first I want to call and thank Sally. How did she know I needed her just at that moment?"*

Jill smiled recognizing God had once again worked in her life. "Thank you Father."

Chapter Twenty-one:
Forgiving Others

Paula was running late, almost. As she rushed through the Center's door she prayed silently that none of the women had arrived. She always felt better about starting the class when she and Karen had taken time to pray together. She knew they both prayed continuously throughout the week for each of the women, but to spend a quiet moment before God had a calming effect on Paula and helped her remember that God was the true leader of the class.

Karen was sitting, with her head bowed, alone in their meeting room. Paula slowed her pace and tried not to disrupt Karen's prayers. As Karen lifted her head, Paula was astonished by the glistening eyes that met hers.

"Are you alright? What's the matter?" Paula said as she rose to move closer to her friend. She was used to seeing Karen serious and concerned, but seeing her close to tears was unsettling.

Karen patted the hand Paula had placed on her shoulder. "I was sitting here enjoying the first moment of quiet all morning when Alice came to mind."

Paula nodded, murmured understanding then asked, "Did she call?"

"No, haven't heard a word."

"That's worse isn't it?"

"Ya know you'd think I'd be used to it by now. How many times have I really connected with someone only to never hear from her again? How many women does my heart know of that are out there still hurting? What can I do, what more can I do to show women that they don't have to live in their pain?"

Paula, feeling helpless to console her friend, remembered the plate of cookies she had made. They usually didn't have snacks at the class, but Paula had worked through some frustrations the previous night by baking. In the morning she was faced with an abundance of peanut butter, chocolate chip cookies, her greatest weakness. She reached back into her canvas carry-all behind her and brought the treats out, removing the wrapping.

Karen smiled and accepted the comfort food. "There are no answers sometimes huh?"

Not wanting to cut Karen short from venting her feelings, Paula asked, "How do you let go of it all?"

"I used to think I could. Today I can't. I thought if I allowed the ache in my heart to well up the groaning of my spirit would somehow reach Alice and prompt her to call. Then I thought, if I'm hurting for her maybe it would lessen some of what she's feeling."

Paula, so used to the unwavering leadership qualities in Karen, was left speechless at seeing Karen's sensitive, vulnerable side. She slowly bit into a cookie.

"I guess I get irrational when the emotions hit. Then I have to quiet my heart by praying, giving it back over to God. It helps to remember that his timing is perfect. But, for Alice, I really do believe this was God's timing. He was trying to bring her to this group."

Paula stopped hiding behind the cookie and responded, "But you know he won't give up on her."

"You're right. He won't."

"Can I pray for you before the others arrive?"

Karen was touched by Paula's request, that she had taken the lead. "Sure," she said and bowed her head, waiting as the voice of her dear friend lifted her up to God.

Afterwards they both looked at the clock then at each other. "I bake cookies and nobody shows?" Paula exclaimed.

"More for us," Karen said reaching for another cookie. Then they heard the front door open and the sound of female voices.

"Guess God's going to teach us how to share!" Paula said with a smile.

The four women entered together, giggling and chatting, their common bond turning into friendship. When they saw the cookies they all cheered and settled in to partake of good food and God's word.

Since everyone was in a conversational mode Paula decided to open with a more general approach. "Before we start today's lesson, let's take a moment to discuss how last's weeks lesson on anger has effected your lives this past week."

Not wanting to turn this lesson into an extension of the one about anger, Karen clarified what Paula was asking, "God is always a gentleman. He takes every step necessary to meet us right where we are, except for that last step. That step is up to each of us. We learned a lot about anger last week. And when we read scripture we have seen the promises God makes to us. But there is always a part we play, an action for us to take. What specific actions have you taken to deal with anger properly?"

"Anger is not a sin but instead what we do with it is," Gail said. She could not believe all that had occurred is just a few short weeks. She had seen so clearly how her outbursts were the product of suppressing her anger or not even acknowledging when something made her angry. Then one small incident would have her foaming at the mouth ready to devour anyone in her path. But she would never have seen that if God had not stayed with her that night she went ballistic in her bedroom. She was awed at how cathartic that evening had been, especially speaking what was exactly on her mind to John.

Since then John had metamorphosed into a chivalrous suitor, sending flowers the next day, brining home a gift when he returned from his trip. At first she thought this was just to make up and after a period of extra attention life would revert back to pre-outburst days. Flowers then sex, that was John's way of making up. So far it had only been flowers, gifts and no sex. John would kiss her lightly before leaving for work. When he came home or as they went off to sleep he would do the same. But other than that he rarely did more then give her a brotherly hug.

She had tensely awaited the normal routine, then felt a tinge of rejection when he didn't "want" her. When that passed, she felt relieved, the pressure lifted, relaxed. She never realized how much she had to prepare herself to "enjoy" lovemaking.

Now, when he gently hugged her, she just rested in his embrace not thinking or worrying if it would lead to more. The "more" she wasn't yet ready to handle. These created a new sense of security, of acceptance, of unconditional love. She didn't have to do anything to have John's love.

As the days proceeded Gail saw a quality of innocence about how John approached her. It reminded Gail of Adam and Eve in the garden before Eve had eaten of the forbidden fruit and how their relationship had been; pure and simple but with fullness. Her heart was becoming more full with John's gentle display of affection. He was not giving to receive, he was purely giving.

It made it easier to identify her own feelings, especially anger, which she had gotten so adept at burying. It felt good to talk it out and let it be done with, put away not hidden to erupt at some unsuspecting moment. She remembered as recently as last night sharing deep inner feelings that, in the past, would have been stuffed until they exploded. The best part was, that as she spoke directly from her heart, she was laying within the embrace of John's arms.

Kalli was wiggling again. None of the others missed it and knew she was eager to share her thoughts. Jill, who was about to speak, relaxed back into her seat in deference to Kalli.

"Feel, think, act!" she exclaimed. "Sometimes it's right to get angry. Sometimes it's something hurtful that makes you angry. It's okay to feel angry. But then you have to deal with those feelings before you act. Think it through, talk it over with someone, pray... whatever helps." Having stated her piece, without the need to go into great detail, Kalli looked over at Jill as if to say, your turn, I'm done.

"I wish I could do that. It seems I'm angry and reacting before I can get a grip on it," Jill revealed. "Running sometimes helps. Drinking used too." She smirked knowing that everyone seated around her knew that wasn't true. "I've almost gotten worse. By being angry at God I kept him at arms length, which then I twisted into he didn't care about me. Now I'm not angry with God, just everyone else.

"I remember as a kid there was this huge snapping turtle along the side of the road down by the reservoir. As cars passed they would slow down to see it, or to avoid hitting it. I had been riding my bike and stopped to watch. That turtle would snap out viciously as tires rolled by it. The people in the cars were not attacking, just curious or trying to help, but the turtle interpreted every action as a threat. That's what I feel like I am doing. Even if someone is slowing down to avoid hurting me, I just snap away at them."

Paula offered Jill some encouragement. "Remember this is a process. Some things take time. Most of us have dealt with our anger in distorted ways. Once we gain the proper perspective, even if we fully understand what it is we should be doing, that doesn't mean we can instantly change. Give yourself a break. You'll get there. We all will, even if along the way we mess up. When you catch yourself just keep lifting the motives of your heart up to God. Let him help you. It is his good work being done in us. You'll get there."

This triggered more sharing of successes and struggles that they had faced over the past week. The women did not shy away from the sometimes-stark insights they had gleaned. Next, Karen introduced that day's lesson.

"We move from anger to forgiveness. Let's spend some time seeing what God showed you in this lesson."

As the women opened their books, Karen acquiesced to Paula who had already been designated to lead this class session. Paula, going around the group, had each person read different verses about God's forgiveness. They moved from the Old Testament through the New Testament. Everyone seemed comfortable in accepting God as forgiving. Then they moved into the area of their responsibility to forgive others just as God had forgiven them.

Gail was the first to speak. "That anger chapter was tough. Telling all of you what I did was embarrassing. But the worst moment for me was the end of class last week when Karen mentioned this chapter on forgiveness. Suddenly my mother's glaring face swooped right up in front of me. And I thought, "No! There is no way I am going to forgive my mother." She paused as she called to mind the agitation she had felt. "Every alarm in my system went off and I knew I would not be coming back to this class. Just the word 'forgive' brought back the one time I had tried to talk to a pastor about my abortion. When I got to my mother's part in it that's what he zeroed in on. In order for me to move forward I had to forgive her.

"He never heard the pain and sorrow in my voice. He never showed an ounce of compassion about what it had been like for me all those years. Nope, just forgive, like it's the Biblical quick-fix for all problems.

"I left his office and I left that church and I've never told another pastor about my abortion. But since then I can't tell you how many times I've heard people dole out forgiveness as the remedy to every aliment."

171

She paused again slowly shaking her head at the memories. "It's not that easy. This is what I know. During the worst periods of my pain, the circumstances in my life and my mother's life were such that our paths never crossed. I saw that as God giving me breathing room, healing room. Not having to do my duty as a daughter was so freeing. It really did help me to deal with things.

"Back then I was reading in the Bible where Jesus says you must leave your mother and father to follow him. That's what I was doing. Not so much physically but emotionally. In order to grow in the Lord, in order to follow God, I had to 'leave' my mother, emotionally…and all the hurt she caused in my life. I figured that when God wanted me to forgive her, my heart and emotions would be ready. It wouldn't be because a pastor, or anyone, said it was my duty to do so." Gail paused and surveyed the room waiting for their reaction. Then she became embarrassed for striking out and speaking harshly. "I'm sorry I'm talking too much."

"No go right ahead," Paula said in such a gentle way that Gail, for the first time, felt affirmation, that her feelings, held inside for many years, were valid.

"Well, ah, where was I. Oh – then last week" Gail continued, looking at Paula's kind expression, "you introduce the forgiveness chapter. I just wanted to bolt out of here. I couldn't get to the door fast enough. I walked out and headed for my car reaching into my purse for my keys. I had no sooner put my key into the lock when I felt washed in peace. The others were saying goodbye, going to their cars and I stood there flooded with peace."

That's what's different, Paula thought as that peace emanated from Gail. To Paula, Gail had always had that kind, motherly way about her. Yet, if you saw into her eyes the grief was just below the surface. But not today, not now. There was peace.

Gail finished by saying, "Then God gently make known to me how small and frightened my mother was back then."

Paula uttered the words of Stephen as he was being beaten and stoned, "Forgive them Father for they do not know what they do."

Gail nodded in agreement then described her experience with the image God had given her that day, "My heart was filled with these waves of compassion. Like the flutter of the wings of a thousand tiny

172

birds, all the remnants of hate that still infected my soul were lifted up and carried away."

After a moment of quiet Karen suggested, "Why don't we each pray the prayer we wrote on page 50."

Renee was the first to speak, "Dear God I forgive Alex for being a jerk and using me. I forgive myself for hating men so much and then for using them and tossing them aside – just like Alex had done to me. I forgive myself for getting pregnant again to replace the loss I felt, even knowing the relationship with Jay's dad, Trevor, was a dead end. I forgive myself for breaking off the relationship and the tremendous hurt I caused Trevor who was in love with me."

"Dear God," Jill began, "I forgive you for not letting me have any other children, please forgive me for all those years I kept you at arms length. I forgive Russ for not rescuing me. I forgive myself for taking the life of my only child."

Kalli shared her prayer, "Dear God I forgive Eric for hurting me. I forgive his mom for making me feel wrong, like a criminal. Even if it wasn't his baby, it could have been. I forgive Christians for not fighting hard enough to stop abortion from becoming legal. I forgive the clinic for their pro-abortion counseling emphasis. I release them to be judged only by you. Amen."

Gail was the last to pray, "Thank you Father for the forgiveness you have buried in my heart to replace the hate I have held for so many years against my mother. That is a miracle I can not fully grasp but accept what you have done. Father, I am bringing to you another list of sins that I need to be forgiven for. Thank you for revealing to me how much pain I caused John and the hardness of my heart toward him… my husband. I have been unloving and unmerciful and I have hurt John by walling myself in – not giving or receiving love.

"I have tried to retain control over my life rather than abandoning myself to you – allowing you to care for me – to take my hurts and anger. Father I grant you, alone, authority to rule in my life and I thank you that you are always in a hurry to forgive me."

Stillness settled over the room. Paula let the peaceful quiet speak to each of them. After a minute or so, she closed in prayer.

Karen picked up the lead, "By this and the other forgiveness prayers written in your books, you have begun the work of cleansing your soul from the roots of bitterness. But, like pulling weeds from a garden, this is an ongoing discipline." Karen asked, "What tools does God show us in Psalms 4 and 139 to keep the garden of our soul weeded and cleared of bitterroots?"

Jill began, "I love that word picture about the garden and weeds. That's the one place I go where I can be quite. In Psalm 4: 4 it says, 'Tremble and do not sin; meditate in your heart upon your bed and be still.' I can probably do that better in my garden than at night in bed. But, being still and meditating – letting God speak to me, not always blurting out requests to him…I can see how that could help."

"I read Psalm 139: 23-24," said Renee. "It was great. But the entire Psalm says so much about God. How He knows where we go, when we stand up or sit down…that he knew us when he formed us in our mother's womb. That really hit me. Can I read that part?" she asked.

"Sure, in fact, read the whole Psalm," Paula answered.

Karen added, "I often read this to clients, if they let me, as a poem from God to them. Why don't we close our eyes and just listen as Renee reads."

"O Lord," came the resonant words from Renee's mouth, "Thou has searched me and known me. Thou dost know when I sit down and when I rise up; Thou dost understand my thoughts from afar. Thou dost scrutinize my path and my lying down, and art intimately acquainted with all my ways.

"Even before there is a word on my tongue, behold, O Lord, Thou dost know it all. Thou hast enclosed me behind and before and laid Thy hand upon me. Such knowledge it too wonderful for me; it is too high, I cannot attain to it.

"Where can I go from Thy Spirit? Or where can I flee from Thy presence? If I ascend to Heaven, Thou art there; if I make my bed in Sheol, behold Thou art there. If I take the wings of dawn, if I dwell in the remotest sea, even there Thy hand will lead me and Thy right hand will lay hold of me.

"If I say, 'Surely the darkness will overwhelm me, and the light around me will be night.' Even the darkness is not dark to Thee and the night as bright as the day. Darkness and light are alike to Thee.

"For Thou didst form my inward parts; Thou didst weave me in my mother's womb. I will give thanks to Thee, for I am fearfully and wonderfully made; wonderful are Thy works, and my soul knows it very well.

"My frame was not hidden from Thee, when I was made in secret, and skillfully wrought in the depths of the earth. Thine eyes have seen my unformed substance; and in Thy book they were all written, the days that were ordained for me, when as yet there was not one of them.

"How precious also are Thy thoughts to me, O God! How vast is the sum of them! If I should count them, they would outnumber the sand. When I awake, I am still with Thee. O that Thou wouldst slay the wicked, O God; depart from me, therefore, men of bloodshed. For they speak against Thee wickedly, and Thine enemies take Thy name in vain.

"Do I not hate those who hate Thee, O Lord? And do I not loathe those who rise up against Thee? I hate them with the utmost hatred; they have become my enemies.

"Search me, O God, and know my heart; try me and know my anxious thoughts; and see if there be any hurtful way in me, and lead me in the everlasting way."

When Renee's voice ceased reciting, eyes opened and heads slowly lifted. Stirred souls just sat in the presence of their Lord. Karen read again verses 23 and 24 reminding them of this powerful tool. "To avoid bitterroots taking hold in your lives remember to ask God to 'Search me, O God, and know my heart; try me and know my anxious thoughts; and see if there be any hurtful way in me, and lead me in the everlasting way.'"

Karen led on by saying, "Forgiveness is powerful, it frees us from that tight fist of bondage that hurts us more than the person whom we are angry at. Inviting God to search your heart is asking him to go beyond your own understanding. As you worked on this chapter did God reveal to any of you someone you had to ask for forgiveness? So often we are so focused on the injury done to us, that we forget the others involved that we may have hurt. Who did you hurt? From whom do you need to seek forgiveness?"

"My aunt," Jill said with a deepened awareness. "All along I was blaming God for not helping me, but He sent my aunt to intervene." Jill briefly shared the memory about the weekend her aunt and she had spent together just prior to Jill's abortion. "I still did what Russ and I had decided. I told my aunt I had a miscarriage. I know she didn't believe me. Yet I've never said a word to her. I totally put her involvement in trying to stop my abortion – trying to help me, stand by me – completely out of my mind. That dear woman... how I must have hurt her."

"I really hurt Jay's father," Renee shared, "He was probably the one nice guy I've ever dated. He wanted to marry me, be a father to our child. All that mushy stuff that I just laughed off. I wrote him a letter asking for his forgiveness. I don't even know where he is anymore so I haven't sent it, but I had to write it. Writing it helped me process my feelings."

Gail nodded in agreement, "Rick, the father of the first baby I aborted, doesn't even know I was pregnant. I treated him so badly when he returned home on leave. I was so messed up...hurting. I couldn't even look at him and see all that love he wanted to give me. I wasn't worth it. But he didn't earn getting dumped so coldly."

Kalli shrugged then said, "I wrote my mom. I guess she was trying to stay close and I pushed her away. Big college girl stuff. She kept asking if something was wrong. I would say, "'Let me grow up mom.' To keep her away."

Karen noticed that the class had gone over the allotted time and brought their time to a close. After introducing the next week's lesson she prayed for the group. None of the women rose to rush out as they had done in the first few weeks. By now their shared experiences and the stark vulnerability each women opened herself up to weekly had created a meaningful union between them.

Karen reluctantly excused herself knowing there were calls to be made before that day's clients came in for pregnancy tests. The volunteer peer-counselor was out sick which left Karen to cover for the day. She had a moment of envy toward Paula who had the time to partake in the unstructured conversations after class. Karen always had a long list of pressing responsibilities. The computer screen in her mind flashed on at the end of each class displaying what awaited her. Sometimes she was able to push those demands aside and chat for a while, but usually she did not have that luxury.

"Bah humbug," she grumbled allowing her self a moment of self-pity. Then she entered her office to do the work that she loved.

Section Three:

New Life

Chapter Twenty-two:
Mandi

Nicole was in tears.

Mandi had no words of comfort. She was the one that needed comfort. It had been two weeks since she and Kip had learned that she really was pregnant. Her resolve to abort had not diminished. The only thing standing in the way was money. Mandi had scheduled the abortion for last week and had to cancel when she and Kip were short by about $75.

As she sat on Nicole's bed at two in the morning she waited for her best friend to stop crying and respond to her request. It was Nicole's birthday. They had celebrated, true to tradition, with a few other close friends doing the shop-'til-we-drop trip to the mall, then pigging out at Le Crème de Crème, trying every combination of sundaes available.

Also part of the tradition was the sleep over limited to just Mandi and Nicole. A best friend ritual they carried out on Mandi's birthday as well. Mandi was experiencing concurrent feelings of being manipulative and desperate. She loved Nicole and would never purposefully do anything to deliberately hurt her.

But she needed Nicole's help. More succinctly, she needed money and Nicole's relatives always lavished presents and money on Nicole for her birthday. She would have the $75 Mandi and Kip couldn't come up with for the abortion.

As her sobs receded Nicole stammered, "How can you ask me to help pay to end the life of your baby."

Oh God, not this, Mandi thought. "Nicole please, I already know you're against this. But, you're not me. You don't know what it's like. This is not make-believe theory on how we feel about abortion. This is real life and mine's about to be flushed down the toilet into the sewer. I'm only trying to survive this. And I need your help."

"But Mand, every year on my birthday, I would know. I would know that I…" She burst out crying again.

Mandi had been listening to Nicole all evening, ever since they had parted form the others after leaving Le Crème. It was wearing on her. "If I can't turn to my best friend when I need help who can I turn to. Quit making such a big deal of it. I'm the one who's in trouble here. You'll just go spend the money on clothes you'll wear once then never be able to find in your closet jammed so full you can't close the door!"

Whoops, seeing the anger and hurt flash across Nicole's face, Mandi realized she had said too much. Nicole struck back.

"Oh and you should talk, miss perfect. But I'm not the pregnant one. And I'm not the one groveling for money to kill my baby. I'm not the one with a spineless boyfriend who can't do the right thing... no, doesn't even know what the right thing is. You do Mand – you do. But, no rather than do what's right, what you know is right, you're asking me for money so you can keep your perfect image."

"Forget this. I'm outta here." Mandi didn't have an answer to Nicole's irrational tirade. She grabbed her backpack and left not even considering how she would get home or what she would say when she arrived there.

But before she left she vented, "Some true friend you are Nicole. When I really need you alls I get is moralizing bull that we both know doesn't apply in the real world."

As much as Mandi wanted to she didn't slam Nicole's door as she left not wanting to awaken the rest of Nicole's family. Nicole watched in stunned disbelief wondering if she ever really knew Mandi.

Chapter Twenty-three:
Gail

It had been a week since Gail had the luxury of sitting at her kitchen table sipping coffee alone. On her second leisurely cup, absorbed in the serenity of the morning, Gail was not in a rush to start her day. John had taken the boys to practice, Mandi was spending the night at Nicole's, for her birthday all-night gab-a-thon. Gail smiled, pleased and thankful that Mandi's teens years were filled with fun, laughter and the good times that Gail had never been exposed to.

Sure there were more times than not that she and Mandi were distant. But everyone with teens assured Gail that this was normal. Mandi was just establishing her own identity. Even John wasn't concerned. The few times he had approached Mandi about Gail's struggles, Mandi had seemed unaware and unaffected. John reminded Gail that Mandi was raised to be self reliant, to think for herself and at sixteen that's what she was doing. Gail just had to let go, to come to terms with the fact that Mandi would turn to her less and less as she grew more independent.

A flutter of heart reminded Gail that letting go wasn't as easy as it sounded.

John and her friends were right of course, but it was hard. Gail missed the confidences she and Mandi had freely shared in the past. Gail couldn't fully accept that some of the distance between them didn't have to do with what Gail was going through. Well, in just a week the class would be finished. And it had definitely been worth it.

After the class on forgiving others, the group had worked through depression, then last week they had done forgiven and set free – learning to accept God's forgiveness of themselves. Both chapters on forgiveness had so cleansed Gail's heart and softened her that she could only believe that her waning relationship with Mandi could be rekindled.

This week's lesson was on acceptance. Gail had begun answering the questions in the workbook yesterday afternoon but had put it aside sensing she could do with a break from the Bible study. She had mentally designated Sunday after dinner as her time to finish off the lesson. This morning was one hundred percent just for doing nothing and doing it exceedingly slowly.

It was just before eleven that Mandi drifted into the kitchen. Gail, realizing that she had not come through the front door but from down the hall, was stymied.

"Didn't you stay overnight at Nicole's?"

Mandi offered a clipped response, "No, I left."

"Was there a problem?"

"Only that Nicole is an immature childish baby who I've obviously outgrown!" She said as she opened a breakfast bar foregoing the warm, freshly made sticky-buns just under her nose on the counter.

Gail doesn't remember a time Mandi didn't hunger after sticky-buns often offering to clean up afterwards so she could scrape off and eat the remaining walnuts caked in the butter-molasses-brown sugar goo. Something was seriously wrong.

"Would you like to talk about it."

"Talk! Huh everyone wants to talk – give me advice. Why don't people just leave me ALONE?" Mandi stomped out of the kitchen and back down the hall.

Boy that must have been a whopper of a fight, Gail thought as she reached to answer the ringing phone.

"Hello." She spoke still shaking her head in bewilderment.

"Gail?" it was her mother's voice.

"Yes mom, it's me."

Oh, you sounded strange. Is something wrong?"

'Nah, just dealing with the unexplainable moods of a teenager."

"Tell me about it. I remember the mouth on you when you were in a snit."

Not feeling at all defensive Gail replied, "Me mom, I thought I was always an angel."

They talked for a good fifteen minutes. Her mother telling Gail about some of the hi-jinks from Gail's teen years. "The way you used to time your return home to arrive after your father had conked out impressed me. You were pretty shrewd for a kid – good instincts. I knew you'd do okay in life."

Gail was astounded and felt flushed with awareness that her mother had just complimented her, "You knew about that? I thought I was so clever in secretly carrying out my master plans."

The conversation was lighthearted yet revealing. As the conversation ended and they said their good-byes Gail added, "I love you mom."

An awkward silence ensued for just a bare few seconds. In the time it took Gail's mother to respond Gail's words replayed in her mind. How many times had she, being the dutiful daughter, said those words in empty closure to one of their conversations. But this time the sincerity rang clear. No wonder her mother was left momentarily speechless.

"Um, I love you too dear. I hope you know that."

"I do mom. I do."

After they hung up, Gail sat, picking walnuts off a sticky-bun and basking in the truth of God's promise as it worked in Gail's heart – a healed heart – a heart of flesh. For the first time Gail had had an exchange with her mother where she didn't feel on alert to defend herself. In reciprocation her mother had been more honest and open than Gail had ever remembered.

This was some kind of quiet morning. Her daughter pushes her further away while she becomes closer to her own mother. Maybe this was time to do that last chapter on acceptance and see what God had to say to her.

Gail refilled her coffee cup and, picking up the pen by the message pad, walked toward the living room. As tears welled up in her eyes Gail realized these were not tears of sorrow, but the long awaited tears of joy.

Chapter Twenty-four:
Kalli

When Kalli first began the lesson on acceptance, she was hesitant to consider where her baby was now, the baby she had aborted. But it became a comfort to envision her little boy, she never doubted it was a boy, in heaven with Jesus. One of her favorite pictures was of Jesus bending down on one knee with arms outstretched and the verse, "Suffer the little children unto me." In the past she would stare at the picture for long periods of time placing herself within the group of children gleefully running into the arms of Jesus.

That's where her little boy was. Not only running, but playing, being held, and growing up in the care of the best parent possible, Jesus Christ.

In tribute to her son she wrote a letter.

Dear Jesus,

Please tell my son that I love him. I know you take perfect care of him and he is always happy. I am excited that one day I will be able to see him and I think that if ever I face death, it will help me to know he is waiting for me with you.

I have been afraid that since he was conceived in sin and didn't have a chance to be born-again, that he might have gone to the devil. But it was my sin, not his. YOU are a loving God and I praise you for loving my baby.

It hurts when I wonder what he looks like. I sometimes think he would be a toddler right now. He would be laughing and playing and calling me mommy and loving me. I will always regret my decisions – to sleep with men so easily – then to get rid of my baby so easily. If I had said "no" to the abortion, I would have my precious son at my feet. I have wanted to name him but Lord, you know my son and I pray that you would give him a name that fits.

I hope he loves me and forgives me. I want to see him play and sing and smile. The little baby I carry inside me now will never know his brother. But I will never look upon this child's face without remembering my son who lives in heaven with you. Thank you Jesus.

Then Kalli took out her calligraphy pen and a sheet of floral stationary and wrote the verse that had most touch her heart in this lesson. That made ten verses, one for every week she had been in the Bible study. The verses framed the mirror in her bathroom. To the previous nine she added, Isaiah 25:8: *"The sovereign Lord will wipe away the tears from all faces. He will remove the disgrace of His people from all the earth."*

She knew she could now tell her mother that she was pregnant. In all this time she had avoided visiting home and the one time her mother had dropped in unexpectedly en route to an exhibition further north, Kalli had been able to hide her swelling figure.

What was the big deal? Her mother knew she was living with Sean. She knew they were planning to get married. Her mother liked Sean and wasn't upset by the living arrangements. After all, her mom had never even bothered to marry these last several guys in her life.

Her deep-seated anxiety sprang up from a sense of disgrace. Kalli remembered how her mother had reacted when, at the age of twelve, Kalli had finally worked up enough courage to tell her mother what Uncle Clay was doing to her.

Uncle Clay was her mother's younger brother. He was the one in the family that had made something of himself. Kalli's disclosure shook the foundation of family pride built on Uncle Clay. On one hand her mother had to intervene to spare her little girl. Yet a part of her seemed not to fully embrace the truth of what she had heard. Of course not, because with all her being she wanted it not to be true.

Kalli grew up in disgrace as if it had been her actions that caused the family to collapse, for the exalted son to fall from his position on high. Yes, her mother had done what had to be done to keep Kalli's uncle from further abuses. But the abuse was never reported to the authorities. Kalli was still exposed to him at family reunions. Although Kalli's mother kept a close eye on her because not everyone knew what he had done, there was always unspoken tension crackling, igniting sparks just below the surface of conversations.

"Kalli why don't you go play with your cousins and Uncle Clay and let the grown ups talk alone," an aunt would say.

"No, Kalli needs to stay here with me," her mother would say without offering any explanation.

"Don't baby her." Another would interject. On and on it would go; all the while Kalli felt disgraced, like she was the one who had done wrong.

She was not a disgrace in God's eyes. He loved her. And He loved her baby boy. Whatever her mother's reaction would be to her pregnancy, Kalli no longer felt like she had to run away and hide from that reaction or the reaction of others.

In fact, she felt ready to talk to Sean about his desire to set a wedding date. Kalli wasn't quite sure about all the thoughts and feelings jumping around inside her head. She was afraid to be alone... and pregnant. How could she financially take care of a baby? Besides, she liked Sean, probably even loved him, but marriage – setting a date. Every time she tried to make that thought sound romantic like a little girl's dream come true, she always ended with a desperate need to flee. She didn't want to end it with Sean but his pushing for a wedding date was too much to deal with right now. She needed Sean but she also needed space – time, and she was ready to ask him for what she needed.

Chapter Twenty-five
Jill

It wasn't going to work.

Jill had everything planned out down to the smallest detail. It was a God given talent; being organized in the midst of the chaos of an event. She kept the food supplies well stocked and beverages flowing. Jill believed that as long as people's stomachs were fed, any event could be a success. Her job was to feed the multitudes. She smiled as she pictured a little boy with two fish and a loaf of bread. Then her shoulders sagged. She wasn't God and this situation was going to take a miracle and then some.

Saturday's event was a celebration for the 75th year since the city was established. The event would honor the mayor and his wife who were relatives of the city's founders. All the people in high places, the dignitaries, had received gold engraved invitations. This celebration was about to test her skills to the maximum. Today was Thursday and the hostess had called to increase the head count. Jill always built in a buffer to accommodate at least 10% above any count given her. But this went far beyond that.

How could people involved in running the city, always in the limelight and used to entertaining, be so unorganized when planning such a big event? Now it fell to her. To make matters worse, she had recommended a menu that would be a feast to the sense of taste, touch, sight and smell. The herb crusted prime rib lent itself to expansion. While the salmon tartar, a stunning presentation of salmon, dill and cucumbers, was labor intensive. Every dish was elegant and stylish, even the dessert penna cotta, a light, silky egg custard.

Russ had, in the past, jumped in to help when Jill was in a pinch. But, his specialties were Swedish meatballs and Buffalo wings, not delicate hors d'oeuvres and artistically presented entrées. Besides his skill level, there remained some unresolved tension between them. Jill couldn't put her finger on it only to note that the healthier she became, emotionally, the wider the gap grew between them.

Up against a wall, Jill did something she didn't customarily do, something she had actually never done before. She called her church. How many times had she heard about a home care group pulling together to help out another person. Or the women's Thursday morning Bible study taking on a project to better their community.

Jill had never taken part in group things, afraid that people would learn of her secret life in the bottle. Once that was uncovered then what the drinking was suppose to cover would probably surface as well. Better to stay in the background and leave quietly on Sunday mornings than to risk having her secrets discovered.

But, she had called. Pastor Andy's secretary Dotty offered consoling words and asked Jill to give her a little time to see what could be done. Jill thanked her and hung up not sure what that meant. It didn't sound like a brush-off but having never made a request for help in the past, Jill didn't know what to expect.

"Now what?" she wondered. Jill didn't have time to waste waiting. She picked up her address book and started with "A" scanning the names of friends and acquaintances that she could call on for help. In the "D's" was Daniels, Jennifer. Gosh, it had been years since Jill had spoken to Jennifer who had worked as a server until getting pregnant and leaving to raise her baby. Hoping that Jennifer might want to make a little money, Jill gave her a call. When she was greeted by an answering machine, Jill left a message and went on searching her address book. At "F," for frustration, Jill took a break and went out into her garden for solace.

She shook her head as she came across her gardening tools left lying by the pots of begonias she had begun to arrange for planting several days ago. Jill, usually so fastidious with her gardening, always putting everything back in its place, knew she was really in trouble now. Leaving tools around was a sure sign that she was losing a grip on her well ordered, well contained life.

Kneeling down she began to arrange and rearrange the begonias under the arbor, around the man-made mini waterfall. When the color scheme and look finally took shape Jill began to dig and transplant the begonias to add to the splendor of her garden.

There was no breeze yet. Usually about mid afternoon the cooling breezes off the nearby lake relieved residents of the heat. But Jill basked under the searing spring sun beating down on her exposed shoulders. As she dug and replanted she talked to her flowers, her voice mingling with the babbling of the water cascading over three feet of rocks into a pond that boasted of water lilies and whimsical ceramic garden creatures sunbathing around the edges.

These were Ross' contribution to her garden of art. The first bequest, a brightly colored bullfrog, had left Jill searching for words that would portray thankfulness for the gesture but convey that it just didn't fit the image she was working to create. Unable to find those words, Jill decided to put the frog aside for a while until the perfect place was found for it to reside.

Never having taken the time to explain her dislike to Ross, a few days later she came out into the garden to be greeted by this outlandishly colored bullfrog staring up at her at the edge of the pond just where the waterfall met the pool of water. Ugh! Jill cringed inside. Now what? She glanced around conspiratorially to see if anyone was watching, then fluffed up a leafy fern to cover the frog, at least in part.

Gradually meandering around her garden she tried to inconspicuously examine the effects. From various angles Jill viewed the focal point of the garden, the hand built rock waterfall, to see how much aesthetic damage the frog would do partially hidden by the fern. She concluded that ugly was ugly even when partially hidden. Which meant that she had to weigh this against the damage to Russ' ego if she was straightforward and told him how repulsive the gaudy creature looked to her. But she knew she didn't have it in her to reject Russ' gift.

It wasn't long until she was plotting the creature's demise, running excuses through her mind, *"Oh Russ, I didn't even see it, barely touch it with the wheelbarrow and it broke."*

A remark made by her running buddy, Sally, had unwittingly saved both the frog's inert life and Russ' ego. Sally, who could be somewhat over exuberant when expressing herself, but whose garden had been on the spring tour last year remarked, " I love it Jill. I just love what you've done back here. This is magnificent. I feel transported away from the bustle of life into a world of glorious magnificence. Oh what comes to mind? There's an experience of... let me see..."

As Sally searched for the right words, Jill's chest swelled with pride.

She had purposefully escorted Sally into the garden to seek her approval. In the back of her mind, Jill had considered competing to be accepted for this year's spring garden tours. She was sure she could hide the frog for the week the tours were held.

"I know!" Sally exclaimed, "Beauty …elegance with a touch of fun and frolic. You've captured it Jill! So many gardens are tributes to perfectly groomed, painstakingly maintained works of art. But you, with a flight of the imagination, using that half-hidden pond-animal, have made a more visually complete experience. I don't just want to absorb the grandeur I want to giggle. And that opens me up to even more beauty."

Jill's head snapped to the left, eyeing, in total disbelief, the abhorrent frog that had instantly been crowned an objet d'art. She too, found herself smiling along with Sally. "You like it…the frog?"

"Oh I love it. I can see more, little touches of laugher, throughout your garden. What gave you the idea?"

As they headed out for their run, Jill found herself telling Sally the life story of her unwanted, under-appreciated bullfrog. That had been over two years ago. Since then both Russ and Jill had kept their eyes open for unusual, but whimsical pieces to add to the garden.

The garden was Jill's hiding place, even more so now as she fought to become whole and leave the numbness of alcohol and death behind. Sadly, she had to admit that it felt like she was also leaving Russ behind. This was not what she wanted but the reality seemed to be knocking on the door of her life.

Digging in the garden, with the sun warming her back, Jill yearned for a reprieve from all the unanswered questions in her life.

She tried to remember how that last Bible study lesson on acceptance had started. She had worked on it a few nights ago after Russ had called to say he would be home late, "Don't bother with dinner, I had a late lunch."

Ah yes, the lesson began with hope and the verses from Isaiah. The Lord would swallow up death and wipe away tears. There would be joyfulness and gladness, everlasting – sorrow and sighs would flee away. Or something like that. Jill wanted to go back and memorize those verses. But for now, she didn't want a mental exercise she wanted to take in the meaning the verse portrayed.

The lesson walked her through trading guilt for joy and then it got to the question that haunted Jill the most. *Do you agonize over what your life could have been like if only you had made different choices?*

That is when she experienced what the other women in the group had been openly experiencing throughout the Bible study, grief. It had been blocked by her anger. There had been so much anger, at God, at Russ, at herself that she never acknowledged the root of that anger, her grief over the loss of her only child.

Part of the acceptance lesson was the first section on letting go. Jill had skimmed over that with perfunctory answers. She did not want to delve into where her baby was now or to bring tribute to her baby in some way. To do that would mean to come face to face with the truth of her pain.

But once again God had gently brought her to the place where she had to assess what she had so skillfully avoided for over twenty years. It was not just the loss of her dreams or the love-hate marriage within which she and Russ resided. It wasn't merely the alcoholic stupor she had sought daily while painting an imaginary picture to those around of a life which in no way resembled the truth of her morose existence.

Fashioned on God's canvas for her life was hope. His brush strokes, wide and expansive, had the dual effect of wiping away guilt while bringing forth joy. He didn't just coat Jill's exterior with the color of joy. He brought if forth from within her soul. And when He had done that God tenderly turned her to face the loss of her baby and caught every tear that she cried in His masterful hands using those tears to thin the color of her pain.

Afterwards Jill had gone out into her garden knowing what she wanted to do next; find the perfect place and in an inimitable way to permanently honor her lost child. Jill stood in silent peace surveying her garden for the place of homage to her child. *"Of course!"* she thought as she eyed the waterfall with the sounds of laugher trickling over the rocks and the frolic of the family of ceramic creatures that had grown over the past two years. This is the place. This is where a child should reside in love and laughter.

But first she had to add her favorite plants, begonias. Then she would find just the right memorial plaque or – well she didn't quite know what it would be. But she would know it when she saw it. For that moment, she needed to add the vibrancy that her begonias could bring.

Jill was setting up her work area to begin planting the begonia when Russ finally did arrived home. He was beat, his eyes almost lifeless. Jill had left her gardening, mid stream, and gone to comfort her husband. But her efforts brought no rewards just more distance as he shrugged her off saying he needed a shower.

Jill found herself jamming her hand-held spade angrily into the ground at the memory. That had been two, no three days ago. Russ' late night meetings and excuses had become fairly routine.

She loosened her grip on the spade to help calm her troubled spirit. Jill's catering extravaganza was about to become burnt toast. And yet, kneeling in dirt, planting begonias could transport her away from the cares of life, even if only for a brief period of time. Pushing aside thoughts of Russ and catering dilemmas, she began to hum and focus on gently planting the begonias. Humming led into mouthing worship songs, which Jill eventually began to sing out loud, and proudly on key, mostly. Twenty minutes later was enough time to refresh her and help her regain her perspective about her relationship with her husband.

The tension between Russ and Jill had shifted from the dual between love and hate, blame and reprisal. Of late it had become the old verses the new. With each step of healing for Jill, Russ was being left emotionally in the past. The thread of guilt and self-loathing that connected them, was no longer part of the fabric of Jill's life. Yet Russ had not been fitted with new clothes. He still resided in the time worn garment of guilt. Their lives had become a contrast of renewal and decline, or if not decline then stagnation.

Karen had explained to the group that loved ones might not fully be able to understand the transformation that God would work in their lives. But Jill had not been prepared for the distance, the ravine that would be carved out between she and Russ.

It hadn't become apparent to Jill until just a week or so ago, when they had moved into what Karen called the victory chapters. The group had been in spiritual surgery for weeks, feeling every cut and stitch that God made. The last few weeks in the victory chapters, they had been bandaged up and were on the mend.

It was then that Jill had first seen the great distance that had developed between she and Russ. Trying to draw him into her new world Jill had shared sections of the lessons after she had worked on them. Russ became resentful and almost adversarial. Now, it seemed to Jill, he was hiding away with late nights at the office. She hadn't even attempted to share her idea about the garden memorial. She was afraid to push him further away. Besides, this week she had enough to worry about with the 75th anniversary of the city looming hungrily before her.

Hearing the phone ring, Jill stood up, brushed the dirt from her legs and walked towards the house. Her spirit calmed even after just a little time of digging, planting, and praising God.

"Hello," she spoke into the phone. When no one respond, Jill realized that she had not been fast enough getting to the call and the call had gone to her voice mail. She would give it a minute and then check for a message.

Feeling dehydrated from the sun, Jill drank a glass of orange juice then dialed up the number to check her voice mail. The familiar but unnamed voice began, "You have one new message and one saved message. First message received today at ten-thirty two." After the tone Dotty's voice came across clearly, "Jill, Hi this is Dotty at the church office. I wasn't having much success with your request. But then I bumped into Vi and Helen." The image of two elderly women from Jill's church came to mind as Dotty's message continued, "They were returning books to the church library. We were chatting and I told them about your situation. Well Vi's face just lit up. Did you know she was once a chef in her father's restaurant right after the Korean War? I guess the place burned down over 25 years ago. Anyway, she loved cooking so much that she and a few of our gray-haired saints signed up for the culinary arts series at the senior center a few years back. They've been cooking up exquisite recipes for each other ever since."

Jill was grinning at the picture of these elderly women puttering around in the kitchen preparing delectable cuisine then dining with china, crystal, fine linen and candlelight. She hoped she was as spirited in her later years.

"They jumped at the chance to help you. Vi, Helen and maybe even the entire senior center will be stopping by your house within the next hour. Gee, I hope you're home then. Well, here's Vi's home number if you miss each other."

Jill jotted down the number, erased the message, then got out her planning book to review the supplies required to accomplish the tasks ahead.

"Imagine," she thought, *"the 75th anniversary will be catered by women who were born around the time when the city was incorporated. How fitting."*

As the tribute to the founding fathers once again took on an air of excitement for Jill she thought of a more important tribute; the one for her child. Jill put aside her daily planner and walked back out into the garden. Standing in the midst of its vibrant splendor her heart became filled with joy. She lifted her arms toward Heaven in praise of her Lord and reaching to touch her child.

She spun slowly around. Children's nursery songs flooded her heart. She began to swoop and glide, spin and sway singing audibly to her child. Finally, motioning with an expansive sweep of her arm across the entire garden, she said, "This is for you my little Christina until we meet in the garden of eternity."

Chapter Twenty-six:
Renee

Done.

Renee closed her workbook, then closed her Bible bringing it up and holding it to her heart. The Bible; a book she had, before this study, barely read but had held in disdain. The Bible; how often had she scoffed at those who had referred to God's Holy Word.

Now she was one of those weak, crutch-needing people but she didn't feel weak. She felt whole, complete, infused with a dimension that was at the core of her being. She had been an undefined hollow cavern echoing whatever the wind blew through her. Feeding on sagebrush and tumbleweed thinking she knew it all. While mice, rodents and other vermin ran undisturbed through the crevasses within her soul. So long Lord, I was empty for so long.

The dark, dank, cold embodiment of her life had been transformed. Jesus had walked out of the tomb, no longer dead but alive, risen from the grave. Renee had, in following the example of Jesus, come out from the grip of death on her soul.

No she was not weak nor did she need a crutch. She was free. She could fly and soar with the eagles. All things good and worthwhile were laid before her, a banquet of love prepared by Christ for her to consume. She would never again hunger after things that did not fulfill her soul, things that only brought decay to her life.

Letting go and acceptance. Yes, those were the victory chapters as Karen had called them. Surprisingly, as she let go she had wondered, *"What now Lord? Who am I to become now?"*

But the answer had already been placed before her. The day before, Liz, the school nurse had called because Jay was complaining of an earache. After they discussed a plan of action Liz had invited Renee to a women's tea being held at Liz's church. Renee had accepted without hesitation. She was ready to place herself in the path of the Lord's.

The image of the career woman that didn't need anyone had faded. Even at work she had begun to hear snatches of "God talk" that she had never heard before. Renee was sure these conversation's had always been there, but her ears had been listening for more important things like the next award-winning news break. Awards – worldly acclaim. The Professional Writer's Society would take another month before they announced the winners. Sure, Renee yearned to be named. But, now, the glory would belong to the Lord.

Daily, as she went about her job, whenever she overheard co-workers mention God she smiled and nodded at them. It wasn't long before she stopped to join the discussions.

So when Liz invited her to the tea, Renee was eager to go and then she shocked poor Liz by asking if she and Jay could join her for church on Sunday. Jay, with a child's curiosity, had often asked about God and heaven. In the past Renee would give a nonspecific answer or change the subject, distract Jay from any issue involving God.

Now, more than ever, Renee yearned to expose her son the loving Father she had come to know. What better way then for the both of them to get involved in a church? Jay thought the world of "Nurse Liz," who cared for him with kindness and little jokes that helped him forget his discomfort.

Renee put away her workbook and laid her Bible on the coffee table. Switching off the light she headed toward her bedroom. Settling into her nighttime rituals, Renee got into bed and laid back against her plumped-up pillows.

Her final prayers took her back, what was it now, two, three months ago. She prayed for Leo and Tessa the young victims of the shooting at the mall. In reverence she walked through the last few months; who she was, where she was and what changes had occurred in her life, in her heart and in her soul. With praise and thanksgiving she said goodnight to God and reached to turn out her bedside lamp.

One day, she thought, I have to write about this. More women need to know how powerfully God can change their lives.

Chapter Twenty-seven:
Karen

It felt good to get caught up on paperwork.

Karen had come to terms with the ebb and flow of her responsibilities. She knew that if the ministry was to be people focused rather than task oriented that meant she had to let go of the tasks from time to time. She was one of those unusual people who got pleasure out of doing paperwork. She often commented that papers talked to her. Just briefly glancing over the mail before passing it on or speed reading through articles and statistics helped her keep her finger on the pulse of pregnancy center work.

One of the first lessons Karen had learned was accepting that the volunteers she trained would not be clones of her. Not that she wanted them to be, but she did want the peer counseling to be consistent with the established standards; providing the truth in love, non-judgmental, or coercive. She wanted the volunteers to be open, honest, genuine and to have their ears attuned to God's leading.

She knew the route she traveled to glean all of that. Releasing others to travel their route meant letting God be the trainer after Karen was done with the classroom segment and had observed each new volunteer. After Karen had done that she was able to monitor each volunteer's progress through the debriefing time conducted before the shift ended.

This time was set aside to be a release for the volunteer from the burdens she had taken on while with clients. It was also when volunteers could evaluate their responses to specific client questions or situations. When a volunteer had not been able to address a client's concern or felt she could have phrased her response better, it was during the debriefing time that they brainstormed as a way to learn and grow.

Karen was also able to point out areas where a volunteer needed personal growth. Her guidance was done for the volunteer's well-being and to assure that every young woman was treated with care and compassion. Eventually, volunteers became adept at covering their shifts and knew Karen's door was always open if they wanted to talk.

Her current staff of seasoned, spiritually sensitive volunteers allowed Karen to focus on administrative duties. By reviewing the intake forms she was able to track the nature and needs of the clients they serve. These forms spoke volumes to Karen, but were often put aside when new volunteers or other demands took precedence.

Co-leading the Bible study meant statistics, reports and intake forms got placed in a 'to-do' pile. Sitting at her desk, Karen felt relieved to be whittling down what had grown to be a tower of paperwork that was at the point of overflowing in her in-box.

This past month seemed to have had an above-average amount of college age young women in for tests. As spring gave way to summer when schools let out and the 15,000 plus college students left the city to return home, there was normally an increase in high school students. Karen made a mental note to see if a shift was occurring.

She initialed the intake form of a 22-year-old education major whose one-night stand had brought her in for a test. The test was negative but the client and the volunteer had an in-depth discussion about relationships and sex. From the client's Exit Form, Karen saw that the young woman had appreciated and taken to heart what they had discussed.

The next intake form was for a 16 year old, Christian young girl. The volunteer's notes were sparse, typical of talking to teens. This didn't concern Karen because younger teens tended not to discuss things as deeply as older clients. The checklist was going off in Karen's mind; intact family, boyfriend was with her, active in her church. She stopped at "intentions." The volunteer had circled abortion.

Karen went back to reread the form searching for clues as to how the client's thinking had led her to consider abortion. Nothing surfaced. Karen glanced to the bottom of the form to see which volunteer had met with the young woman. Seeing the initials of a veteran volunteer, she gave a sigh of relief and turned the page over to see how the rest of the session went. Did they discuss abortion – the procedure, the emotional risks? Because this client had shard her faith, did they discuss the spiritual aspects of abortion?

Karen was dismayed that the client had not been open to any

198

discussion. True to the integrity of the center, volunteers, as a matter of procedure, asked permission before discussing sensitive subjects and always respected the wishes of the client. They had not discussed the abortion procedure, the emotional repercussions, faith – none of the important aspects of making such a crucial decision.

Now I remember, Karen thought. This was the young girl Darlene had talked to me about. We prayed together and had written the situation on the prayer board. Since all of this was done in a way to protect the clients' confidentiality, no names were used. The same held true for women in the Bible study. Prayer requests were put up on the prayer board, but the names of the women were not written to maintain their confidentiality. There were many small habits and details that the staff and volunteers got used to doing to assure that records were confidential and those helped at the Center remained anonymous. It was a learned discipline for new volunteers but a fairly routine way of life for Karen.

Karen turned the form back over to the front and looked at the name on the top of the page. The name did not immediately prompt a connection in Karen's mind because Mandi's last name differed from Gail's. It was the address that brought recognition pouring down upon Karen. *"Oh God, no,"* she cried within herself as she sat alone in the quiet of her office. *"No. No. No."*

Darlene was scheduled to come in that very afternoon. But Karen could not wait. She had to know if Mandi had taken Darlene up on her offer to come back and talk more. *"How long ago was she in?"* Karen thought, *"Three almost four weeks ago? Did she abort already? Does Gail know?"*

Karen's mind raced with unanswered questions as she reached for the phone and began to dial Darlene's number. Before entering the last digit she hung up the phone.

"I can't call Darlene. I can't break Gail's confidence about being in the Bible study. What could I say? Wouldn't it seem strange that I have a sudden interest in a client she saw weeks ago?"

Karen was pulled between wanting to take action and working within the statutes of confidentiality. She wanted to do everything to save the life of that baby and prevent Gail's daughter from repeating the destructive choice Gail herself had made.

"How Lord, how do I do this," she prayed.

She could talk to Gail. Ask how she's doing, how the kids are doing. Even bring up Mandi's name. Hadn't Gail talked about Mandi in the group; feel her out, see if she knows. But what if she doesn't know, then what do I say?

"Lord help me here. You've got to help me."

But, the truth was already before her. There was nothing she could do. The destruction continued. Whether it was Mandi or any other young woman. The lies promoting abortion had been around for close to 30 years. Now they were part of this current generation's truths. Abortion was as quickly decided upon as what movie to see on a Saturday night. With about as much angst or forethought. It was only afterwards that the comparison to movie-going fell apart. Or more accurately, turned into a horror flick.

Karen saw, all too often, how the cycle played itself out. The young woman emerged from the abortion clinic with the "problem" taken care of, and began to regain a sense of normalcy. No longer in self-preservation mode, she becomes more aware of feelings she had stuffed down. That's when the reality of what abortion did looks her straight in the heart. That unadulterated, unmodified, raw fact rips through her nurturing nature, a tornado gripping and tearing at her insides.

In the months that follow, she may talk about it. But at some point it becomes too much and she takes shelter from the tornado burying herself, her feelings, deep under the earth, hidden from the starkness of day and hopefully protected from the assault of the raging storm.

This is post-abortion syndrome.

The first phase of this is denial, stuffing down the reality because it is just too horrendous to look at. After three years of counseling clients who have shared the pain of their past abortion, Karen knows that two out of three women suffer with and live lives that have been effected by the post traumatic stress of their choice.

Without fail during every volunteer training she had conducted, when the class covering abortion and post-abortion syndrome was conducted, a new recruit would ask, "Do you think all women are hurt by abortion?"

Karen would share about what she had observed, explaining the emotional reactions of two out of three women who have experienced abortion. "As for the other third," she would say, "I believe that there probably are some women whose level of nurturing is extremely minimal. Then there are others whose connection to the truth of what they did will never rise to their consciousness. I don't know how that can be, but I have seen women so untouched by abortion that the experience had very little impact. But, for most of that remaining third of women I would imagine that somewhere down the road they will come to terms with the loss created when they chose abortion. Once they acknowledge the loss the layers covering the other emotional and spiritual aspects of abortion will probably begin to surface."

Staring at Mandi's name on the top of the intake form it was evident that even with all her experience nothing could truly prepare her, or anyone, for the reality that a baby was about to die and a young woman's life was about to be irrevocably changed. Yes, God could restore lives but why do we have to walk down that destructive path to begin with?

As Karen sat at her desk, half in thought, half in prayer, God reminded her of Eve. How much better could life have been than in the Garden? Yet Eve had a diet problem, an eating disorder; her eyes were bigger than her stomach.

Karen smiled as she thought through that analogy. Eve was in a perfect world but her appetite was not satisfied. She thought she was capable of knowing as much as God; seeing with His eyes. Eating the apple represented just a fleeting glimpse of what God sees, but it was too much. Eve's lack of satisfaction has become our legacy.

Karen thought of how often people have tried to see with God's eyes, to know all He knows, not satisfied with the piece of the picture He, in His infinite wisdom, allows us to see, knowing it is not humanly possible to grasp more.

Like spoiled defiant children people run ahead of God making decisions and choices that will eventually bite back. Instead, God wants people, His children, all those He has created to run to Him.

With a sigh, Karen considered the outcome of defiance; the broken lives, the hurt. But worse, how people then knot up all their painful emotions into a fist and shake it at God, like He was to blame.

How often had she seen that? How often had she caught herself close to doing just that? Thankfully she had learned that the hurt, the broken parts of life will never cease, will never be given the opportunity to heal and be turned into something better, deeper, more useful until that fist is unclenched and held open to God.

She thought of church during worship thinking of how many people lift their hands, palms open up to God inviting His irrevocable will into their lives.

Sadly, at some point during these past few weeks Mandi had clasped her hands into a fist. Karen prayed that Mandi had released her tighten hands and become open to hearing God's voice and leading for her life and the life of her unborn child, Gail's grandchild. Her prayer did not come without an impression of sorrow. This was not a prediction of the outcome in Mandi's situation as much as the acknowledgment of how well abortion has been sold to the unsuspecting pubic in general and young women in particular.

"And Lord," she concluded to herself, "for those who promote abortion, specifically in my community, please remove the blinders from their eyes. Let someone today begin to see that they are in the business of death. Let them understand that this is not compassion, this is not helping young women by teaching them to take the life of their child. Oh Father, remove the veil that prevents them from seeing that you are the giver and maker of life and they should not do what is yours alone to do."

Karen moved on to the next intake form and began to read about a young mother of two who was having marital problems. The prospect of being pregnant only added to the tension at home. One by one Karen made her way through each form reviewing, stopping to pray, writing comments and jotting down points to discuss with specific volunteers.

Chapter Twenty-eight:
Paula

The end.

Letting go.

Farewells.

As Paula drove to the Center she struggled with the fact that this would be the last class. Oh, she was tremendously encouraged by the growth and healing she had seen in the lives of the women in the group. But Paula got attached to people quickly and easily. Knowing that after today they would no longer be getting together every week tugged at her heart.

Well, she told herself, if it's tugging at my heart, I am sure some of the women in the class would be feeling like I feel. I have to remember to let them know that their feelings are normal and acceptable. After all, they have shared their most intimate inner selves. They have been open and vulnerable. Bonds have been formed that now must take on a different expression.

Seeing an available parking space, Paula zipped her van into the spot, audibly thanking God and turning off the engine. After fishing through her purse filled with notes, gum wrappers and her son's latest piece of artwork, Paula found some change for the meter.

She plugged the meter, headed into the Center and found Karen at her desk working through a large stack of papers.

"Wow, I almost didn't see you behind all that paperwork," she chirped, trying to buoy her spirits for the class ahead.

"Done," Karen exclaimed, "Finally." She neatly stacked the client files and placed them in a file box marked 'to be entered.' "Well, for the time being anyway. Are you ready for this last class?"

"Did you ever consider that the last class is on acceptance and letting go. Isn't it ironic that we're letting go of each other, also? I still find it hard to do."

"Good," Karen responded in an almost abrupt manner. Seeing Paula's expression she expanded, "It shows you have a tender heart.

That's what I love best about you."

Paula was touched by her friend's ready expression of their close relationship. Karen, always the teacher, continued, "I was just thinking about the letting go process. Do you realize how often we do that? Look at Wes and I. In a month our first born, our dear sweet daughter will get married. I am overjoyed yet at the same time inside there is this smidgen of grief swirling around my heart. My baby will be making her own home somewhere else. What will our relationship be like when she's a wife?"

Paula nodded recognizing the validity of how lives are always in a state of flux. She thought about how things had finally settled down at home and within her greater family since the sowing season was over. The mood was lighter, the tension of deadlines dissolved, everyone was getting along again. Planting was something Paula was glad to let go of, with the group it wouldn't be as easy.

"I guess there's no easy way to move from one thing in life to something else," Paula stated.

"Easy, no, but gracefully yes. You know, like how I handle change!" Karen said poking fun at herself.

"What about me. Remember how I cried after I dropped Holly off for her first day of school? I think I drove right here in tears. The new volunteer thought I was a client," Paula said thinking back to almost two years ago.

"We are funny with our emotions. To me it is important to affirm that what we feel is real otherwise what we will fall into is a seemingly inconsequential form of denial. We've both seen how that leads to not expressing what is truly going on inside our hearts."

"Not a good habit," Paula added.

"Let's not forget that in today's class. We should prepare the gals for the mixed feelings they may experience," Karen said.

With that the two women began to set up for the class each aware of the other but somewhat lost in their own thoughts. Karen was mentally preparing herself for seeing Gail. She prayed that God would continue to keep her heart at peace and focused on what He brought forth during the class.

Paula was making sure there was enough boxes of tissues within easy reach of where the women sat. She knew she'd need a few herself today. She stopped at the seat Jill usually chose and was reminded of an underlying concern that she had not been able to shake.

"Karen, are you concerned at all about Jill?' she asked.

"In what way?"

"Well, she was so full of anger in the beginning of the study. A lot of that has past but she still seems to be holding a lot inside. There's something there. Everyone else seems to have broken through their walls, you know, that major obstacle that allows God to work. Even with all her progress, there seems to be something holding Jill back."

"Now that you mention it, I can see what you're saying. I kind of figured the study wasn't over yet. I kept thinking about that one group we led where not one, of the five women involved, had any major breakthroughs until that last class. It was like suddenly it all became clear for each of them."

"You're right, but were any as composed as Jill seems at times, almost shut down? I mean she was open about her anger. But, it's like she has no feelings about her baby."

"She's never grieved either, has she?" Karen said trying to recall some of Jill's responses over the last few weeks. "It's the letting go process again but on a spiritual level. For instance, you have to let go of your will in order to have God's will in your life. Or you have to let go of bitterness before God can pour forgiveness into your soul. You and I don't know what Jill is holding onto, but there is something. She has to let go of that for God to pour in something better. "

"Have you ever led with someone who wouldn't let go and the Bible study didn't help them?"

"What I try to remember Paula, is that this is just the beginning of God working. It continues on even after the Bible study ends. If we can get women to move toward a closer relationship with God, to recognize how much He loves them and wants to direct their path toward wholeness, then that's a lot. Most women who have been in this study leave it seeing God in a completely different way, more approachable. They also know how to reach out to Him and to see His involvement in their lives. That goes with them when they leave which allows God to continue what was started."

"Good. I guess I just wanted to know that Jill would be okay."

"Yeh, have all the loose ends tied up. But, again, it's not our work it's God's. I do remember one gal took years to come forward after hearing about the Bible study. She walked around with the brochure in her purse but never called. When she was finally part of a group she was a raw open wound. Every week her struggles were all consuming. Yet in the midst of her pain was this wonderful hope that she saw within each lesson. She movingly spoke of God bringing peace to her internal melee.

"But then the strangest thing happened when we got to the victory chapters, the last few lessons where the focus is on accepting what God wants to do in our lives. She started to regress. She knew God wanted her to surrender to Him so He could restore her life, but she was so accustomed to who she was with her pain, that she didn't want to give it up. She was afraid of the unknown, not knowing who she would be if she wasn't carrying around guilt, regret, sorrow and self-hatred.

"What was worse is that she saw what she was doing, talked about it openly but still wouldn't let go and allow God to refill her with a new spirit."

"Did she finally give in?" Paula asked hopefully.

"Not in the class and I've never seen her since. I think of her from time to time, which leads me to pray for her. It sure would be nice to know that she was able to respond to God's leading."

"Bummer. I don't think Jill's like that woman."

"No, I don't think she is either. Besides, God is bigger than our greatest obstacles. And He's persistent. It's not over yet."

In fact, the end was just beginning as the women began to arrive for their last gathering. Their faces portrayed the mixed emotions Paula herself had been feeling earlier. So after prayer that is how Paula opened up the discussion, "Your abortion experience aside, what other times in your life did you have to deal with letting go?"

Their comments and musings set the tone for the final class lesson. Although their discussion throughout their time together was introspective the healing and changes that had taken place in each of the women's lives buoyed it.

Paula watched Jill's reaction, noting that she seemed more at peace. What had happened, she wondered. But held back from probing too directly just to satisfy her curiosity. She did not need to have a verbal accounting from Jill to know that God had once again delved into a life

206

and refined it. Her lips moved slightly as she mouthed *thank you Lord.*

As they came to the end of their time together, Karen led them into a discussion by asking, "What will you remember about this time of healing? And how will that help you in the future?"

Jill started but stopped abruptly reaching for a tissue to catch her tears. Paula glanced at Karen her eyes relaying the care she felt. "I'm sorry," Jill murmured, "This has been a hard week."

"You need to cry Jill. Go ahead, we've each had our turn," Gail said lovingly.

"It's just my baby, my precious little baby," Jill stammered between audible sobs. No one rushed her or became impatient. Several reached for tissues as tears of sympathy filled their eyes.

A good five minutes later, Jill blew her nose then gestured for someone else to share. "Can you come back to me later?"

Kalli, having been the one most uncomfortable by the long silence and Jill's tears began to share, "The most important thing that I learned is that my child has always been safe in heaven. All along it was me that was suffering."

Jill nodded appreciating Kalli's attempt to minister. Kalli continued, "I realize nothing I can do will save me, only Jesus' death. I now have the joy of feeling God's love. So when I am confronted with painful things I will give them to God."

Karen thought how simple Kalli's words were, but how true. Kalli wasn't finished, "I was walking across campus yesterday. It was right after the recycling truck came by and picked up everyone's trash. But, on the ground was a corner of a ripped up picture. A few steps further was two other pieces and then another corner. Here were these ripped up faces staring up from the gravel at me. I thought about the times somebody hurt me or rejected me and I tore up letters, or pictures or whatever to vent my anger and rid my life of them.

"Funny how quickly I destroy things; memories of people who hurt me. Or I try to reclaim the past with scotch tape and glue. That was my life but nothing was doing a very good job of holding it all together. Not until Jesus anyway. I can look at the picture of my life and I can't even see where the rips used to be. That was done by Jesus."

"When I look at my life," Jill began softly testing her voice and resolve, "I see two wide-eyes kids not even thinking beyond what's directly in front of them. By having that abortion it was like we invited the spirit of death into our lives. It has resided with us ever since. Killing our love, our marriage, and my soul. Talk about Satan prowling around to steal, kill and destroy. He found fertile ground in our lives.

"No matter what I tried to do, on my own, or even seeking God's help, it was never powerful enough to overcome that spirit of death that had consumed our lives.

"During this Bible study I was so entirely submerged in God's Word coming specifically against that demon of death, that I finally feel purged, released from the grip of it on my life.

"I can not describe the torture of that death grip tearing at me every single day for all these years. And now it is gone. There are no claw marks. There is no hot, vile breath carrying utterances of hatred to fill my thoughts. There is no longer a weight that is so unbearable that I interpret depression and the call to end my own life as my hope.

"This," Jill paused to wipe a tear. "This is freedom in Christ."

"I was in the store last week," Gail said, "and saw a display of angel merchandise; statues, books, sayings, pictures. Usually I don't pay attention to those things because it offends my sense of the role angels really do play in our lives. It's commercializing God. But there was this small, delicately framed picture of four angels that caught my eye. As I looked at their sweet, innocent faces I thought of my four little ones. The babies I aborted.

"I bought the picture and have hung it just above my favorite reading chair. Next to it I have the verse from Romans 6:21-22: 'What benefit did you reap at that time from the things you are now ashamed of? Those things result in death. But now you have been set free and become slaves to God, the benefit you reap is holiness and the result, eternal life.'

"God brought me into holiness and gave me a picture to remind me of my four children that are with Him. When I gaze at that picture I don't feel shame, I feel such love; my love toward my children and God's love towards me."

Murmurs of agreement softly rang out. In further unison the women turned to face Renee who had not yet answered the last question. She was ready to respond, "My abortion served as a barrier between me and God. It made me feel badly about myself. It held me back. The lies tied me down, the bitterness wore me down and I turned my face from God so He wouldn't notice. Or so I thought! This made me a prime target for that prowling, roaring Satan. I heard his voice in my own recriminations and rebellion.

"Now I've stepped into the light. I am God's. All my thoughts are brought captive to Him. I look, not with dread, but with hope and eagerness toward my other past iniquities. I know God can help me deal with those too. My face is toward God now. The light is on and we can both see what has been lurking in the shadows. I used to worry that I would get to heaven and be turned away. No longer!

"I have to confess, when I first heard about post-abortion syndrome I just thought it was a guilt trip that affect religious people. I guess you could have classified me as an atheist or at least an agnostic. Guilt and regret had no place in my life and I looked down on people who let the past hold them back.

"Funny how I never saw that pretending I had no regrets had such a hold on me that it dominated and controlled the focus of my life. It took a great deal of effort to keep that philosophy alive and to not face the truth. This is a far more peaceful way to live. I am not afraid of the truth and letting God search out my soul."

When Renee had finished Karen was about to wrap up but Gail jumped in, "I have to tell you all what happened." She started to flip through her workbook. "I think it's on page 82."

The other women followed her example and began flipping toward the end of their workbooks.

"Yes, there it is, the question about what areas of your life have you found new hope that sprung up out of your abortion grief? My marriage!" she exclaimed.

Gail's face was beaming but there was also a hint of mischief, "You all know how kind John has been to me lately, courting me and being so patient. It struck me just how blessed I was to have such a wonderful man. My heart overflowed with genuine love for him. I mean, I haven't felt like that in… I don't know how long.

"I figured since he was being so good I could be a little naughty. So I lured him away from his office to the Renaissance Hotel for lunch. But we started with dessert up in the honeymoon suite I had reserved."

Gail blushed and glowed simultaneously, then said, "The courtship is over. But I sure want the honeymoon to last for a long time to come."

A sudden eruption of girl talk reminded Paula of how special the unity in Christ was. These women, besides being ministered to by God, had developed a closeness that was a reflection of Jesus himself.

It's hard to let go and move on but it was time to bring the last class to a close. They did so by holding hands, most had their tissues near by, and praying with sincere thankfulness, lifting each other up to God. They ended by praying for those women who have experienced abortion but have not yet felt God's healing touch; that they too would find the courage to come forward, to break the silence, to move past their fears and to let God work within their hearts.

As they reluctantly rose to leave, hugs, tears and promises to stay in touch we exchanged. After thanking Karen and Paula the women gathered their purses, books, Bibles and belongings and headed out into their new lives.

Karen and Paula stood, not speaking, each in her own thoughts. After a few minutes Paula moved and Karen followed suit.

"I guess I'll head out. Vince and I will be at Lisa's wedding. We're looking forward to it."

"Oh so am I. If we live to see it! I am glad most of the major work is done. Now it's just the small details and waiting. Lisa does not do "waiting" well."

"Gee," Paula teased, "I wonder who she gets that trait from?" She embraced Karen, whispered thanks and left.

Section Four:

Fight For Life

Chapter Twenty-nine:
Kip

Kip said good-bye to Mandi and hung up the phone. He sat on the edge of his bed staring vacantly out his window. Cash of varying denominations lay neatly beside him. It totaled three hundred and thirty dollars the amount needed to secure Mandi's abortion. A motion caught his attention to the left bringing him out of his blank state of mind. Two squirrels were running along the top of the backyard fence. As Kip watched, the squirrels ran and played up and down the fence, jumping onto branches, moving easily from tree to tree then adeptly dropping back down onto the fence.

His life used to be that carefree. That was eons ago. Before his parents' divorce and now this thing with Mandi. Why – how had his life gotten to this point? He admitted that he had no answers to the many questions pounding within his mind. Reluctantly, he pulled himself back to the task at hand. He and Mandi had been combining their funds for a few weeks now. Finally the last seventy-five dollars had been added to the envelope that Kip kept hidden in the back of his junk drawer. One place his mother didn't clean.

The appointment was set. By tomorrow at this time it would all be over. Life would be back to normal, if that was possible. And he and Mandi could do something more than worry about "the problem."

Kip remembered the first time he had ever met Mandi. It was the night Ryan had finally talked him into going to youth group, which he had done partially as a joke but too, Ryan was an excellent b-ball player and Kip sorely needed diversion from all the disruption at home.

Home life was the pits. School was the same 'ole same old. Why not hang out with Ryan, he could put up with a little talk about God. So he had gone.

It was Nicole that had caught his attention at first. Mandi was pretty and all but Nicole was a natural flirt and exuded a magnetism that peaked Kip's curiosity. Well, until Mandi came back onto the court and he found himself challenged by her complete absorption into the game.

She was good, darn good. Without knowing it, she challenged him during the group discussion later on that night. It had made him uneasy, this self-assured, church chic unsettling his thought processes. How could a distant God, if there even was a God, mean that much to her. She didn't seem weird or afraid of life and she didn't act better than him. It was like God being in her life was just a matter of fact.

Nicole attracted him but Mandi challenged him. A challenge always drew Kip's attention stronger than alluring charm. That's probably why he was big into sports. In response, Kip took on the challenge of Mandi as an amusing distraction. She began to swing by his school while he was hangin' out before class. The first time she had said she would come by on the way to her school, Kip had noticed her almost a block away. He deliberately waited until she was almost past the group before acknowledging her.

No matter what slick moves he conjured up there was no denying or avoiding that he wanted to be with her, needed to have her in his life. She elevated him out of the squalor his life had drifted into since his parents' split.

At times he saw Mandi for who she was and what she brought to his life. Her goodness, her pure, open honesty, the no game playing straightforward talks they always had. She was good for him and Kip knew it. Why then did he sometime revert back to his old ways like he was dating just any chic, the party-fun thing where the "no, no, maybe" was merely a precursor to sex. He knew with Mandi that she really meant no but he rarely stopped pushing her.

Sometimes he depended on her stronger resolve to keep them in line. Sometimes he just wanted to cross the line, pure and simple, without regard for her. Which time was it that had led to this?

He absent-mindedly fingered the money at his side. Pregnant. A baby. He shook his head sending his thick blonde hair back and forth across his forehead. I can't think like that. The problem.

When Mandi had first told him – he could still hear the quiver in her voice – that her period was late, he had just about choked. He knew if she really was pregnant that his future was over. Being a father at 17 was a dead end but he knew Mandi well enough to know that abortion was out of the question. Odd how the thought of fatherhood had seeped into his subconscious stirring up a pride and desire he never knew existed. An urge to protect Mandi and the baby welled up from time to time. Then he had begun thinking about how he could manage being a teenage dad but still having a life. When Mandi had responded to the positive test by saying she wanted to have an abortion, her voice was so firm that Kip did not share all the dreams he had conjured up in preparation to becoming a father.

He picked up the three hundred plus dollars knowing without a doubt that this should not be. But as an act of contrition for his sexual responses to Mandi – pushing her when she really wasn't ready – he would not push her to have a baby she didn't want to have.

Chapter Thirty:
Mandi

Everything was set. Having spoken with Kip, who sounded ready, Mandi felt relieved. In less than a day this whole nightmare would be over, behind her. Her parents would be away for the weekend, which made things even better. Although she had to watch the boys, there would be no one watching her.

She sat on her bed, leaning back on a mountain of pillows nibbling on the chocolate covered raisins she had taken from the candy bowl in the living room. Catching herself frantically popping the tiny candies into her mouth Mandi thought, nervous energy and chocolate – not a good combination.

What she needed was to talk to Nicole. Nicole always calmed her down or at least distracted her. Well that was the old Nicole. She was no longer an option. This was going to be a long night.

A few hours later Mandi had finished the candy, a bowl of cereal with bananas – something healthy – and was now eating popcorn; lightly salted but smothered in butter. The clock was taking its sweet old time. Seconds taking hours before turning into minutes. How could Mandi tolerate twenty-four hours done in slow motion?

I know how to make it go quicker, Mandi thought. She got up and went into the hall. She heard her parents in the living room. Good she thought, mom and dad are involved watching television. She quietly made her way in the opposite direction to her parents' bedroom and their master bathroom. Mandi began rummaging through her mother's medicine cabinet for the prescription that her mom had stopped taking because it had made her sleepy.

She felt like a thief but kept on carefully finding her way through the clutter of vitamins and old nail polish. It wasn't there. Mandi was wound too tightly to give up. She began pulling open draws and scrambling through them, searching, digging, and cursing when she would come up empty. With each unsuccessful foray she became more consumed. Under the sink she pulled out an old shoebox that held discarded hairpins, outdated lipsticks and a variety of ancient beauty treatments, but no pills.

It's gotta be here. Mom never throws anything away. Mandi thought as she stood up and started again with the medicine cabinet. There they were right in front of her.

"Oh, Mandi!" her dad said surprised to come upon her. Mandi was startled and yelped then tried to hide her look of guilt.

"Um, I, um – I was borrowing some of mom's nail polish."

"No problem, I'll use the other bathroom," her dad said cheerfully, oblivious to anything unusual going on.

As he turned to leave Mandi grabbed the pills and stuffed them into her pocket. Then, living out the lie, took one of her mother's polishes and quickly headed back to her room. She noiselessly closed the door, leaning against it with a sigh of relief.

The polish was subtle melon, not at all her taste in color. She tossed it into the pile of stuffed animals cuddled together by her closet. But the pills, with its bright orange warning label – may cause drowsiness – were exactly what she wanted.

She read the dosage, removed two from the container, then one for extra measure and reached for her can of pop to help wash down the relief she yearned for.

Within a few minutes Mandi began to relax, not so much from the pills as from the promise they held. True to the bright orange warning, in less than half an hour Mandi began her descend into a state of unconsciousness.

"Oh, I wonder if this will hurt the baby?" she thought. She didn't catch the irony of her thought before fading into a drugged sleep.

Chapter Thirty-one:
John

John was a happy man. The happiest he had ever been in his life. He marveled at how good could come out of a struggle. These last few months with Gail taking that class had been unfathomable. Daily their lives had been like a roller-coaster ride through hell. Finally it was over. More than over, it had brought he and Gail to a wonderful place in their relationship. Then last night seeing Mandi borrowing Gail's nail polish signaled to him that even the mother-daughter relationship was on the mend.

John had suggested to Gail that they get away together, alone, after the Bible study was finished for a long weekend. It would be his graduation present to her. Gail had readily agreed. Today was the day.

Everything was in place. John was leaving work early. Mandi would watch the boys for the weekend. The reservation had been made and he had even thought to have champagne and flowers put in the room. He was taking Gail to a rustic lodge that was similar to a bed and breakfast. He had found it on the Internet and it looked to be very cozy nestled up against a mountain on a remote lake. Their room had a fireplace, hot tub and balcony with a view. The lodge had canoes, kayaks and even wave-rider's available for the guests. He and Gail could do as much or as little as they wanted for the next four days.

Life was just perfect.

Chapter Thirty-two:
Gail

She was packed and ready. Well, almost. Now to take time to pamper herself with another cup of coffee while she filed her nails and put on some polish. How long had it been since she had done that?

She had an even better idea. Rather than use one of the many shades of peach polish which she owned she would use one of Mandi's more sparkling, alive colors. She was feeling more like a teenage than a mother anyway.

Gail went into Mandi's room and over to her dresser. Along the top, which could use dusting, was the trophy Mandi had won last year for basketball with a doll propped up against it. Next to that was a small tabletop flip calendar that showed one day per page with a Bible verse. It had not been flipped for more than a week. One vial of passion purple polish was there as well.

Gail continued her searched laughing to herself at how John would react escorting his purple-nailed wife to dinner. He probably wouldn't notice unless she reached out to hold his hand across the table. Mandi's nightstand held more promise. There was a neon lime green, midnight blue madness and pumpkin. Close but not quite the "look" Gail wanted.

Where does Mandi keep her ten million polishes? Gail thought as she absentminded opened first one nightstand drawer then the other. Nothing, just candy wrappers and papers. The last drawer was stuffed to almost overflowing. Gail tried to close it but the papers caused the drawer to jam.

She wiggled it without success. Then pulled it open and tried to shut it again. It stuck again. This time Gail couldn't get the drawer back open. Just then she saw a pink plastic basket on the bottom of Mandi's bookshelf. More than a dozen white long necked orbs signaled that Gail had found what she was looking for – the nail polish cache.

With one last strong pull and push Gail righted the nightstand drawer only to force some of Mandi's papers out and onto the floor.

Bending down to pick up the mess she had created – like Mandi would notice with the disarray of her room – Gail noticed the partial image of a logo on a business card sticking out from a folded piece of paper. It was the women's health clinic logo. A design that had always irritated Gail because it was so appealing but the health clinic had only one purpose, abortions.

More curious than alarmed Gail unfolded the paper thinking, Mandi must be doing another pro-life report. On the folded paper that held the business card were guidelines for a woman about to get an abortion. This would make for a good paper, Gail thought, and began to refold the paper. As she slipped the card back into the folds she saw that it wasn't a business card at all but an appointment card. Gail turned it over and saw that the blanks for the appointment information were not empty. It held the day, the time and the date of few weeks ago.

"Oh God no!" Gail cried as the possible reality stuck her. "Oh God let it not be true. Let it not be Mandi. Was it just part of research – or maybe for a friend? What friend?"

She ran to Mandi's dresser top calendar and flipped back a few weeks to the date indicated on the card. There was nothing there that gave any further information but Gail had a gnawing uneasiness that did not diminish. She went to the teddy bear calendar hanging above Mandi's desk. Just about all the boxes representing each day of the month held a reminder or scheduled event. The only indication that something was to occur on the date from the card was a red circle around that day's number. It was crossed out with a small "no" written next to it.

Gail was starting to feel relieved when she noticed a pencil mark, a faint line drawn from that day diagonally across the calendar ending in the box marked 26 – Thursday – today.

Today!

Gail's heart was about to lunged into sheer terror when she was overtaken by anger so forceful it brought a calm clarity to Gail. With exacting and deliberate motion she retrieved the card and headed toward the phone. Her mind rapidly reviewed what she would need to do to stop the clinic from destroying lives – Mandi's life and the life of her first grandchild.

Neither cool, detached inquiry nor flat out threats broke through the wall of silence at the clinic. They would not provide any information nor answer any questions. When Gail countered by saying she was on her way down there, the nurse manager came on the phone to advise Gail that the police would be waiting for her when she arrived.

The arsenal of hateful words that Gail had absorbed under her mother's parenting rose to the surface of her tongue. They tasted bitter and repulsive – quite appropriate for the clinic manager that supervised the destruction of lives. Instead, Gail heard herself say, "May God have mercy on your soul," before she hung up the phone. Gail pressed the automatic dial for John's office. It took all her effort to suppress the sobs welling up inside of her.

"Hello my sweet," John said lovingly, "Can't wait to see me huh?"

The tears caught in Gail's throat made her voice sound husky, "John, please come home now."

John, thinking Gail was flirting, responded in kind, "Honey, I can't wait to be with you either. Give me an hour and I'll be on my way."

When Gail didn't come back with a flirtation retort John said, "Gail, are you there?"

"John, it's Mandi."

He heard Gail's desperation, "Is she hurt? Was it an accident?"

"No – just come home. We need to talk."

"I'll be right home."

Although John didn't know it, he made the twenty minute cross-town trip in record time. He only knew where he had to be – with Gail.

It wasn't until John walked through the front door that Gail released her tears, babbling incoherently about an appointment with death. On the phone she had said that no, Mandi was not hurt. John was confused wondering who had died?

Gail finally unclenched her hand from around the tissues she had been crying into. Also in her hand was a mangled piece of paper, which she handed to John.

Was it a letter about someone who died? John unraveled the paper, which also held a business card. No, it was an appointment card and it was from the women's clinic downtown. It was dated for several weeks ago.

Gail, between sobs, whimpered, "Mandi."

"Mandi had an appointment at this clinic?'

221

Gail nodded affirmatively.

"For what, a check up?"

"No."

But Gail was still not able to tell him so John offered his next thought, "Birth control pills? Do you think Mandi is having sex?"

Gail was just shaking her head no, then yes, then no again. "Gail tell me, what is it? What's going on?"

"An abortion," was all she could offer.

"An abortion, who, not Mandi?" If there was one person he knew would never fall into that trap it was surely Mandi. John had a brief sense of reprieve until Gail managed to say, "Yes, Mandi."

With those words the dam broke and more disconnected thoughts spilled forth from Gail as John listened in stunned disbelief, "How could this have happened. I thought we had taught her – I thought she knew. It's all my fault. I haven't been there for her. Who is she dating seriously enough to get pregnant?"

Finally John had a focal point for his emotions, primarily of which was anger, "Kip – that arrogant good for nothing jock violated our little girl. Wait 'til I get my hands on him. I'll show him what he gets for messing with Mandi's life."

For a good hour Gail and John went back and forth between consoling one another and venting. They ran the gamut from anger, to hurt then self-pity, revenge, confusion and doubting. The pendulum of their emotions swung wide and vast but eventually the arc became less drastic until it came to a standstill several degrees left of rational.

John was at a loss of what to do next, "Mandi will be home within half an hour. Should we let her know we know what she did or wait for her to come to us?"

"No, John, we can't pretend we don't know. And she won't come to us. It is too horrible an experience. She'll try to bury it just to survive. We have to let her know we know. That is the only way we can help her now."

"Can I still wring Kip's neck?" John's tone alerted Gail that he was not joking.

"No John, Kip is as much a victim as Mandi, if not more so. Mandi knows that abortion is wrong and why. Kip probably has no idea. He needs our help too. Besides, we don't know for sure that Kip is the father."

"I need a cup of coffee before she gets here. How about you?"

Yes, there's coffee already made. But it's pretty old by now."

"Old is good," John said and headed to the kitchen. Gail went down the hall to wash off her face and regain her composure. What lay ahead would not be easy. Both had forgotten that they should have already been on the road headed for the lakeside lodge.

Chapter Thirty-three:
Evelyn, R.N.

Some days you just know it's going to be a bad day. From the moment you stumble out of bed you know the gods are against you. But not today, thought Evelyn, today her new trainee would start and in a few weeks the hectic pace at the women's clinic would be eased.

They usually ran a nursing staff of at least six but had been down to just four nurses since Mary left over a month ago. Worse still, they had done more abortions in this last quarter than ever before. The docs were talking expansion while the nurses were running ragged. As the nurse manager, Evelyn had finally been able to get the docs to give her authority for hiring nurses and filling the two positions.

This nurse was hand picked by Evelyn and would be a far cry better than some of the so-called nurses she had been saddled with in the past. Men, humph, they weren't worth a nickel when it came to hiring a nurse. They think, if she's perky she's fit. Then Evelyn would get stuck trying to train them. Not this time. Fate shined favorable upon her.

Evelyn went in early to prepare and was mentally going through the training schedule for the new hire, Joyce. Let's see, she thought, I'll take her on a tour and while doing so explain not only where everything was but also some of the must-know policies. After all this was different than working in an OB/GYN office. First there's the security measures. Then there's how to deal with the people in the waiting room.

Evelyn was making mental notes as she began to set up the rooms for that day's procedures. Most were first trimester abortions but the clinic also did second trimester abortions as well. There weren't many of those but today was the second day of one that had been started yesterday. Good, she thought, the new nurse will get to see how we handle the procedure.

It was messier and there was more product of conception to remove. She'd be glad to hand that over to an underling. It wasn't that Evelyn was squeamish or anything like that. She just hated grunt work and would relegate it to whoever else was available. Unfortunately being short staffed she hadn't been able to avoid some of the clean up work of late. Because new people were always so eager to please, especially since she hired this trainee, Evelyn felt she wouldn't catch any slack when she handed off the dirty work to her.

Basically it was a matter of sanitizing the table, throwing the soiled sheets into the laundry-service bin, taking the bucket into the back bathroom and flushing everything down the toilet. No matter what, and this always astounded her, once a nurse began cleaning up after procedures and doing disposal duty, they avoided the back bathroom for personal use. Evelyn could never understand that but caught herself avoiding that room as well.

Ten hours later Evelyn finally found time to linger over a cigarette in the smoking room. Joyce, her trainee, had done well but she sure had a million questions. Evelyn took a long drag on her cigarette, then released it slowly. All in all the day went well, mostly. There was that irate mother trying to push her weight around and get answers. When will parents realize their kids are old enough to make their own decisions. They don't need interference from over-protective meddling mothers or fathers.

Well it wasn't the first time Evelyn had to rescue the receptionist and it wouldn't be the last. Luckily the police were just a phone call away. Protests and clinic violence had its rewards. Now the police were very responsive. No police department wanted a clinic shooting that would make national headlines in their jurisdiction.

Crushing out the stub of her cigarette Evelyn lit another deciding she had earned an extra few minutes of break before finishing up the paperwork on her desk.

Yeah, she thought, that mother was a piece of cake. The only real snag to a perfect day was the patient who started to freak out a bit. What was it she said – something about her darkest hour. Man the little twerps could get so dramatic. Joyce's interference had been the sticky part. Evelyn would have to let her know, in no uncertain terms, not to jump in when she was working with a patient. She knew how to handle last minute jitters. And that's all it was.

Her darkest hour, what a silly comment, Evelyn thought shaking her head. The kid didn't even realize what it meant to have a screaming infant to take care of day and night. Sometimes they just refused to use common sense. Evelyn felt good that she provided firm direction when a skittish teen was vacillating.

Yup, overall it was a real good day, Evelyn thought thanking her lucky stars that she was smart enough to not be saddled with any unwanted kids. Working at the clinic not only paid good money, but also the benefit of free abortions made it worth it. Tomorrow she'd have to fill Joyce in on all the "extras" that come with the job, like abortions at no charge.

But for today it was time to wrap things up and meet with some friends for a few drinks during happy hour at the local watering hole. Gee, she thought as she laughed dramatically, this could be my darkest hour! Stupid twerp! She ground the remains of her cigarette in the ashtray and walked out of the smoking room.

Chapter Thirty-four:
Mandi

Mandi sat in numbed silence as Kip drove toward her house. For brief moments she was afforded the luxury of the dense void that overtakes ones mind when there is far too much to fathom. Unfortunately, the reprieves were fleeting as Mandi's mind shouted back at her, demanding answers that she was not able to proffer.

How did I get to this? I knew the truth. How did I ignore what I knew? And what about Kip so willing to go along with whatever I wanted?

As they neared Mandi's house she became aware of her father's car in the driveway. At first it struck her as normal until she remember that it was only mid afternoon and too, that her parents were suppose to have left for their long weekend.

Oh, she thought dully, maybe they decided to take mom's car.

Kip eased his car into the driveway pulling up behind her father's car. "I thought your parents would be gone?"

"Yeh, they probably took mom's car." She couldn't look at Kip knowing what she knew and without any justification to give him.

She had wanted to rent a few videos to keep the boys occupied and out of her way over the weekend, but realized her video club-card was in her other purse. "I'll be just a minute," she said reaching to open the car door.

Kip left the car running and turned the radio on to the local game. Anything to distract his thoughts.

Walking toward the house Mandi briefly wished her parents were home so that she could tell them, talk it all out, look to them for answers to her questions, her fears, her aching heart.

It's probably better to wait until Sunday after they've had their time away, she assured herself. But how will I even say it then, she wondered.

Inserting her key into the front door lock Mandi didn't even notice that the door wasn't secured. Simplistic thoughts kept her moving forward; get the club-card, get a few videos and soon she could surrender to sleep and halt all the questions.

Gail and John had been praying, their heads bowed when they heard the car door close. Looking across the living room out the front window they saw Mandi approach the house and Kip remain behind. John's face tensed as his eyes fixed on the car. Gail gently spoke, "Dear, let's hear Mandi out first then see where God leads us." John nodded in agreement but his face didn't relax.

At first Mandi didn't notice her parents sitting quietly together on the living room sofa. Her dad cleared his throat just as her mother softly called out to her, "Mandi?"

"Oh mom – dad, I didn't, I thought you were gone." The words stumbled out of her mouth.

Gail gripped John's hand, "No, we uh…" she did not know how to continue.

"We were just praying and having a cup of coffee before we left," John offered. "Come sit down a minute."

Mandi was almost relieved that they were home. Maybe she could tell them. She walked into the living room and sat in her dad's favorite chair, close to the couch. Yes, maybe she could tell them. She wanted to, needed to.

Suddenly her mother was crying which made Mandi cry. Something she had been too numb to do all afternoon, since leaving the clinic.

"Mom, dad, I've done something… I have something to tell you. It's not good. You won't be very proud of me."

John protectively put his arm around Gail and pulled her tight against him. "We're here for you Mandi. Whatever it is, we're here for you," he said.

Gail just nodded as tears streamed down her face only able to murmur agreement. She couldn't bear to hear what she knew she had to hear, what she knew needed to be said before any else could happen.

Kip was getting restless waiting out in the car. Not that many minutes had past but because not even a good ball game could distract him. He opened his door and stood leaning on the doorframe.

Since Mandi was sitting adjacent to her parents and the window, Kip's action made Mandi notice him. Following Mandi's gaze John realized that Kip had not driven away.

"Uh, do you mind if Kip comes in? He's kind of part of this," Mandi said.

She started to get up but John signaled for her to stay seated, "I'll go out and get him," he said heading toward the door. He wanted a face to face with him.

"John?" Gail said meekly.

"It'll be okay," he reassured her as he reached for the door.

Kip heard the door open and turning toward the sound was caught off guard to see, not Mandi, but her father walking toward him. This is not good, he thought.

But when he looked into the face of Mandi's dad slowly approaching him, Kip thought, maybe he doesn't know.

"Kip?' John said extending his hand.

"Sir," Kip responded, shaking John's hand.

"Let's go inside and talk." It was a temperate command to which Kip just nodded affirmatively. Just the same, Kip was ready for this to be out in the open even though he was afraid of how Mandi's parents would react. There was a degree of relief that it would all come out and he could share the heavy weight that had been crushing in on him.

He followed Mandi's father. He was no longer looking for answers, instead he was looking for forgiveness, clemency, exoneration. For some reason Kip felt he would find it within this man's home.

Epilogue

In like a lion out like a lamb was a lie, at least in the mid-west, Karen thought as she eased out of her driveway. I sure hope the office parking lot was plowed.

The landlord was pretty good about maintaining the building. It was only if the forecast was for unrelenting snow that he would wait before having the lot plowed. Unfortunately Karen could not wait out this storm. Well, if the lot isn't plowed I'll park on the street and plug the meter, she resolved.

Life didn't come to a stand still just because of a few white flakes. And today she and Paula were putting getting together to pray before heading to the local radio station where they would be interviewed about post-abortion syndrome. No silly snowstorm was going to stop them from taking advantage of this opportunity.

Karen thought about the many times she had offered to talk about PAS to the public but the topic was just too controversial for the local media to accept her offer. But God is always at work. A new board member attended a church with the radio station's program manager. It took a little priming, but the right door had opened.

Karen had received many offers to debate the issues surrounding abortion but had turned them down saying, "We are not a political organization here to debate abortion. Our heart is to create a safe place for women to seek help when facing a possible unplanned pregnancy. Or to receive healing from a past abortion."

As much as she wanted women who have experienced abortion to know that they didn't need to carry the hurt alone, that they could let it go, she didn't want to impart the information in an adversarial setting. Today she and Paula would finally have the opportunity to reach out to women in a discussion format, not a debate. No snowstorm would hinder that chance.

Karen had no sooner found decent curbside parking than Paula pulled up driving her husband's big four-wheel drive mud racer. The contrast of mud with virgin snow, of big huge wheels giving way to petite Paula climbing out of the cab made Karen laugh out loud.

"Making fun of my ride?" Paula said as she scooped up some snow and threw it toward her friend. Giggles, laughter and snow were thrown between the two friends for several minutes.

"Hey, aren't we suppose to be talk show personalities? What kind of image is this?" Paula chided as she hurled another handful of snow at Karen.

"Image? You ought to see yourself! There's not an ounce of curl left in your hair," Karen said as she dodged Paula's throw.

Paula instinctively turned to look in the truck's mirror at her hair as Karen sneaked up behind her depositing a double scoop of snow on top of Paula's head.

"Absolutely gorgeous!" She said and ran to let herself into the office before Paula could retaliate.

After drying themselves off with paper towels they made hot chocolate and went to Karen's office to prepare for the upcoming talk show.

"Is Renee still a go?" Karen asked.

"Yes. I talked to her this morning and she'll meet us there. Her office is only a few blocks away, so the snow won't be a problem."

Being invited to be a guest on the popular talk show had brought more blessings than Karen would have imagined and they hadn't even done the show yet. In planning for it she and Paula had discussed several of the women who had gone through the post-abortion bible studies over the past years to choose someone who would be willing to share their story.

This had given them each a reason to connect with past class participants which led to getting an update on their lives. As much as you would think otherwise, most often, when a class was completed, the women usually lost touch with each other. Just like with clients, there were a handful that Karen heard from regularly. But most often the women were off pursuing life, from a healed perspective Karen was sure, and she never heard from them.

There were always those few that remained close to Karen's heart and were often in her thoughts for years afterwards. Gail had been one of those women. Although it had been last spring when that class had ended, Karen found herself praying for Gail and her family often. In a way she wanted to use this radio prospect as a reason to contact Gail. But then the dilemma of confidentiality surrounding Mandi's pregnancy nagged at her. Karen never made the call.

Paula did not have any restraints that hindered connecting with the gals. She was actually very good at keeping in touch with many more of the women from past Bible studies. It was Paula that was usually the first to offer, "Guess who I saw this weekend," or "Guess who just called." Then she would go on to fill Karen in on what that woman was doing and what she knew about the others that had been in the same group.

Thank God for Paula, Karen thought. She keeps me informed and gives me a sense of connection. This time, even though it had a purpose – the radio show – was no different. Not only had Paula gotten several women willing to speak publicly about their pasts, she had also gotten a thorough update on many of the women.

The past few weeks had been too busy for Karen to chat with Paula beyond the task at hand. This morning, as Center activity was lulled into quiet by the storm, Karen and Paula had time to chat.

"So tell me whose doing what, I'm dying to hear," Karen asked.

"Did I tell you Renee's boss is letting her do an article on post-abortion syndrome?"

"You're kidding, really?"

"I kid you not. You know she won that professional writer's award?"

"Yes, I read about it and sent her a congrats note,"

"Well after that her boss wanted to fast-track her to bigger and better things,"

"Great. I know she wanted that,"

Paula shook her head no, "Not anymore. She said after the Bible study she started to evaluate her life, her priorities and realized she didn't want to lose what she had gained from the study. She became friends with her son's school nurse who goes to Calvary Cross Church. Renee is going there now. She's in a Bible study and says she's found a creative outlet by teaching Sunday school for kids – her son's class,"

"Wow, who would have guessed. Career woman was written all over her,"

"Well turning down the fast track didn't hurt her any. I guess she and her boss have a good relationship. He gives her lots of leeway on stories."

"That's fantastic. Who else did you talk to," Karen asked as faces and images of women went through her mind, "How about Jill, they were in the same class weren't they?"

"That's not all good news."

"Oh, why not?" Karen became concerned remembering that Jill showed real evidence of growth during the last class. Had she lost it, slid back?

"She and her husband have split up," Paula offered.

"No. Oh, how sad."

"That's how I felt at first. But maybe it's not that bad. Jill still has hope that they'll reconcile. She said that they had lived such a convoluted dysfunctional life together for so long that they couldn't sort out what was good and what was detrimental to their relationship. It sounded like this was a mutual separation. Jill says she not interested in other men or divorce just having time to heal and giving Russ time to also."

Karen just nodded then began her update from the few calls she had made, "I wasn't able to reach Kalli. Her phones been disconnected."

"I reached her!" Paula exclaimed then continued, "She had lived with Jill for a while."

Paula noted the shocked expression on Karen's face but didn't pause, "Yea, and she had a baby boy, named him Ezekial. No wait… Isaiah, that's it, Isaiah David!"

"But she was living at Jill's?"

"Yup, for awhile. Remember how they kind of bonded? Well a few months after the class ended Kalli's boyfriend…" Paula paused to remember his name, which came to Karen faster, "Sean?'

"Yes, Sean. Anyway he really wanted to get married but Kalli wasn't sure. And she didn't feel right about them living together, even though by then they had stopped having sex."

Karen rolled her eyes. "How can you live with a guy and not have sex."

"Beats me, but that's what Jill told me. Kalli moved out of Jill's. I got her number and I finally reached her." Paula was now beaming.

"What?" Karen prodded.

"They got married, Sean and Kalli. But first Kalli wanted to be sure. I guess she and Jill had stayed in touch and Jill invited Kalli to live there until she was sure."

"Isn't that something."

"It gets better. Jill helped arrange and cater the wedding at Sheffield Estates."

"You're kidding?" Karen gasped knowing that Sheffield's was one of the more exclusive historic homes in town set aside for grandiose formal affairs. She felt under dressed just driving by the place. "It must have been like a fairytale to get married there."

"I made Kalli promise to come by the Center when both you and I are here, to show off her baby and the wedding pictures."

"Oh I can't wait," Karen said swooning with anticipation.

"Who else was in that class?" Paula thought out loud, "Oh yes, Gail. You were going to call her weren't you? Or was I suppose to?"

"No, Gail was on my list to call," Karen said trying to sound matter-of-fact. Then tried to steer Paula in another direction by saying, "I wasn't able to reach her. What about the gals in last fall's class?"

But it didn't work, as another thought found its way forward, "Wait, Gail's the one who became a grandmother. Let me think, when was that?"

"She what?" Karen stuttered, "What do you mean became a grandmother? Are you sure?"

"Oh, I remember now. It was Renee that told me. She had seen the birth announcement in the paper. Gail's daughter had a baby."

* * *

Gail refilled her coffee cup and sat down to finish writing out birth announcements. Her sweet precious grandson, Calvin, slept soundly in the kiddie-kradle perched on the table bedside her.

Grandmother Gail was babysitter two days a week while Mandi took high school classes at the community college. It was a special program for teen moms. Mandi could have continued at the private Christian school that she had attended all along. But it was agreed that in everyone's best interest Mandi would be better served with schooling that offered more flexibility.

It wasn't an easy life for two teens but Mandi and Kip worked hard to be responsible and care for their child. Initially Kip had offered to quit school and get a full time job. But, neither Gail nor John would hear of it. Kip's mother was relieved that Gail and John were being extremely kind and understanding about the entire situation.

Both teens attended school, work part time and coordinated their schedules to assure that they, as parents, were the primary caregivers. For Kip his son gave him purpose in life, a goal outside himself, a reason to push harder and do better. For Mandi it was bittersweet. She loved her baby dearly but, even knowing God's forgiveness, felt that she had fallen from grace. In doing so she had gained a son but lost the self-confidence she had once possessed. She didn't know if that was a good thing or not. Most of the time she was too tired to give it much thought.

Nicole came around but it could never be like it was before. What could they share together, all nighters? Mandi did those every night for Calvin's two a.m. feedings.

She was proud of Kip though. He amazed her and probably a few of his rowdy friends. Funny, she thought, I'm the good girl from an intact family and Kip's the one who shines. What's wrong with this picture God?

She had a lot of questions. Thank God for her mother. She kept reassuring Mandi to look to God and the answers would follow. Quite often Mandi would find a scripture verse written in her mother's delicate handwriting stuck inside a schoolbook. It was always just what she needed. How did her mother know?

Gail knew her daughter was struggling but felt it was a good struggle, if on the other end her relationship with God became closer. Gail also knew the struggle was between Mandi and God and she would only be a hindrance by interfering. She restrained herself seeking John's advice often when she felt the need to jump in and try to fix Mandi's life.

Even the birth announcements were an exercise in self-control. Mandi wrote notes, addressed and mailed the ones for relatives and her friends. The ones Gail was doing were addressed to friends' of hers and John's.

Thank goodness I'm done, she thought. Then as one more person came to mind she thought, almost!

Taking out a blank announcement she began to think through the short note she would write inside. No, brevity would not work for this one, she thought and went to get a piece of stationary.

Calvin fussed for a moment, stretched his tiny arms, squirmed then fell motionless again. Gail, pen in hand began to write.

Dear Karen,

I have thought of you often over these past months. There were so many times I came close to calling but always seemed to get distracted.

I want to thank you and the Center for being there. First for me and then, without me knowing it, for Mandi.

Mandi doesn't remember the volunteer's name that talked to her when she came in. But she does remember how kind she was to her. Mandi also told me that she was set on aborting. Praise God for the words He gave the volunteer.

Mandi and Kip, he's the boyfriend, were at the clinic. She told me how shut down she felt, like she was on automatic pilot, about to collide into the side of a mountain, and she couldn't alter her course. The clinic nurse called Mandi in and directed her to undress and get up on the table. There was a second nurse there with a badge that said trainee. Just before leaving Mandi to undress, this trainee nurse asked, "Are you alone?" Mandi answered, "No, my boyfriend is with me."

When the nurses walked out, the words that your volunteer had said came back, "Mandi, in your darkest hour when you are feeling really scared and alone, always remember that you are not alone. God is with you. He loves you and Kip and your baby. And He has enough love to help you get through this."

The nurses returned to find Mandi, fully dressed, sitting on the edge of the table. The nurse in charge asked brusquely, "Why haven't you undressed?"

Mandi just quietly said, "I don't want this to be my darkest hour. Can I please leave?"

The nurse, she must have thought it was just last minute jitters, began to try to talk Mandi out of leaving. But the trainee interceded by moving to Mandi's side and saying, "I think she really wants to leave," and showing Mandi to the door.

Mandi later learned, to her astonishment, that Kip had accepted the idea of being a dad. Their next hurdle was to tell us – the parents. Except that I had found out, just that day, that Mandi was having an abortion, or so I thought.

John and I were in prayer beseeching God for His wisdom on how to console Mandi when she arrived home after her abortion.

There we were the four of us; me, John, Mandi and Kip. John and I thought Mandi had had an abortion. Mandi was trying to tell us she was pregnant not knowing we knew about the abortion.

All our emotions were so heightened – not to mention the river of tears that flowed – that it took several minutes to sort out what each person was saying and to realize that Mandi had not had an abortion.

It was almost a month later when Mandi and I had a quiet moment together that she explained the whole story and how the Center had helped her. She also told me that she had written that the volunteer could not make contact with her. I realized then that you probably knew about her pregnancy.

I am so sorry for taking this long to write. It has been a whirlwind and the months came and went as quickly as the flash of a lightening bug's tail. Now, thanks to God and how He used one volunteer, I sit next to the joy of my life, little Calvin.

May the work of your hands and all those at the Center, be blessed mightily by God. It is because of the work done there that we celebrate life here.

In His love,
Granny Gail

For more information about Post-Abortion Syndrome (PAS) or for assistance in dealing with PAS please contact any of these organizations listed below:

Forgiven and Set Free
CARE NET
109 Carpenter Dr. Suite 100
Sterling VA 20164
703-478-5661
703-478-5668 fax
Care-Net.org

Ramah International, Inc.
1776 Hudson St., Englewood, Florida, 34223
Telephone 941-473-2188
Fax: 941 473 2248
EMail: Sydna@aol.com

American Victims of Abortion
419 7th St., NW Suite 402, Washington, DC 20004
202-626-8800

The Elliot Institute
P.O. Box 7348, Springfield, IL 62704
217-525-8202

Healing Hearts
P.O. Box 7890
Bonney Lake, WA 98390
htohhdqs@integrityol.com

Institute for Pregnancy Loss
P.O. Box 27937, Depot Road Stratham, NH 03885
USA Voice: (603) 778-1450
E-mail: rue@nh.ultranet.com
PregnancyCenters.org

Project Rachel (Catholic group)
St. John's Center, 3680 Kinnickinnic Ave., Milwaukee, WI 53207
414-483-4141
800-5WE-CARE

Rachel's Hope
P.O.Box 17363, San Diego, CA. 92177
(858) 581-3022
Email: rachels_hope@juno.com

Rachel's Vineyard Ministries
1-877-HOPE-4-ME
Email: rachel@rachelsvineyard.org

Safehaven - Post Abortion Counseling
Victims Of Choice, Inc.
PO Box 815, Naperville, IL 60566-0815
630-378-1680 Telephone
630-759-5030 Fax
Email: maggsies@bazillion.com

You can reach the author at:
Email: t-cthomas@telcomplus.net
Web page: WonderfullyMade.Info